SIEGE NETWORK

J.W. CLAY

Published 2024

Printed in the United States of America

ISBN-13: 978-1-950342-15-0 (softcover)

ISBN-13: 978-1-950342-14-3 (ebook)

Editing services provided by: John Paine

Editing services provided by: Jenna Love-Schrader

Proof Reading services provided by: Katherine Stevens

Cover design provided by: Dissect Designs

 Created with Vellum

ONE

NEW YORK

THE SUBWAY TRAIN SLOWS, AND THE BLUR OF ONCOMING faces becomes clearer. Jen Yates looks through the window, past gang symbols and graffiti etched with razor blades, scouting the mix of pedestrians assembled on the platform. Ten o'clock in Manhattan. Hard-boiled executives are barely standing, eager to cap off their sixteen-hour days. Freaks hard-wired into the city's club scene might be thirty feet underground, but they're soaring a mile high.

But Jen is looking for someone very important in between those two poles on the spectrum. Liev Frankel. He's invisible in the crowd, but this is his stop. Frankel is an Israeli citizen living in Brooklyn. The intense surveillance he's under has nothing to do with either of those details though. Frankel's DNA was found on Isla De Sangayah, a tiny island off the coast of Peru.

That connection put him on a short list. For the past two months, Jen Yates and her team have been scratching lines through it, and the ink is made of the blood they've been spilling. They've been inching closer to the criminals responsible for the horrific killings that occurred in Mexico City. And it's Frankel's turn to help with the search.

Tonight, Jen and her team will detain him. Ask some not-so-polite questions regarding his affiliation with the *zakonny vladelets*—the rightful owners. The Founders. What he'd been doing in Peru. Plots to kidnap members of the United States government. And most importantly, his organization's understanding of quantum computers.

Passengers exchange places through the subway's open doors. As Jen observes the traffic, the Whisper planted on the back of her ear vibrates. The bone microphone is synced to her cell phone via Bluetooth. Transmissions occur automatically, detected by the cell phone in her pocket.

"Target is preparing to board . . . second subway car . . . handoff in fifteen seconds."

Al Hastings. Recently retired from the U.S. Army's most elite counterterrorism unit and now a member of Jen's Technical Access Group—a term used to describe elite, compartmentalized teams of hackers.

On cue, Liev Frankel emerges from the crowd. He boards the subway one car ahead of Jen.

"Successful handoff," Jen states.

At the chime, passengers stand clear before the subway departs. Jen moves before the train does. Maintaining visual contact with Frankel is pivotal. After three short days of observation, they're finding disturbing anomalies, and his behavior is becoming erratic.

A forged passport was his ticket into the United States. Fake name. Ditto on his country of origin. His lack of employment is another sign of trouble. This city is expensive, and without a steady source of income, most people end up dining in soup kitchens and sleeping under cardboard.

Frankel is also displaying other unusual quirks. Tonight, he took the subway from his Brooklyn apartment all the way to downtown Manhattan to throw away a bag of trash. Only it wasn't trash; it was a bag of electrician's tools. Valuable items to leave in a dumpster, especially when they could lead to gainful employment.

Her Group retrieved the bag. During the search they found plastic tubes stripped from wires. Bits of fiber-optic cable. Rolls of electrical tape. Mr. Frankel has been working after all, and Jen is bursting with curiosity about his secret project.

Closing in on Frankel, she understands that she's not tracking a paranoid individual but an intelligence operative. One with excellent tradecraft along with levels of motivation high enough to achieve results.

She nears Frankel's car. The accordion bonding the two cars flexes as the train gathers speed. Frankel is ten yards ahead, sitting among a cluster of passengers. He's wearing denim and plaid, New York's hipster de jour, and snow is melting off his boots. A layer of thick, black scruff covers his face.

Before Jen enters Frankel's car, she conceals her mouth and radios Hastings. "Two, what's your position?"

The reply is prompt. "Car five. Coming toward you."

"Copy."

Jen opens the door and steps inside. She avoids eye contact but snatches a quick glance in his direction. Cagey. He's bouncing a knee, and it rocks his slight frame in the seat. Grabbing an open section of handrail, she turns her back to him and locates his reflection in the plexiglass.

MS-13.

Thirteenth Street Crips.

Messages cut into the glass.

She's reminded of another: *Couldn't have done it without you, Ms. Yates.* The message was delivered to Jen as she worked to gain access to the Founders' network in Peru. Painful reminder of what was taken. She stares at Frankel's distorted reflection.

Some not-so-polite questions coming his way . . .

Frankel's eyes jerk in her direction. She's staring too hard, sending too much hatred his way. Before he disregards her, he checks out her ass, and Jen marks him as a sucker for it. Tonight, she's just another pretty blonde New Yorker in a black leather jacket with jeans to match and All Star Chuck Taylors. He doesn't recognize her, but his agitation confirms something else: Frankel is nervous about something, and he has decided to flee.

———

Gabriella Martinez is monitoring the team's work inside a small tactical operations center in the CIA's Manhattan field office. New York is one of the most heavily surveilled cities on the planet, and she doesn't need a Predator drone or satellites to observe this battlefield.

A digital map of Brooklyn has multiple marked locations. Jen's team is stalking Frankel through the streets as he returns to his apartment building. He hasn't deviated from his assumed route—a good sign as he nears a preset choke point. "Ms. Hamilton, give arrest teams authority to detain Frankel."

Sloane Hamilton gives her boss a nod. She's a skilled hacker, and this is a script she's familiar with. "Yes, ma'am. Ten minutes and he'll be wearing bracelets."

———

"Handoff successful."

Charlie "Animal" Keats watches as Jen crosses the adjacent street and breaks off from Frankel. He's in an unmarked Crown Vic. Detective's special. It's worn after a few hundred thousand miles and haunted by the smell of New York's more charming residents. A detective named Sam Herbert sits behind the wheel and, much like the car, he's worn in just right.

Animal gets a visual on Frankel as he walks down the sidewalk. Snow is falling, and it's windy. He's using the collar of his jacket to shield his neck. Animal's eye is trained, refined, and he's already finding angles, weaknesses. Cold is good—zaps the will to fight. But the jacket could conceal a weapon. When Frankel passes the Crown Vic, he activates his handheld radio. "Thirty seconds."

A response comes in from a unit at the opposite end of the street. Grayson "Gray" West and Salvador "Coco" Garcia, both retired Delta operators like Animal, along with a second NYPD officer. When the time is right, they're going to box Frankel in. "Copy."

Animal rechecks the street. He sees only headlights shimmering on the Brooklyn Bridge a few miles away. It's late and it's too cold to linger on the sidewalk; no pedestrians, which translates into witnesses. A trap door will soon open under Frankel's feet. The black hole waiting for him is deep. Best that no one sees him tumble inside.

Herbert keys the Crown Vic and hacks the steering wheel until it bottoms out. Quick U-turn in the making. Before he can hit the gas, an expensive black Audi turns onto the street and speeds past the Crown Vic. "Got an issue."

"They're gonna block our approach," Animal replies as he twists in the passenger seat to get a better visual. He finds a bigger problem than he expected. The Audi honks and stops next to Frankel, who approaches the vehicle. A conversation begins.

Animal remains cool. The function of a decade's worth of combat experience. Holding the radio up, he says, "All units, hold. Let's ride this out."

"Got it. Head count incoming," Gray replies. After a pause he adds, "Suspect vehicle has three occupants. All males."

Animal continues observing the conversation. It's casual. Friendly. Frankel knows the men in the vehicle. He's comfortable, and they're goading him into the Audi's warm cabin. "Just tell them another night . . ."

One man exits the Audi's rear passenger door. He's large, wearing a blue Adidas track suit. He gives Frankel a bear hug, then shoves a silver flask into his hand. After a quick nip, Frankel follows him into the Audi.

It's Animal's call, and he needs to make it quickly. If he lets Frankel leave, he may never see him again. Tangling with three potentially armed men isn't appealing either—but only in the career sense. New York has laws against gun violence, after all.

Animal lets his mind shift from a potential letter of reprimand back to Mexico City. To the blood that was spilled. Just like what comes next, and as a soldier, he's fine with that. "All units, go on Frankel. Do not let him off the block."

Animal activates his cruiser's siren. Herbert jerks the Crown Vic out of the spot and nails the accelerator. As he careens toward the Audi's rear end, Coco and Gray do the same from the front. The Audi's driver cuts his wheel, attempts to squeeze between two parked cars and jump the curb, but it's too tight.

"That's right! Keep resisting!" Animal says as he drops an NYPD detective's badge over his Kevlar vest and draws his pistol from under his hoodie. His weapon is a Staccato P 2011 chambered in nine-millimeter. Not quite standard issue with a Trijicon red dot sight and a threaded barrel, but it's suited for the task ahead.

"Jerkoffs always do," Herbert replies. He brakes late. Lets the Crown Vic's bully bar crease the Audi's rear bumper. Locked in.

"Driver! Put the vehicle in park and turn off the engine!" Animal shouts as he exits the car and takes cover behind the door. The call echoes several more times as his team surrounds the vehicle. Blinding lights cut through the tint, and silhouettes are shifting. He drops his RMR's red dot on a silhouette in the back window.

Everything happens out of order. The Audi's four doors boom open, and the occupants step out. The vehicle's engine continues to run, and it's still in drive. When the driver's foot separates from the brake pedal, the Audi smacks against Coco and Gray's Crown Vic.

Frankel bounds into the oncoming traffic lane, which is blocked, and sprints up the street. Animal should be chasing him or radioing his direction of travel, but there's no time. All three of Frankel's friends are armed. One of them, wearing a track suit, has exited the rear passenger side with a pistol pointed in Animal's direction.

"Drop your weapons! Now!"

Time slows. Snowflakes hang in the red dot's glass aperture. Slack disappears from the 2011's trigger, and an orange fireball chases the snowflakes away. A bullet strikes Track Suit's chest. Then another. Then another. The Glock in Track Suit's hand discharges as he falls, striking the Crown Vic's headlight.

Gunsmoke and bloody mist hang in the air. Three men are bleeding, dying on the street, but Animal is unfazed. He's not here for them. He runs after Frankel, just in time to see him disappear into an alleyway. "Frankel is heading east on foot. I'm in pursuit!" Animal shouts into his radio.

———

Jen peeks into the upcoming alley, expecting to find Frankel. When she handed him off, she kept moving in his expected direction of travel, and it looks like her foresight will pay off. Making use of the spare time, she exposes an NYPD detective's badge from under her leather jacket and draws a Staccato P of her own.

Frankel stumbles out of the intersecting alleyway, struggling to get his bearings. Looking for a place to run, hide—anything to get clear.

Jen shouts, "Liev Frankel! NYPD! Get down on the ground, now!"

Uninterested in following instructions, Frankel looks in the direction opposite Jen. Al Hastings is standing at the far end of the alley. Another box. Without options, he sprints for a nearby apartment building and tries the back door. Someone left it unlocked, and he disappears inside.

Jen signals Hastings ahead. If Frankel emerges from the building's front door, he needs to catch it.

She runs down the alley, zigzagging past piles of trash, litter, and icy puddles. She arrives at the back door and enters. The interior is familiar. Black-and-white linoleum checker the floor. Dim lighting, some of which flickers. Tile and moldy grout chase down the hallway. Old Brooklyn.

Jen clears a nearby laundry room before stopping at the entrance to the main hallway. The building's front door has just clicked shut. The sound hangs in the corridor. She listens for footsteps in the stairwell but doesn't hear any. Could have been someone leaving, but Hastings would have called out the movement.

Frankel is close. Jen's focus heightens.

Rows of mailboxes, unclaimed packages on top. A moth clinks against the burning light bulb over her head. Weapon raised, she approaches the stairway. She scans between slats in the banister but doesn't see Frankel. Before she can radio an update, a door pops open under the stairwell. No force behind it, just a latch that failed to catch.

Jen's gut draws her to the door. Only cracked an inch with a slip of black running floor to ceiling. Smells like cleaning supplies and dirty mops. Her muscles tense as she reaches for the knob. Before she can grab it, it crashes open, and steel flashes. Jen has just enough time to raise her arm and block the blade from slashing her face.

Frankel heaves himself out of the janitor's closet, preparing to take another swipe. Jen steps back and angles her Staccato from the hip. As Frankel tries to swing again, she puts a double tap into his abdomen.

Muzzle flashes fill the space between them. Heat sucks oxygen away. Jen's ears ring. She kicks out his knee and, as he sags to the ground, plants her own in his face. The back of his head cracks the tile and splits his scalp. Frankel hits the ground, dazed, as blood traces the moldy grout.

Jen kicks the knife away before kneeling to render aid. Frankel has links to the Founders, and she needs him *alive*. She places her hands over his abdomen, applying pressure to his gunshot wounds. Blood spurts through her fingers, and she realizes that she's bleeding too. Frankel's blade bit through her leather and split her forearm.

The front door swings open and Hastings runs through. "Heard the shots! You good?"

Jen nods, remains focused on Frankel. "Fine, but we've got two GSWs to the abdomen here. I need a hand."

Hastings extracts an emergency medical kit from his pocket and kneels next to Jen. "All right . . . let's keep this guy breathing a little while longer."

Two

Blood drips onto the hardwood floor.

Jen's arm was bandaged by Gray, their medic, but the dressing is already soaked. The shock is wearing off, and pain levels are rising. Only the night's first failed medical intervention. Liev Frankel is dead. Bled out in the lobby before an ambulance could arrive. While he fled the arrest teams, he bricked his cell phone, which the Group is considering a blow to their investigation. But there's an upside.

Warrants to search Frankel's apartment were in the team's possession before the arrest attempt. The search has yielded information about what he may have been doing inside the United States.

For months Jen and her Group have been circling the edges, looking for deeper lines of access to the Founders. They've found one inside this old Brooklyn apartment. The decision to arrest Frankel tonight had been the correct one. His suitcases were packed, airline tickets stuffed inside. This was his last night in the city, and he was bound for St. Petersburg, Russia. A place where he'd have been untouchable.

Jen is standing with Gabriella Martinez and Sloane Hamilton in his living room. The furnishings are spartan. Plastic tables, camping chairs. Tubs of ammonia are empty, their contents spread along the floors and walls—or anything Frankel may have touched. He'd been serious about removing traces of DNA from the scene, and it's an ode to his tradecraft.

Sound traps were also in place on windows—stacks of coins in front of downed shades. A Corona bottle stuffed with metal jacks was placed by the front door. Easy to imagine it resting on the knob when he was sleeping. An intruder would have caused the bottle to fall and break, scattering the jacks. They'd prevent the door from opening easily, if it all.

More of what most would consider paranoia, but in reality it was simple caution.

Martinez is tall and slender, with sleek black hair that matches her suit. Had her life gone a little differently, she'd be on the cover of fashion magazines. She regards the specks of blood on the floor, which Jen has failed to notice, and taps Sloane on the shoulder. "I think she's trying to elicit sympathy."

Sloane has a DSLR camera strapped to her neck. She'll be photographing Frankel's possessions as they conduct a more thorough search. His suitcases are unpacked, contents spread along the floor. Folders full of documents are laid out individually. "Probably just wants more time off," she remarks casually.

"What's next?" Martinez asks. "Going to pop a bunch of aspirin for show?"

Jen runs through her list of smart-ass responses, but none of them seem to fit. Truth be told, she's hurting. Nauseous from shock and blood loss. Disappointed by Frankel's death, though she won't be crawling into a bottle over it. Staying focused on work has always been her way through. "Enjoy this. When I'm stitched up and back to one hundred percent, you're both screwed."

Sloane angles the camera cradled over her chest toward Jen and snaps a photo. The flash startles Jen. "Oops."

"Way to seize the opportunity, Ms. Hamilton," Martinez remarks as the flash bulb's zing fades.

"Yup. Thought she was going to cry for a minute. Had to document it," Sloane replies. She smirks, tosses her wavy brown hair over her shoulder. A Southern girl from Georgia, she's tan, well-mannered, and charming—scratch one or two of those, depending on her mood.

Jen blinks away the stars and laughs. They know her too well. Which buttons to push. How to put a smile on her face. Yes, they're a team, but they're also family. "How about these documents?"

"On it," Sloane snaps.

Martinez is already wearing latex gloves and starts the inspection with Frankel's travel documents. "Passport and airline tickets are falsified. Fake names . . . country of origin."

"That identity is also different from his entry documents," Jen observes. Frankel's first alias was flagged. Had he tried to use it, authorities would have detained him at JFK. Mix a clean passport with a hundred thousand daily travelers, and he'd have had the recipe for a clean exit from the United States. *Enjoy St. Petersburg, Mr. Frankel.*

Martinez glances up at Jen. "He knew he was flagged."

Jen nods. "Would explain why he was so spooked."

"That means handlers. Good ones too," Sloane says, snapping a photograph of the passport book as Martinez holds it open. Same with the airline tickets. "What's in the file marked *Void*?"

Martinez plucks the file off the floor and opens it. Photographs of beautiful women are inside. As she flips through the photos, Sloane snaps one of her own. She stops flipping when they reach a marked image. *Remove* is written in big bold letters over a young woman's body. "Guesses?"

Sloane snaps a photograph before replying. "They're all wearing lingerie. Skimpy clothes. Escorts maybe?"

Jen's brow crunches. "I can buy escorts, but why name the file *Void*? Seems odd . . ."

"Very," Martinez agrees. She pulls the photograph of the young woman out of the stack and sets it aside. "We'll ask Herbert about her. This is his city. If she's a working girl, he might have seen her."

Jen doesn't reply, but she knows what Martinez is thinking. Herbert is with the Major Crimes Division, and if she's dead, he'd have seen the body. The girl is—maybe was—young and pretty. Someone worth crawling into a bottle over. "Two items left."

Martinez assesses a matchbook for the Waldorf Astoria hotel. Nothing of interest written on the flaps. The second item is a business card. All black. *Lust* is written boldly on the front, and a website is printed on the back. That's the Advanced NeuroNet Engine's turf. She extracts her phone, activates the camera, and hovers it over the website. "Anne, pull up this website."

Their quantum computer was waiting for direction. It's linked into their tech, and like an operator on call twenty-four seven, it's always there to help. Anne's voice is feminine but synthetic, and echoes through the cell phone's speaker. "One moment, Ms. Martinez."

Martinez grimaces as Anne's results populate her screen. She turns the phone to face Jen. "Short-lived hopes."

"404 error. The website was taken down." Jen speaks a little louder, allowing Anne to pick up her voice. "Any info on the original host, Anne?"

"No longer active, Ms. Yates."

Jen and Martinez exchange a look. Something is very wrong, and they're not sure what.

"Why do you think he kept the photos?" Sloane asks.

Pervert. Jen's answer doesn't need to be spoken. He had contact with these women. Something work-related—the Founders are into organized crime. Human trafficking and prostitution are cornerstones of that world. Free tastes are part of the job. Photos keep memories fresh long after the work is through. "Any word from Herbert?"

Martinez shakes her head. "We're up to date. The Audi was stolen, and the three dead guys didn't have licenses or IDs. Going to take a little longer to figure out who they were."

"Let's hit the morgue. Check on the autopsies," Jen states. "We need to figure out who Frankel was working with in New York."

Martinez looks at Sloane. "Good here?"

"I'll keep sifting through everything. Let you know what I turn up."

THREE

WEATHER IS FINALLY SETTLING. NO MORE SNOW, AND THE wind has stopped battering Brooklyn's skyline. Jen and Martinez are standing in front of the city morgue. Nerves are eating at them, and they'd rather shiver and smoke than sit in their Suburban. They both sense that they're on to something, and they haven't had that feeling since Peru.

Jen's motto is *people first*. Martinez may be her superior officer, but she's family. One of the first battles after the Peru raid was to save Martinez's career. She made serious errors in Mexico City, and people suffered for it. An Office of Inspector General board was prepared to obliterate her life's work upon returning to the United States.

Retrieving three kidnapped Americans helped wipe her slate clean. Information on the Founders was another crucial factor. Their existence was news to the Agency—an organization shocked both by their cunning and by what they'd been targeting: the Advanced NeuroNet Engine. Those revelations gave them a target—a unified cause to rally around. Martinez was, and still is, the officer at the center of it all. Her experience was too vital to throw away. The OIG board thought it best to leave her career intact, and resettled itself in Langley's shadows.

Anne may have been the target, but Terrance Kline is the Group member who suffered the most. He and two other members of the army's Combat Applications Group, or Delta Force, were abducted in Mexico City. During an escape attempt, he was shot and recaptured. The bullet nearly took his life but stopped short, settling instead for his ability to walk.

His recovery is only just beginning.

Jen has stood shoulder to shoulder with him along his journey. Watching Terrance struggle through surgeries and rehab sessions has been gut-wrenching. Morphine has also been a silent reaper, blotting out his pain in exchange for the spark that made him one of his generation's greatest computer engineers.

Jen has firsthand experience with the damage opiates cause. She'd never turn her back on Terrance, but she senses she may lose a person who she cares for. Losses like these . . . they're worse than any physical injury she has ever sustained, and they never fully heal.

A colossal figure emerges from the mortuary. Detective Sam Herbert. A twenty-year veteran of the New York Police Department, he's a member of the city's Major Crimes Division. These are the detectives that solve the city's most serious crimes. He's also been an instrumental part in the Group's investigation of Frankel.

Langley has a substantial presence in the city. As one of the world's largest melting pots, it's ripe for penetration by criminal and terrorist groups alike. The Agency conducts investigations through men like Detective Herbert. They act as liaisons, or front men, making arrests and fastening handcuffs where Agency intelligence officers cannot.

"You two don't have the sense to come in from the cold?" Herbert asks in his typical gruff tone.

Martinez flicks her cigarette butt away and straightens her overcoat before entering the Suburban purring behind her. "Your mother didn't teach you not to keep ladies waiting?"

"Ladies?" Herbert grunts. "Get what you get when you got me working double shifts."

Jen tosses away her cigarette and steps aside so the detective can enter the Suburban first.

"Fine you for that, ya know?" Herbert scolds.

Jen's brow arches, and she stares him down. "Go get your little ticket book then. I'm not going anywhere."

Herbert chuckles and settles into the warmth. "No news on Frankel, but I've got some serious juice on the three thugs we killed." He pulls out his cell phone and opens a series of photographs. Bodies on mortuary slabs, bullet holes marking vital organs like textbooks. "Recognize the tattoos?"

Martinez takes the phone first. The tattoos are cheap jailhouse-style markings. They're *X*s with dots between the crossed lines. She shakes her head before passing the phone to Jen. "I'm blank."

"Same," Jen replies before passing back the phone.

"They're members of the Lika Syndicate. Albanian organized crime." Herbert tucks the cell back in his jacket. "I'm not exaggerating when I say that they're the city's worst."

Jen's neck tingles. Hits on hits. Alex Varga was the worst Mexico City had to offer, and he was the Founders' pet. They exercised silent control of Alex's cartel and reaped massive profits from it. The Lika Syndicate could be the same in New York. Then the photograph from Frankel's apartment pops into her mind. *Remove.* "The Lika Syndicate run girls?"

Herbert nods. "Girls and a lot of cocaine—which has been notably absent lately."

Martinez gives Jen a slanted grin. Mexico City . . . a lot of cocaine there too. The man who sold it is dead now. Unfortunate result of a late-night meet and greet. "We need specifics here."

"A guy named Sandro Lika runs New York's Albanian crime scene. His nephew, Ceno Lika, is his number two. They're based in the Bronx, but we can't touch 'em."

"Why can't you?" Martinez asks.

"We've come close, but these guys don't play. Italians would intimidate judges, maybe turn one into a headline. The Albanians will whack the guy's entire fucking family. Sit in court and smile at him while he makes arrangements to bury his kids. Nothing, and I mean nothing, sticks to these guys."

Martinez hands a file from the dashboard to Herbert. "You recognize that woman?"

"Remove," Herbert mumbles before nodding. "Jane Doe number . . . x-x-thousand. Major Crimes kicked her to Homicide after we couldn't link her to anything organized. Turned up floating in the East River."

"Recent?" Jen asks.

"Two weeks back. Harbor Patrol got her before the crabs did. Allowed us to get clean pictures."

"We think she was an escort of some type," Jen states.

"We reached the same conclusion. Recent vaginal and anal intercourse. Semen present. But we couldn't link her to an agency or a pimp."

Martinez hands him a small evidence bag.

Herbert studies the business card inside the plastic. "Lust is a known escort service in the city. Very exclusive, invite-only service. Top-dollar girls that serve Wall Street types, politicians . . ."

"We found all of that in Frankel's apartment," Martinez informs.

"The hell did he want with an escort service? Or a dead hooker?" Herbert asks.

"Tell me where the Lika Syndicate operates out of, and we might be able to get you an answer," Martinez says.

A hard smile cracks Herbert's face. He chuckles. "Y'all are the only mob worse than the Albanians. Got an address for a brake shop in the Bronx." He pulls out his phone, punches a name into Google's search bar, and hands it to Martinez. "You can find them there."

"Old Town Brake and Muffler," Martinez says while jotting down the address. "Now's the time to look the other way."

"Was hoping you'd say that," Herbert replies as he steps out of the Suburban. "Just do me a favor . . . no bodies. City's had enough for one night."

Jen winks at Herbert. "We'll take your request into consideration."

FOUR

PORT MORRIS. THE INDUSTRIAL ASS-END OF THE BRONX. OLD
Town Brake and Muffler is a block away from the East River with a
picture-perfect view of Rikers Island—one of the United States' most
notorious prisons. Ironic, given the city's deadliest organized-crime
outfit is headquartered on the prison's doorstep. All they need is a
nudge in the right direction.

Jen is happy to provide that nudge. She approaches the target with
Hastings and Animal at her back. Street clothes like before. She's still
got her black leather. Hastings wears blue jeans with a Vietnam–era field
jacket. Animal in his baggy zip-up hoodie. But they've lost their NYPD
badges in favor of a few extra weapons: saps, brass knuckles, and stilettos. Street tools that leave hard scars. This incursion will be off the
books. In crime-scene photographs, it'll look like common criminals
who took a score. But the methods will be unusual, the culprits obscure,
their motives murky.

They're not the first ones to walk Port Morris's streets with bad
intentions. Parked cars line the curb, windows busted out. Others are
propped up on cinder blocks. Business owners have taken precautions.
Their operations are hidden behind fences. Tall, made of corrugated
metal, stretching from one end of the block to the next.

Jen opens her jacket and extracts a compact drone. Roughly the size of a CD with propellers on its four corners. Without breaking her stride, she holds it casually by her shoulder. "Anne, drone is free to launch. Proceed to our target."

The propellers spin up, and the miniature aircraft zips out of her hand.

Thirty seconds later, Jen's Whisper is buzzing with a message from Anne. "Drone on station, Ms. Yates."

Up the street, Coco and Gray round the opposite corner. They were circling the block, checking for witnesses. Silence over the radios means they didn't find any. She gives them a nod as they close on their target.

At the fence, Jen pulls out her cell. The drone's camera feed is displayed. Old Town Brake and Muffler has a relatively large parking lot, which is doubling as a junkyard. A dozen vehicles are in various states of disrepair. Four garage doors lead to individual service bays. From the outside, it looks like a functioning business.

The lights are out, but that's a red herring. Tire tracks mark the snow. Fresh, from the two vehicles parked by the shop's entrance. She zooms in on the vehicles, starting with a BMW M8. The coupe's body is coated with grime, but the windshield is clean. Defrosters haven't been off for long.

The condition of the black Acura parked next to the BMW is similar.

"Anne, lower the drone." A drop in elevation allows her to evaluate the footprints between the shop's door and the vehicles. Deep impressions. Sharp edges. Fresh, like the tire tracks. Someone is working late tonight.

She catches movement in the corner of the camera frame. Two Rottweilers. They'd been asleep in one of the wrecked cars. They jump out and rush to the center of the parking lot. The buzzing propellers roused them, and they stare up at the drone, growling.

"Return to seventy-five feet, Anne," Jen orders before she stows her phone.

Weighing the raid's risk, she tastes salt in the air. Easy to imagine members of the Lika Syndicate stuffing the dead escort in the trunk of a stolen car. Taking her the short distance to the East River before dumping her body in the water. *Remove.*

Like a beacon, Terrance Kline flashes in her mind. All the touch-and-go nights. Surgery after surgery. Permanent paralysis.

Couldn't have done it without you, Ms. Yates.

Jen won't let this trail go cold. No way. The risk is worth the reward. "Masks."

On cue, they drape balaclavas over their faces.

Jen gives Hastings a nod. "Milk Bones." With a look toward Animal, she says, "Prepare to breach."

"On it, Z." Hastings grabs a plastic bag out of his coat. As he approaches the fence, the dogs lunge at him. They're shivering and their fur is raised. But they relax as he feeds treats through the gaps. "Eat up! Uncle Al's got all the fixin's."

Animal extracts a pair of bolt cutters from under his hoodie and dices the chain. Carefully, he unwinds it from the gate and lowers it gently into the snow—silence is golden. Finished, he eases back the gate.

Wagging tails greet them, and Hastings is flush with Milk Bones. He dumps the entire bag in the snow and falls into position as the team rushes toward the brake shop.

Coco heads straight for the Bimmer. He slips off a glove and rests the back of his hand on the hood, then whispers to Jen, "Still warm."

Something got these guys out of bed. The Brooklyn morgue's newest residents might have something to do with it.

"Let's go hot," Jen orders.

She prepares her weapon while the team does the same. Same Staccato from earlier, only with a suppressor screwed onto the barrel. The red dot sight mounted on the slide is glowing at a high setting. Too bright for the current ambient conditions, but if she uses the weapon, it'll be accompanied by her weapon light, which will drown out the red dot.

The dot is also doped in for use with the suppressor. Oftentimes, muzzle-mounted devices affect a bullet's point of impact. The red dot is set for accurate suppressed fire while the iron sights are aligned for unsuppressed work.

Animal is the last team member to finish his prep. A compact twelve-gauge shotgun is concealed under his hoodie. Slugs in the tube can punch through hardened doors if the need arises. Satisfied that his weapon is ready, he gives Jen the nod.

"Let's keep it quiet," Jen hisses as she kneels in front of the door. Extracting a Lichi lock-picking set, she begins working the tumbler. It's cracked within thirty seconds. Hastings angles his suppressed pistol as she twists the knob. At her nod, he rushes into the darkness.

FIVE

A BROKEN CELL PHONE BROUGHT SANDRO LIKA INTO HIS brake shop in the middle of the night. The phone was Frankel's, and it wasn't actually broken but bricked—rendered totally useless by a specialized program that turned its CPU into a hunk of silicon and metal.

Frankel didn't get a message off before he bricked the phone, but he would have only done it for one reason: imminent danger. That three of Sandro's best soldiers are missing only adds to his anxiety.

Sandro barges into the strong room with two armed men at his back. The space is fireproof, and there's no ventilation. The heavy steel door has multiple deadbolts, chains, and lock bars across it. He beelines toward the giant steel safe in the corner.

The dial clicks like a machine gun as he turns it. His gold chains and matching Rolex flash. He is in his mid-sixties, and his laborer's frame is covered in a silk shirt, which matches his gold-rimmed glasses. On the final digit, he twists the wheel and the vault door swings open.

Close to half a million dollars cash is stacked on the top shelf. The neatly bound hundreds are quickly transferred to a duffel bag.

His two men are his relatives, relatively. Both men are distant family from the old country, Albania. But family is family, and it's the corner-stone of his criminal enterprise.

Sandro hands off the cash. The man who takes it switches a MAC-10 machine pistol to his weak hand and clutches the satchel. "Go straight to the lawyer's office," Sandro orders. "Put it directly in his hands *only*."

The armed man nods. He is honored to be trusted with this much cash.

Sandro tells the second man, "Rexhep, see him to his car and watch the door."

"All right, Sandro."

As they leave, Sandro activates two paper shredders. Unloading stacks of documents from the safe, he thumps them on the desk.

These documents are the reason he came here tonight. They were an insurance policy of sorts. Now he's second-guessing his decision. The shredder eats up the first bushel and asks for seconds. Sandro Lika is in an obliging mood, and he feeds in another batch.

———

The service area of the brake shop is far from low-rent. In the spare light, Jen makes out Ferraris and Lamborghinis and Porsches. They're parked in service bays, which are surrounded by boxes of tools and equipment. Some are elevated on lifts. A nearby Jaguar has half its body stripped away.

Chop shop. Another hallmark of organized crime.

Jen leads her team into a service bay and takes cover behind the rows of toolboxes. She peers through the stripped-down Jaguar's frame. More warehouse space yawns open to the right of her position. She can't detect any movement, but light fills a plastic-sheet-covered door. She points toward the light. "Gray, Coco."

Before the two operators can move out, they hear voices. They drop back into cover and the team waits for the threat to emerge. Before long, two large and well-armed men emerge from a hallway to the left. They stroll through the shop, familiar with their surroundings.

Jen signals the team. About to get "hands on," the team makes silent kit adjustments. Their targets are armed and will be hostile, but they're still operating on U.S. soil. These men could be citizens. Zipping nine-millimeter bullets through their unsuspecting heads is beyond the pale unless the goons shoot first.

The targets pass the service bays, unaware of what they're walking into. When their backs are exposed, the team members pounce.

Animal wraps his arms around the neck of the first man. The choke-hold locks in, and he gets perfect elbow placement in front of the target's Adam's apple. The angle cinches both of the target's carotid arteries and he fades rapidly.

Jen and Hastings work in unison to neutralize the second man. Hastings rushes first and delivers a kick to the back of the target's knee. In the same motion, he latches onto his leather jacket and thrusts him to the ground.

Jen's sap is waiting. Twelve spring-loaded ounces of "the best sleep you ever had" connects with the side of the target's head. The sap's leather doesn't act like a cushion—it only protects her hand from the seismic shock of the impact. Police officers were banned from carrying saps decades ago, and as Jen's target slaps against the floor, she understands why.

That's *first contact*, and it generated a few decibels. It's time to move, and quickly.

"Gray, Coco! Clear the right side of the warehouse," Jen whispers. She turns to Hastings and Animal, who have just finished zip-tying and stashing the two unconscious men in the shadows. "On me."

Jen leads her element toward the hallway from which the two men emerged. She peeks around the corner. An armed man is standing in front of a door, an ear cocked in her direction. Sandro Lika, recognizable from photographs, is fully alert.

"Weapon!" Jen shouts as she dives back into cover and presses her back into the wall.

Sandro raises his MAC-10 and lights into Jen's position. A dozen .45 caliber slugs rake the cinder-block wall. Each impact pulses through her back. When the shooting stops, she angles her pistol around the corner. Smoke is curling around Sandro's position as he runs for a nearby room. She takes a shot at him but it misses.

"Press!" Jen shouts.

"Moving!" Hastings races forward along the hallway's far wall. He presses the Staccato's trigger, making use of the twenty-one-round magazine as he closes in. Rounds snap against the metal door and launch cinder-block dust in the air. They reach the door and stack up along the wall as deadbolts shoot into place.

Jen nods to Animal. "Do it."

The twelve gauge comes out and the safety clicks off. Animal rests the muzzle against a deadbolt that's yet to fall. Someone's night is about to get much worse.

———

Sandro keeps his weight against the door as he works the strong room's locks. Bolts shoot, sealing him in. He's cornered, but getting out won't be as difficult as it appears. At worst, he'll only have to wait several hours until the shop opens. Meantime, he'll destroy documents, certain that the people trying to kill him won't be able to stop him until he's finished.

Metal shears open and sparks explode out of a deadbolt. The shotgun blast obliterates Sandro's hand. He steps back, raises the shredded appendage in front of his face. There's no pain. Just shock and confusion, which leaves him paralyzed in front of the door. Successive blasts cut through the door's remaining locks. One. Two. Three.

Sandro's silk shirt sucks up the orange sparks, metal, shrapnel, and whatever is left of the one-ounce shotgun slugs careening toward him.

A boot lands against the door with enough force to rock the entire building. It punches Sandro back, and he topples onto the desk behind him.

Blinding white light follows the impact.

A few seconds tick by. Sandro remembers where he is, what he must do. He angles his machine pistol toward a white light as it draws nearer, but he doesn't have time to get a shot off before he's introduced to eternal darkness.

———

Jen sidesteps into a corner, pistol raised. Smoke is curling out of her suppressor. She uses her weapon-mounted light to search the space for remaining threats, but it's clear. One down, hard. Sandro Lika—and he's a high-value individual.

With the space clear, her focus shifts to what was transpiring in the room. A shredder is running, with photographs and documents piled nearby. She took a risk bringing her team into this building tonight, and those documents may well be the reward.

Hastings approaches Sandro Lika, his 2011 leveled at the mafioso's head. Dead, and a safety shot isn't warranted. Instead, he removes the MAC-10 from Sandro's hand, drops the magazine, and eases the bolt forward. Passing Animal, he says, "We need to clear the remaining office spaces."

Jen's mind clicks back into conflict mode as the two operators retreat to the hallway. "Three, you good?"

Coco's reply vibrates Jen's Whisper. "Good, Z. Got something you'll need to see though."

"Solid copy," Jen replies. "TOC, any gunfire reported on my POS?"

Martinez responds from the Agency's Manhattan field office. "Nine-one-one's lines are buzzing, but not for you, Zero. Give me an update."

Jen takes a breath, allows her adrenaline to subside. Another body, and she hates to have made Detective Herbert an empty promise. "One hostile down; two in cuffs. I'm preparing to conduct sensitive site exploitation. Stand by for a potential intel dump."

Six

Sandro Lika wanted to shred documents, and Jen is planning to oblige him—only after she photographs every one of them. She hasn't left the brake shop's strong room since entering ninety minutes ago. What she's found has been revelatory, borderline shocking.

Frankel and the Lika Syndicate were conducting surveillance on an important individual: Tony Mitchell, Chairman of the Federal Communications Commission. Telecommunication and internet service providers purchase bandwidth from the FCC, along with their operating licenses. Mitchell oversees it all, which is why he was targeted.

It appears Mitchell was a gatekeeper to what the Lika Syndicate—and the company who employed them—was after. Surveillance was conducted on behalf of a company called Gombe Wireless, an upstart internet service provider based in the Democratic Republic of the Congo, attempting to procure a license to operate in New York City.

Gombe's first attempt at gaining a license in the nation's capital, Washington, D.C., ended with rejection. Fearing another round of failure, they asked the Lika Syndicate to step in. With the help of Liev Frankel, they sniffed out Mitchell's weakness and exploited it.

Like many men, Mitchell has a soft spot for beautiful women. They uncovered his travel itineraries and, during his visits to New York, planted escorts at places he'd frequent. Restaurants. Hotel bars. Night-clubs. They were Lust's—and the Lika Syndicate's—most beautiful women. Before long, Mitchell swallowed the bait.

An escort enticed him into her hotel room at the Waldorf Astoria—only the room was a sophisticated surveillance post. Married men are easy to exploit, and Frankel obtained graphic images, video, and audio of the high-ranking official's infidelity. Even so, the Lika Syndicate didn't consider the leverage strong enough.

Jane Doe was the woman Mitchell fell for. *Remove.* Found floating in the East River by New York's Harbor Patrol. Infidelity is wrong, but links to a murder victim are a different set of problems. The Lika Syndicate killed the escort less than twenty-four hours after her rendezvous with Mitchell. The semen found in her body no doubt belongs to Mitchell, permanently tying him to her corpse.

Did you kill her to cover up the affair, Mr. Mitchell?

Natural question. Type that men like Detective Herbert specialize in. Also the type of interrogation a square like Tony Mitchell would do anything to avoid.

Despite how callous these documents are, they're advancing her understanding of what's happening in New York City. Already, her focus is shifting away from the Lika Syndicate to Gombe Wireless.

Victor Orlov was in Mexico City to study Anne's capabilities, and if the Founders have made the leap to quantum computing power, an internet service provider like Gombe Wireless would go a long way to flexing that muscle. They would have access to the internet through what is called the "backbone," the internet trunk lines that traverse the entire planet.

Access on that level would give them the ability to send and receive information with an unparalleled level of security—like the cellular network Alex Varga was using in Mexico City, but on a global scale. Alex's cellular network shielded his entire cartel, allowing him to operate in the digital shadows. Tools like that kept Varga safe for a long time. But those are just defensive capabilities; it's the offensive ones that make Jen nervous.

The thought only adds to the urgency she's feeling. The brake shop opens in two hours, and they'll show up early to prep for work. She needs to finish and return to the Agency's field office to begin a deeper analysis into Gombe Wireless.

She pulls her latex gloves tighter and makes a last sweep of the documents. This opportunity will not come again. Certain that she's taken photographs of everything, she feeds the documents into the shredders.

As the blades gobble up the Lika's dirty laundry, she cleanses the space of her presence. Strands of stray blonde hair are picked up, along with anything else linking her one-hundred-ten-pound frame to the crime scene. Her bullet killed Sandro, and she uses her stiletto to pluck it out of the brick wall behind the desk. The corresponding shell casing is also in her pocket.

One more thing before she goes: car keys. Three sets are available, and she takes all of them. Sandro Lika already bagged up a nice pile of cash, and it's waiting in the service area.

Hastings is headed in her direction as she exits the safe room. Compared to the other retired CAG operators, he's the smallest. But he makes up for his size with an ample supply of attitude. He keeps his wavy red hair slicked back, and his wild blue eyes convey his intensity. He flashes two CDs, each in protective cases. "Surveillance footage from the past two weeks."

Jen nods. Her plan is forming up.

Coco appears several seconds later, several cans of spray paint in hand. When he retired from the Unit and joined up with Jen, he brought two capabilities: sniper and pretty boy. Women may be his forte, but he's uncompromising behind a rifle. Coco holds up the two cans, red and black. "Wanted to make sure you were finished before I started."

Jen peels back her sleeve and taps her Submariner. "We don't need a Rembrandt. Keep the timeline tight."

Coco gives his rattle cans a shake. "Got it, Z."

Jen and Hastings hurry to the service area. Exotic cars have been lowered on their lifts, and their trunks are open. She peers inside a trunk and finds it stuffed with home-made weapons. UZIs or MAC machine pistols. Just stamp metal with bolts and triggers sandwiched inside. Kits to manufacture them are available on the internet. Most are composed of old Israeli parts, waiting for a shop like this to fuse them back together. Two hundred bucks and some know-how can build a modern-day bullet hose.

"What's the count?" Jen asks, awestruck by the sight.

Animal drops a box into the back seat of the Ferrari. "Twenty-eight weapons. All full auto. They were making suppressors too." The giant stands six foot five. Tattoo sleeves roll down his arms; one of which was badly burned in Mexico City, leaving the tattoo wavy and disfigured. His black hair is short and parted. He uses his hands like crowbars, prying open a box full of weapon kits. "Weren't finished either."

Gray, the Group's medic, is a Californian. Tanned skin. Laid-back demeanor. Equally at home on a beach as behind a rifle. He points at a line of green ammo cans in the car's footwell. "Stocked for the zombie apocalypse."

"Photos?" Jen asks.

"Tons," Animal states.

Jen looks in the strong room's direction. "Hey, Rembrandt! You done in there? We're waiting on you."

"Coming now, Z," Coco says over the Whisper. Several moments pass, and he comes trotting out from the hallway, a satisfied grin on his face. "Who's driving what?"

Jen tosses him the keys to a Porsche. Hastings lucks out with the Lambo. She saves the Ferrari for herself. "Beer's on the first guy that blows a clutch."

They laugh as they open the service bay doors. Neighborhoods from here to Manhattan are about to get early wake-up calls. As the gates rise, the two Rottweilers come rumbling in, bodies shivering from the cold.

Jen doesn't have the heart to let the dogs suffer through another night. She unlocks the Ferrari and invites the dogs into the passenger seat. They climb in, enthusiastic, crowding the space. "What's a little Italian leather between friends?"

She drops into the driver's seat and presses the ignition button. The twelve-cylinder engine purrs, and she flicks on the heat, giving the dogs some respite. "Hey, back seat."

The two Rottweilers jump into position, eager to obey their new owner. She puts the luxury vehicle in drive and eases out of the bay. All told, the team is driving away with close to a million dollars' worth of cars. The cash is a bonus, along with the weapons. When members of the Lika Syndicate arrive, they'll reach a single conclusion: robbery.

As far as false flags are concerned, it's imperfect. But it will take the Likas—and the organization handling them—time to untangle. That narrow window will be all it takes for Jen's Technical Access Group to exploit what they learned from Sandro Lika's documents.

SEVEN

SNOW ACCENTS THEIR HEADSTONES PERFECTLY.

Daniil Ionov stands in front of two granite headstones in one of Russia's largest military cemeteries. The ground is frigid under a blanket of gray clouds. Winds howl as they sweep through gravestones and mausoleums dating back to the 1940s.

Sixty. Just a number loosely associated with Daniil's age. Throughout the nineteen-nineties, his peers used vodka to experiment with cirrhosis. Daniil remained sober—at least by a Russian's standard. With a clear mind and healthy body, he propelled himself to the top of the nation's military leadership.

His princely frame is light and agile, and as he kneels in front of a headstone, he's in complete control. He rests a bouquet of roses onto Elizabet Ovechkin's headstone. Ladies first. When the flowers are properly settled, he places a second bouquet over her twin brother's headstone, Nikolai.

Death. Could there be a more potent symbol of change?

Mourning death has always been easy for Colonel General Ionov. As the commanding officer of the Main Directorate of the General Staff of the Armed Forces of the Russian Federation—known as GRU—he's experienced tremendous amounts of it. Death is meaningless to him now, but he knows that something inside him is rotten, just like the bodies under his polished shoes.

Unlike death, he's always struggled with change. After watching the Soviet Union crumble, he associated change with chaos—a harbinger for terror, suffering, and poverty. The fall of the Berlin Wall, which he witnessed as a young KGB officer, horrified him. Only a few years later, when the Soviet Union collapsed, that same level of desperation visited his home in St. Petersburg. That's when he made a vow: *My beloved Russia will never return to that place.*

But that vow will soon be broken.

Just like the Soviet Union of the nineties, the Federation of Russia is about to endure drastic change. Decades separate those two chapters in history, but they'll both be described in similar terms: folly.

Daniil recently left the Kremlin. Listened as the military's top brass discussed their plans for war with the president. Invasion. Victory, which was considered inevitable. Sweetened with memories of the Soviet Union's glory days. When he saw the confidence glinting in their eyes, he recognized them as fools.

Russia's citizens will suffer for these men. And they won't be alone.

Daniil Ionov will pay too. Just like Elizabet and Nikolai did.

With a hand as pale as the snow, he sweeps snow away from Elizabet's headstone to reveal her military commendations. *Hero of the Russian Federation.* Russia's highest honor. Nikolai never reached that level of success, but he was a force, like the frigid wind sweeping through the cemetery. Together, they were unstoppable.

Daniil lowers his head and forms the sign of the cross over his chest. When he's ready, he whispers a prayer for them both.

Straightening to his full height, he adjusts the overcoat covering his dress uniform. Seeing them both has brought back so many memories. Elizabet and Nikolai were two of Russia's most loyal guardians. Murdering them was the challenge of his career, and he's still unsure of how he found the strength to do it.

And the most terrible part? He'll need that strength once more . . .

EIGHT

DOWNTOWN MANHATTAN IS HOME TO LANGLEY'S NEW YORK field office. It's one of the Agency's busiest intelligence hubs, in stark contrast to what many would consider the CIA's core objective: foreign intelligence gathering. Yet terror has a way of creeping onto sacred ground, and it's a last line of defense against hardened jihadis and malign governments seeking to harm the United States.

Martinez is standing in a below-ground detention center, observing an interrogation from behind a two-way mirror. Sam Herbert is taking on one of the Albanian mafia members arrested earlier in the night.

Half a dozen cameras are pointed toward the mobster, who holds an icepack over the knot Jen stamped on his head. Medical treatment has been provided, including pills for nausea. The cameras observe the blood flow to his face and pupillary responses. Microphones are used to detect unusual vocal intonations, which are another powerful indicator of deceit. Despite the technology, the interrogation is going nowhere.

"Take a look around," Herbert states as he extends his arm to show off the lavish interrogation suite. "You aren't in the Bronx anymore. You might not even be in the United States . . . Only one chance to get this right."

The mobster's eyes are stone. He adjusts the icepack on his head with his free hand and replies, "Phone call."

Martinez chuckles. There will be no phone call. Unique laws are in place for situations like these. The mobster was detained during an active intelligence operation. Jen's discovery may be connected to an ongoing national security threat. This individual will not be permitted to contact anyone outside this building, period. Only when the investigation is concluded will he be allowed to call his family members—or warn elements of his criminal organization.

"Phones here are broken," Herbert replies, a shit-eating grin across his face. In a deep, dark recess of his soul, he enjoys these moments with the CIA—an organization where the rules have a little more flex. Typically, criminals abuse the system. When the Agency is involved, the system abuses criminals.

"My lawyer won't like that," the Albanian says as he tosses the icepack on the table.

"Must not need that anymore," Herbert says as he swipes the pack away. It skitters along the floor, and the Albanian lets out a sigh. Sam opens a file on the desk. The escort. *Remove.* "You recognize this woman?"

The Albanian leans forward. Doesn't flinch at the grisly image. In fact, he smirks toward Detective Herbert. "No."

Herbert can't hide his disgust at the Albanian's obvious lack of remorse. He was involved, somehow. May not have pulled the trigger, but he knows the man who did, and why. Another photograph. This one of the file marked *Void*. "Tell me about this. What's Void?"

The mobster's jovial attitude vanishes. Struck a nerve. "Lawyer."

Herbert extracts a business card from his pocket, taken from the Albanian's wallet. He holds it up for the Albanian to read. "This your lawyer?"

"That's my lawyer."

Herbert rips the card in two. "Not anymore."

The Albanian leans forward and spits in Herbert's face. What he says next is in his native tongue. Martinez reads the translation on a nearby computer monitor and considers the slur unworthy of repeating.

Herbert stands up and wipes the spit off his face. Before he exits the room, he says, "You fucked up."

"This isn't the Ritz-Carlton," Martinez says, and a nearby CIA psychologist gets to work. The interrogation room has independent temperature and lighting controls. Thermostat adjustments are made. Eighty-five degrees Fahrenheit, the legal limit. Soon the interrogation suite will be a sauna. Martinez's mobster will get more than cozy in his heavy leather jacket. Excess light will worsen his migraine.

Detective Herbert storms into the observation room, fighting mad. He's still wiping saliva off his face with a handkerchief, which he tosses in the trash. "To think I was pissed your people dumped another body in my backyard."

"Won't make it to a homicide detective's desk. Sandro's people will handle it," Martinez replies.

Herbert looks through the two-way. Sweat is already dripping down the giant's cheeks. He smirks. "Got real funny when I mentioned Void."

"I noticed," Martinez agrees. "Man couldn't care less about catching a murder charge, but there would be consequences for letting that secret slip."

"What are we doing about his lawyer?" Herbert asks.

Another specific set of protocols Martinez must follow. The detainee is not a U.S. citizen, but he still has rights. Counsel will be provided. But the officer of the court will be cleared by Langley, possess a top-secret security clearance, and understand how these investigations unfold. The lawyer will notify the mobster of his rights—despite how limited they are—and depart.

Martinez checks her watch, noting how long the Albanian has been in custody. "We'll make a call. Give him twelve hours of chair-apy first. Then take another crack at him."

"Twelve hours in that room in that position? Shoot me."

It's on the edge of legal, but Martinez wants answers. She laughs as the psychologist amps up the lighting. "It's like they say, Detective: truth dies in the darkness."

Nine

Doctors. The smell of antiseptic. Strange machines strewn about the Manhattan Field Office's infirmary. Jen eyes the gash on her arm and regrets it. Going to require seven, maybe eight staples. But the nausea is worse than the needle.

After all the injuries she's endured while serving, most people would think she's developed a tolerance, but the opposite is true. Each new injury brings back memories of the old ones. Excruciating pain, both during the ordeal and after, in recovery. Psychological scar tissue is the toughest of them all, and Jen's struggles are no different from the others who have answered America's call to serve.

Taking a deep breath, she fights past the harsh memories and repeats one of her favorite maxims: *Better me than them*. She wears these scars so that the people she loves won't have to. That's what service means to her and her family—the thing she values most in life.

That thought brings her to another: Terrance. She hasn't heard from him since . . . yesterday. That's too long for a close friend in need. Extracting the cell out of her pocket, she tries him on FaceTime.

Jen is both relieved and a little disappointed when he answers the call. He's in a hospital gown, watching television in the wee hours. The lighting isn't the greatest, nor does the TV help, but he looks ashen. The spark she's used to seeing in his eyes is gone. *Morphine.* If this call wasn't meant to cheer him up, she'd cry.

"Why do I already regret answering?" Terrance groans as he struggles to sit up in bed.

"This is serious, *Terry,*" Jen chides, knowing full well he hates being called Terry. Her spirit sinks again when he doesn't look at the cell phone screen or respond to the insult. Clearly, the television is more important. "Think I've got something big on the horizon."

Terrance sighs. "Yeah . . ."

Jen notes his disappointment. He's not out chasing action with his Group, and even though she's trying to clue him in, he'd rather count himself out than be reminded. She decides not to push. "Got any personal projects you're coding up?"

"It's late, Jen. And I already mentioned my regret at the start of the call."

"I got a new *dag,*" she says and forwards him a photograph she snapped of Bullwinkle, one of the Rottweilers from the brake shop. "You like *dags*?"

Terrance rolls his eyes and looks at the phone. "That thing looks disgusting. Clearly, you didn't wash it before you brought it into the office."

"How dare you insult him."

"How dare you," Terrance jabs, making hard eye contact with Jen. "First off, *Snatch* is a modern art masterpiece. Second, your hillbilly accent is butchering the line."

"Hogwash."

"Dawgs-uh," he says in a ridiculous, overextended drawl.

Jen laughs hard, and Terrance joins in. When he stops, recognition lights in his eyes; her call worked as planned.

"Your five minutes is up."

"Whatever, *Terry.*"

"*Terrance.* Get it right, for once."

Jen's hand rushes for the screen, hanging up on him before he gets the chance. It's not a second too soon; there's a knock on the door, and the Agency doctor swoops in.

"Ms. Yates . . . Back again, and so soon."

Jen grunts and tosses her phone onto the table. "Let's just get this over with."

TEN

JEN'S OFFICE ON THE THIRTY-SECOND FLOOR HAS VIEWS FOR
days, and she's taking a personal moment to enjoy them. The office is
dark, silent. Gives her time to rest after a long night—and some one-on-
one time with the doctor.

Once she was patched up, she floated out of the infirmary on a
cloud of painkillers and returned to Rocky and Bullwinkle. Names she's
given the Rottweilers from the brake shop, her new pets. Rocky is the
serious one. He's not interested in sitting on the couch with Jen;
instead, he sits between her and the door, guarding. Bullwinkle is the
goober sprawled across her lap on the sofa, enjoying the type of affection
he hasn't been shown much of in life.

Both of the animals relax her, along with the city lights. Another
one of her favorite crutches is set on the glass coffee table—Tennessee
whiskey, and she's drinking it neat.

Beginning to feel rejuvenated, she snatches a file from underneath
Bullwinkle, who kept it warm for her. He licks her face, which has more
than its share of scars. But they add a unique layer to her beauty and
accent her ruggedness—a trait she's got in spades.

The file is a refresher course on a battle that America's intelligence
services waged inside the continental United States. Their opponent was

China's vast network of telecommunication and internet service providers, which had locations stateside. While they soaked money from U.S. citizens, they used their position to conduct espionage operations inside of the country.

China's efforts centered on a hacking technique called BGP hijacking. Border Gateway Protocol—or BGP—controls how internet traffic flows. There's a U.S. Postal Service analogy, coined by Professor Yuval Shavitt, that illuminates how the process works.

If a person in New York wants to send a letter to a recipient in California, it passes through multiple hubs before reaching its final destination. Internet traffic operates the same way. Data travels through various servers before reaching its intended recipient. Those servers forward internet traffic by choosing the next closest system, which increases transfer speeds.

Unlike the postal service, different entities control servers along a piece of data's path. In the United States, Verizon and AT&T are the top dogs, and they forward a tremendous amount of internet traffic via their servers located across the country. But other companies, like China's, are also part of that network.

The internet was designed for efficiency, not security. Before an internet service provider forwards a piece of data, it consults a routing table. These tables are like digital address books, telling servers where their nearest neighbors are located. When the next nearest server is found, the data is forwarded.

But routing tables can be manipulated—and this is where Border Gateway Protocol hijacking comes in. The internet's address books can be changed, making servers appear closer than they are.

When China Telecom, the CCP's largest telecommunication provider, began altering routing tables, thus performing BGP hijacks, it signaled that its internet servers were in close proximity to vital interests in the United States. Those vital interests began *forwarding* digital intelligence to America's greatest adversary. Reams of data were intercepted and stored in China's servers before being forwarded to the intended recipients.

The result was devastating, and it became a cornerstone of China's industrial espionage campaign against Western corporations.

It was this scenario that had Jen concerned in Sandro Lika's strong room. With an internet service provider like Gombe Wireless, the Founders could conduct these attacks in the United States. With one pivotal difference: this new enemy has likely made the quantum leap, and there's no way to predict the damage such a powerful computer could cause.

Finished reading, she slaps the file shut and consults her Submariner. Thirty minutes in the office is going to turn into an hour if she doesn't get moving. The Group is conducting an analysis of Gombe Wireless, and she needs to get herself into the mix.

Eleven

Jen keys into the Sensitive Compartmented Information Facility behind Martinez. Sloane Hamilton and Andrew Xiao are working on overdrive, along with a dozen other analysts. The energy in the room is frenetic, and that can only mean one thing: progress.

Andrew is wearing his worry. Brows about as thick as his glasses are squeezed down into the frames. Every few seconds his beard seems to turn a little grayer. He folds his arms over his chest and tells Martinez, "Something is happening in London. We need to start waking people up."

"Hold tight. I want a full picture," Martinez responds. The alarm clock Andrew would use for that task is a complex one, involving top-level executives from the CIA, NSA, and their counterparts in London. These men value what little sleep they get, and if she's going to rouse them, she needs to be damn sure about the decision. She looks at Sloane. "Ms. Hamilton, that starts with you."

Sloane gives one of her analysts a nod. Their findings appear on the room's center screen, which occupies an entire wall. Information on Gombe Wireless is laid out. "They've established a very, *very* clean corporate structure, ma'am. We've completed background investigations on the company's C-suite, and they're all legitimate businessmen."

"Show me the key personalities," Martinez orders.

Sloane enlarges several photographs on the center screen. They were taken off of LinkedIn, one of the open sources they've been using to gather intelligence. Others are from motor vehicle databases and law enforcement channels. "The CEO is Matthew Erickson. South African national, just like the chief technology officer, Raymond Bligh. They've been working together for close to two decades, and they've got a track record of successful tech-related startups."

"How are we doing with Gombe's employees?" Martinez asks. "Any links to Victor Orlov? Or the woman we're assuming is his twin sister?"

"No, ma'am. All told, they've got around five thousand employees globally, and we're still scratching the surface there."

Jen crosses her arms and sighs. *We're way behind on this.* "Is the corporate headquarters in Kinshasa legitimate?"

"Global Connectivity, Local Sustainability," Sloane replies with a chuckle. "The company's tagline. Taken at their word, they've run around fifteen hundred kilometers of fiber-optic cable through the Democratic Republic of the Congo. They appear serious about connecting the country to the outside world."

Jen doesn't doubt the claim. The Founders had functioning networks in Peru and Mexico City. The world turned a blind eye to Africa decades ago, and it's possible the Founders crept in and used the neglect to their advantage.

She thinks back to the pile of shredded documents she first uncovered in Sandro's strong room. It's worth assuming that he started with the most important evidence first, and to her, that can only mean one thing. "Has there been any contact between Tony Mitchell at the FCC and executives from Gombe Wireless?"

"Everything has been strictly professional, ma'am," Sloane states. "And as of right now, we don't have reason to believe that the Lika Syndicate made contact with Mitchell either."

Martinez looks at Jen, eyebrow raised. "They may not have pushed that button yet. Jane Doe only turned up a couple of weeks ago."

Sloane nods. "Their first attempt at gaining a license in Washington,

D.C., was a rubber stamp denial—too close to U.S. government interests. Had they applied in New York first, they may have already been operational. I think they panicked and overreacted."

"Sloane?"

She looks at Andrew, gives him the nod. "You've got good timing. Pick it up."

Andrew clears the C-Suite bios from the center screen and replaces it with a global map. Key cities across Europe and Asia have orbs nestled in or around their capitals. "Gombe Wireless already has functional points of presence in Frankfurt and Paris. Singapore is another location that I'm currently concerned about, given its proximity to Japan."

Another glass of whiskey would be nice right about now, Jen thinks. Gombe's progress can only be described as stellar. Points of presence, or PoPs, house the servers internet service providers use to supply customers with internet access. Gombe is establishing a global footprint, and until now, nothing has slowed it down.

"Have these presences been linked to any BGP hijacking attempts?" Jen asks.

Andrew purses his lips. He punches several keys at his computer station, brings up a log of the internet's routing tables—a virtual map of how internet traffic flows, so long as a person can read it. "In France and Germany, yes. It was in the aftermath of a Russian military exercise on the Ukrainian border. My assumption is that whoever is controlling these PoPs was looking for insight into a potential U.S. response."

"Were these attacks reported to us?" Martinez asks.

"We don't have any communications to that effect, ma'am," Andrew replies. "But we also know the French are lax on cyber, and the Germans are stuck on Russian appeasement policies. They may have seen it and decided not to increase tensions."

Jen looks at Martinez. "Both locations are a threat to Europe's security interests."

"But neither rise to the bar of a national security threat to the United States—"

"That's because there's a point missing," Andrew interrupts. "He presses a key, and another orb settles atop the United Kingdom. "Gombe Wireless has gained an operating license in London." He pulls up a webpage that offers sign-up discounts for people who switch to their new service. "They were scheduled to go live one week ago. Technical delays set them back."

Jen's first question typically would have been about the delays. Why were they late? And with what types of equipment? That could have been a way in to their network, but she's stuck on the launch date—the service activates today. When those servers go live, they'll have the ability to compromise a host of assets linked to the British government: MI5 and -6; GCHQ, Britain's equivalent of the NSA; and New Scotland Yard, the country's chief law enforcement agency.

Alone, it would be a catastrophe. But the United Kingdom is a Five Eyes ally. GCHQ is intimately linked to the NSA. Just like MI6 and the CIA. Top-secret intelligence flows between those agencies every day. Within the next several hours, those channels will be compromised.

Andrew hitches his arms to his belt, which is consumed by his stomach. He glares at Martinez and repeats his statement from earlier, this time with more force. "We need to start waking people up."

Martinez has a phone in her hand before Andrew can finish the sentence, but her reply goes to Jen. "Get your team together. I want you standing on the tarmac in Heathrow within twelve hours."

TWELVE

Bronx

Dogs. Morning after morning, they're the first sign to Bajram Lika that the shop is safe. He's standing at the gate to Old Town Brake and Muffler, wondering why the animals aren't nipping at his fingers while he surveys the parking lot. Was freezing cold last night. Weather could have taken them. Wouldn't be the first time. The shop averages four dogs a year. Most die off within months. But the survivors? Well, they seem to linger forever. Whenever one goes, he snatches a stray off the street to replace the one that was lost.

The old Albanian mechanic sighs, thinking of having to carry the frozen carcasses to a dumpster. Arthritis has already gnarled his hands, elbows, and shoulders. Two aspirin a day beats it back. Add some back strain, and it'll be four. That'll mean Pepto for his stomach ulcer.

Bajram fishes keys out of his pocket and searches for the lock. Funny. The chain is missing. That's when it clicks; something is very wrong. Forcing open the gate, he rushes to the front door and finds it unlocked too.

Cars are missing. He rushes to the armory next, finding its secret doorway exposed. By the time he reaches the strong room, a four-alarm fire is raging in his head. Though he is no stranger to violence, finding Sandro Lika's body is shocking for reasons most people would fail to understand.

Bosses like Sandro aren't meant to be killed. They're meant to die in their sleep, or in a cancer ward—anywhere that symbolizes peace. A bullet to the head can only mean one thing: war.

Bajram pulls his cell, dials a few numbers, and expects the emergency line to pick up on the first ring.

———

Seven people missing.

One of them is Ceno Lika's uncle, Sandro. Could be a fluke. Members of the Lika Syndicate enjoy their liquor, their women. Hangovers amongst Ceno's closest friends tend to be severe. But it's not that, and the certainty is in his bones.

If the old country has a tradition, it is the expectation that bad things inevitably come. People don't just learn to accept it; they harden themselves against it. When that bad luck arrives, it usually affects someone it will regret finding. Men like Ceno have not only learned how to make fate regret its decisions, but to change its course entirely.

So, he sits. Patient. Stoic. Sipping an espresso, waiting for his cell phone to ring. When it does, he calmly reaches over, answers. "Yes?"

The caller is frantic. Bajram. The brake shop's manager. A distant cousin, two or three times removed.

"Slow down," Ceno says. "Start from the beginning."

When Bajram finishes his explanation, Ceno nods. "Fifteen minutes."

He hangs up and reflects on what he just heard. His uncle's loss is devastating, personally and professionally. Sandro Lika was . . . everything. Adding up all the gifts Sandro gave to him would cause an error on the calculator.

Men like Sandro leave a big impression, and now Ceno must fill the gap. As of today, he's in control of the Lika Syndicate's New York operations. He's taking charge during what will be a bloody war with whoever harmed his family.

Steam rises from the espresso, and Ceno won't let it go to waste. That would be an insult to his upbringing. Grabbing the cup's miniature handle, he sips it. Slow. Controlled. Processing his emotions like a man from the old country.

He's sitting at a table in his deli, one of his family's many businesses in the area. Doesn't make much money, even with the city's endless foot traffic. But Ceno Lika is an expert at slicing meats. One pound of ham never made more sandwiches. Money laundering made easy. Like the laundromat he owns across the street, which seems to bleed detergent and fabric softener.

Wind whips the snow across the front window. Weather matches the sadness today will bring to him and his family, which has spent generations enduring needless suffering. Sandro was his uncle. One of three brothers who, decades ago, carved out a substantial chunk of the criminal underworld between New York, London, and Albania.

Of the three brothers, Sandro was the least talented. Never got as much attention as the youngest brother. Failed to earn as much respect as the oldest. He was prone to "wearing it," as it is called in the underworld. Silk shirts and exotic cars. Gold Rolexes and women draped in diamonds.

In this, Ceno and his uncle are opposites.

Ceno wears the same outfit almost every day. Pair of crummy blue jeans. If it's hot out, he'll opt for a pair with holes over the knees. A brightly colored windbreaker stolen from a coked-out eighties television commercial. The Nikes on his feet were white once upon a time.

Forty-two, and his muscles still bulge. Gray hair? Ceno's thick, black mane never heard of it. Like his clothing, his hair is unkempt, and his face wears a perpetual five o'clock shadow. Another dirty New York immigrant rubbing pennies together to stay warm in the winter.

Espresso finished, he carries the cup to a nearby sink and rinses it under the faucet. Dries his hands on the way to a back office. An old metal vault takes up one corner.

He unlocks it, grabs a snub-nose .357 magnum revolver, and stuffs it in his pants. Perfect carry pistol for New York. Small enough to hide from the cops, and the magnum round has a reputation for settling disputes.

An old .32 caliber CZ70 sits on the shelf, glistening with a fresh coat of oil. The bluing has faded, but there's not a speck of rust on the pistol. Thirty years have passed since his father died. On that same day this pistol became his, and he became a man, responsible for protecting his family.

Ceno's father was the family's oldest son. Biggest of three brothers. Meanest too. Ceno remembers Sandro walking into the family home in Albania, face heavy and tear streaked. The three brothers had gone out to settle a *gjakmarrja*—a blood vendetta. The law was established by the Kanun, the old country's sacred, governing religious text. Traditions immune to modern law and polite society. Some feuds stretch back hundreds of years and remain unsettled despite endless rounds of losses.

A rival clan had insulted Ceno's family, and the three brothers had gone to settle the score. Ceno's father killed three men with the CZ before succumbing to a gunshot wound. Sandro and Ceno's younger uncle, Isa, made sure there were no survivors.

Sandro had forced the pistol into Ceno's palm and curled his fingers around it. Together they held it, mourned. *The family's survival is in your hands.* Every blood feud that Ceno has entered since that day has been settled with the gun he's holding. It will settle his family's most recent tragedy. Sandro is dead, and New York belongs to him. The Lika family legacy will endure in his hands.

———

Ceno approaches Old Town's gate, and without a word, the enforcer standing guard slides it open, letting the boss inside. Spare chain has already been cut, and the enforcer winds it around the gate, locking them in the razor wire. A body is just feet away. For men like Ceno, law enforcement is too. Getting Sandro back to Europe is a delicate act that could land them all in prison.

Ceno hardly notes the missing cars as he breezes past the service bays. Financial losses are trivial. He only hesitates when he reaches the strong room, but he forces himself to go inside. He'd refused to show emotion today, but seeing Sandro's body forces a tear. So many memories with this man. Loyalty and respect and care. When Ceno's father died, he gained two more in the form of his uncles.

Ceno removes his coat and drapes it over his uncle's body. With a hand on his uncle's chest, he makes a silent vow, committing himself and his family to finding *hakmarrja*—revenge.

With respects paid, Ceno examines the rest of the room. When he notices the bags of shredded paper, his pulse races. He tears open the nearest bag and runs his fingers through the shredded documents. The photos are recognizable, but only because he's seen them before. This is the work they were doing for the zakonny vladelets. The Founders.

He didn't think that his spirit could sink any lower.

Sandro Lika, a man he admired, was keeping records. There would have been only one reason: the documents would have gotten Sandro out of anything, anywhere. Law enforcement, state or federal, would have granted him immunity from even the most severe prosecutions with information like this.

Ceno's mind drifts to days gone by. A hundred conversations about the old country, the strength it gave them. They were men forged in a crucible, and it made them capable of resisting anything, including the United States' most violent prisons. In the end, his uncle was all talk.

Worthless talk.

Ceno is shaking. He runs his thumb along the shreds of paper in his palm. It means so much more . . .

If these documents are discovered, it will destroy his family. Only one other entity Ceno Lika refuses to cross, and it's the zakonny vladelets—a name that still sends tremors through the old country. If they found out, there would be bloodshed, and the family's few remaining survivors would live out their lives in disgrace. It would be the end of the Lika Family bloodline.

Which is why no one will hear of this. To the Lika Family, Sandro was a hero, and his legacy will remain intact. Ceno will bear the weight of this for his uncle, and more.

He rams the shredded documents back into the trash bag and ties it shut. Within the hour, these bags will be ashes. Sooty memories. Drifting amongst their own on New York's polluted horizon.

Cinching the bags in his hands, Ceno stands and prepares to conceal them in the hallway. But the vault in the corner stops him cold. Open. *Empty*. A gut feeling tells him that the safe is still keeping secrets.

There's no way . . .

Ceno pushes past the thought. He'll get to it, in time.

After concealing the bags in the hallway, he returns. He seals the vault and twists the dial. The jacket he draped over Sandro's body isn't removed, but he peels it back to expose his dead uncle's face.

Cell phone in hand, he works the angles. Slugs penetrated the steel door, and his phone's camera lens follows their trajectory to the blood-stained walls beyond Sandro's body. Another shooter stood in the corner. A divot in the brick is decorated with copper jacketing. The killer's position, documented with technical precision.

Ceno's knuckles whiten around the phone as he reviews the photographs. All he needs, but there's one more left. He stands in the doorway. Distance enough for a wide-angle shot. His vision turns red like the spray paint on the wall.

Written in Albanian, the message is a slur against his family. The man who said it, Artur Dibra, also killed his father. Artur is dead. Sandro and Isa Lika saw to that. But the Kanun's laws are immutable, and the blood feud was never fully settled; it only simmered, until today.

The messaging application on his phone uses an encryption standard that's impossible to break. At least, that's what he was told. He attaches the photographs to a message and sends them to his business partners in Russia. Delivery is instant. The zakonny vladelets are now aware of the situation. Ceno leaves the room, eager to start where Sandro finished.

THIRTEEN

ST. PETERSBURG, RUSSIA

THE PHOTOGRAPHS ON ANASTASIA ORLOV'S PHONE ARE disturbing. Direct from the Bronx, they paint Sandro Lika's murder scene in vivid detail. Liev Frankel's phone was also bricked around ten hours ago. After examining New York's 911 call logs, her assessment is that he was gunned down on Brooklyn's streets, along with other members of the Lika Syndicate.

She's been spearheading the surveillance efforts on Tony Mitchell to gain Gombe Wireless's operating license in New York City. Both men were integral to the project, but they played different roles. Frankel was her asset, working directly for the Founders. Sandro Lika was a business partner, much like Alex Varga was in Mexico City.

She paces in her office, which is at the top of a high-rise in downtown St. Petersburg. It's midafternoon, and the sun is warming the snow-covered city. Stellar view, worth admiring, but she drops into her office chair instead. Tension from the past ten hours has settled in her injured shoulder, and it's getting painful.

The injury occurred during her escape from Nogales, Mexico. A high-velocity rifle bullet fragmented before striking the joint and slicing her rotator cuff to ribbons. Parting gift from Alex Varga's foot soldiers, and she was forced to hike across the U.S.–Mexico border with a gunshot wound.

Russia's best orthopedists removed the copper and lead fragments from her shoulder, and they worked with a singular goal in mind: keep the procedure minimally invasive. Scalpels can do just as much damage as a bullet, and Anastasia had every intention of returning to field work.

Results on and off the operating table have been excellent. Physical therapy has helped her achieve a full range of motion, and every day her pain levels are decreasing. It looks like she'll get her wish, but if not, that's okay—the sacrifice is nothing compared to what she gained in Mexico.

While she stretches her shoulder, she inspects Ceno Lika's photographs.

Professionals breached the strong room with a shotgun and finished the job with precision. Took that straight out of a special forces manual, and once the shooters were finished, they went to great lengths to cleanse the crime scene of their presence. Shell casings are missing, and so is the bullet that killed Sandro. Everything they touched has been wiped down.

Graffiti behind Sandro's body is a nice touch, but she discounts it too; spray paint is a weak medium to relay messages. Real mobsters would have carved a love note into Sandro's forehead for his nephew to find.

Anastasia grows certain that Jen Yates pulled the trigger. And if it wasn't her, it was another one of Gabriella Martinez's acolytes. They've got the skill, the motive. More importantly, it's the *safest* assumption.

This is where she counts her blessings. Had either man been arrested, they'd have been interrogated. Once they were deemed high value, they'd have been sent to an Agency black site outside the United States. Under those conditions, they'd have broken.

Trigger-happy Americans killed their only links to her organization in New York. She got lucky, and like any wise bettor, she's going to keep the gift fortune gave her. Jen Yates will remain in the city's relative darkness. Anastasia's work there was only beginning, and it can be jettisoned. But the United Kingdom? That's well underway, and disruptions in London won't be tolerated.

Ping.

Anastasia doesn't need to check the text to know that her time alone in the office is through. She hops out of her seat and checks her appearance. Everything she wears is casual, and today it's blue jeans and a black T-shirt. Simple, but they accent her slender frame. Her hair is a shade of auburn that trends closer to brown than red. Freckles decorate high cheekbones before collecting on the bridge of her nose. Her blue eyes are piercing and, in the right light, nearly translucent. She's got genuine beauty, something that has been both a blessing and a curse throughout her life.

She steps into the hallway and is surrounded by vacant offices. On paper, the office suite is home to a shipping company called Precision Logistics. If a person were to take a tour of the suite, they'd likely wonder if the company was on the verge of bankruptcy. Phones are silent. Computers aren't just off; they're unplugged. Furniture is gone. And if there are desks, they're behind locked doors.

But lights on the cypher locks are glowing. Arriving at a door at the center of the suite's floorspace, she enters the combination and steps into a dead zone—a room between rooms. Just ceiling tile, cheap carpet, and a dozen cameras that capture her body from every angle. The door across from her buzzes automatically.

It leads her into the center of a multibillion-dollar cyber warfare campaign that is gaining traction by the day. There is a large center screen. Three hackers, all subordinate to her, sit behind individual computer stations. From within this cramped little room, she's got access to every one of Gombe Wireless's points of presence. Frankfurt. Paris. Singapore. But that's just a fraction of her capability.

"Leo, give me a status update, please," Anastasia says.

Leo's face appears as a series of blue lines on the center screen. Its voice echoes from speakers planted around the room. "We're still waiting on London, Mrs. Orlov."

Anastasia nods but doesn't reply—the Founders' new quantum computer doesn't need acknowledgement. Leo isn't an acronym but a personality, artfully based on the great Russian novelist Leo Tolstoy.

Alexander Gribov grabs a legal pad from his desk and approaches Anastasia. He was once a member of GRU's cyber weapons arm and was recruited by her personally. It wasn't the pay that lured him into her orbit, but the chance at peeking behind the veil and learning what *truly* drives Russia. "Mrs. Orlov, we've just gotten word from Victor. He's ahead of schedule."

Victor. Her twin brother. Normally, his name forces a smile out of her, but that's not possible after what happened in New York. The Americans are lurking, and she's going to remain vigilant. How could she do anything else with her older brother's safety at stake? "I don't want to keep him waiting much longer, Alex."

Alexander nods, but his spiky blond hair remains still. His personality is upbeat, but he takes his job seriously. High intellect paired with an insatiable curiosity. He's in a challenging job, working to solve complex problems. "We're ready and able to move when London comes online."

Anastasia checks a countdown clock. London. In ten minutes, Gombe Wireless will launch its servers and begin broadcasting its signal to customers across the city. They'll surf the internet and ogle their social media feeds, and she'll gain another powerful foothold in the West. She smiles toward Alex. "It's time to work. Get ready to bring Void online."

FOURTEEN

EVEN BABY STEPS FEEL LIKE MILESTONES FOR HOWARD Hamlin—the identity Victor Orlov is using in London. This old man—with long gray hair and a thick, white goatee—has been living in London long enough that it's starting to feel like a second home. Of course, nothing can compare to St. Petersburg, his actual home, but exploring new cities is always exhilarating.

And Mr. Hamlin's work in London *is* exhilarating.

He's spent two months working on a single project. Decked out in a hazmat suit, he performs a final inspection of an extremely powerful internet server. He's wearing the suit for several reasons. The site is sterile. Fragile circuitry wouldn't respond well to dirt, dust, mildew, or anything else that may be introduced by human activity. He's also concerned about leaving DNA evidence in the workspace.

Half a dozen server racks are organized neatly around him. They're liquid-cooled. Connected with nearly twenty-five miles of fiber-optic cable—spools of which are coiled at Victor's feet, along with tools and a bucket full of trash generated during the installation process.

When he leaves, the site will be airlocked, a feature enabled by dense plexiglass walls and seals. Like the tools he deployed in Mexico City, the internet server is compact and designed to remain concealed. The equipment hidden in this tiny cell is worth tens of millions, and the project it's supporting is worth even more.

Another man in a hazmat suit descends the ladder into the work space. Identical gloves and booties. Heavy white suit. He's a notorious hacker. In the digital ether, he's known as Conscript 19, but Victor knows him as Jonuz Mitrovica. He's a member of the Lika Syndicate, and he'll be monitoring this program once Victor departs London.

Victor has read Conscript's file multiple times. But Conscript only knows Victor by his fake name: Howard Hamlin. Victor's disguise shields him from the authorities and associates alike.

Victor admires his work for what will be the last time. Individual wires connect hundreds of server blades. Each one ends in the proper destination. Perfection. Achieved through months of painstaking labor.

Victor's phone buzzes. A text from Anastasia. The only person with his number.

Nearly there.

Victor replies: *We're in the cleanup process and ready to begin.*

Each of the messages turns to pixelated fragments and scatters across the screen—digital dust storms disappearing into the ether. Leo's part in protecting sensitive communications.

Lessons Jen Yates taught Victor are also operating on the device. While she was hacking him in Mexico City, he was studying her. The phone is using frequency-hopping cell signals that confuse cellular towers and make calls impossible to trace.

Finally, Porosha is in place, acting as a firewall and encryption tool. Only it's upgraded to match Leo's quantum capabilities.

Victor turns to Conscript. The hacker's face is partially visible behind the hazmat suit's helmet. An ethernet cable is snaking up his cheek, and the plug terminates half an inch below his eyeball. "Hop out. Stand by at the liquid pumps."

"Okay." Before leaving, Conscript takes a last look at their work. Once this airlock closes, he won't return for some time. "It's really something."

"It is."

Conscript grabs Victor's tools and a large bag of trash before heading up the ladder.

Another message buzzes Victor's phone. This time he doesn't look at the screen but to a unique router planted in the space. It's flashing green. His servers are now exposed to the internet and functioning as they should. Gombe Wireless's point of presence has just gone live in London, and he's moments away from completing the assignment that brought him to the city.

FIFTEEN

An IP address flashes on Anastasia's center screen. It belongs to a computer in Gombe Wireless's London headquarters. Victor intercepted the computer before it was shipped. He installed a remote-access trojan on the device. Now that trojan is broadcasting its presence to the internet—a signal only Anastasia's team knows how to find.

"Gombe just went live in London," Alexander informs. "And we've detected the ping from our RAT."

Anastasia is standing in the center of the action. Alex has returned to his desk, and three other hackers are working at their own stations. Four people and a quantum computer—the picture of efficiency. She nods. "Let's bring our command-and-control server online."

The team acknowledges the order and launches an obscure website. It's going to serve as a medium. They'll send commands to their remote-access trojan through this website, which is being hosted in another European country, far away from Russia.

She's going to perform an array of criminal acts within Gombe's internal network, and they'll all be executed from this site. If, or when, their website is detected, it can be deleted, severing her team's link to the attacks.

The website becomes available. Its main address is almost one hundred characters, and they're randomized. Gibberish to anyone but the team in this room.

"Let's attempt a first login," Anastasia orders. "Leo, enter our credentials."

"Yes, Mrs. Orlov."

The quantum computer attempts to gain access to Gombe Wireless's computer network via the remote-access trojan.

"Our login attempt was successful," Leo says.

Anastasia nods. The command-and-control server is in place to protect Gombe Wireless as well. In the event British authorities detect the illegal activity in London, they'll think that the crimes were completed outside Gombe's network. How could a legitimate corporate entity be blamed for the actions of a malicious organization half a world away?

Anastasia addresses a hacker sitting at a nearby station. "Ms. Vistin. The next part is yours."

"Yes, Mrs. Orlov," Kamila Vistin replies before she begins the next phase of their operation. She navigates through Gombe's system and generates a new customer account. Fake names. Fake residential addresses. At this point, a technician would be standing by at the customer's home, waiting to help Kamila find the wireless router and sync with it. But in this instance, Victor Orlov is waiting at a remote location, ready to activate a powerful piece of technology. "I'm signaling Victor's router, Mrs. Orlov."

"Just waiting on a handshake," Alexander adds.

Kamila looks back to her superior officer. "We're connected, Mrs. Orlov. Victor's servers are now connected to the internet."

Anastasia nods. "Good work, Ms. Vistin. I want you to encrypt the IP and MAC addresses associated with our new account." She turns to another one of her hackers. Roman Dyatlov. "While Kamila works, I want you to conceal the account. Make sure none of Gombe's employees can stumble onto it."

"On it, ma'am," Roman replies.

Anastasia gives Alexander a smirk. "I'll leave the confirmation to you."

Alexander opens a unique application on his computer. The screen turns black, and a green vial fills with a bubbling, gooey liquid. Ten percent. Fifty. One hundred. The vial overflows and the initialization screen disappears. He turns to Anastasia with a grin. "I think it's time to tell the world Void is online, ma'am."

Sixteen

From the city's tallest vantage point, things seem clearer to Gabriella Martinez.

She came here for several reasons. In a way, this is where her intelligence career began. Like many in her generation, she watched in horror as two Boeing 767s struck the World Trade Center. September 11th. And as the second tower fell, she knew she was going to serve her country.

The daughter of immigrants who came to sow seeds in the world's richest soil, she saw how moving to a country so great improved the lives of her parents and gave them a chance to build a future for their children.

Bucking her parents' wishes, she rejected a shot at an Ivy League college and opted for the U.S. Naval Academy instead. She wanted to become an officer in the greatest navy the world has ever known. And she could never forget her first day in uniform. Eyes misty, she regarded herself in the mirror, admiring the lieutenant's bars on her shoulders. She'd never been so proud.

She took an oath to safeguard the country, and she looks upon the city with those words in mind: *I will support and defend the Constitution of the United States against all enemies, foreign and domestic.* Those enemies have breached the homeland, and from her position, she can see where they'd have tried their worst to compromise the country she loves.

Gombe Wireless's slated point of presence is several blocks from One World Trade. The location would have put Gombe, and the Founders, within miles of Wall Street banks, news organizations, other telecommunication providers, and major interests associated with the United States government—including the CIA's Manhattan field office. Were they all targets? Did the Founders have something specific in mind?

Impossible to know with certainty. But she does know that the Gombe license has already passed through a shredder at the FCC. Pressure will also mount against Tony Mitchell, the FCC's chairman. Retirement will be the only option for him after an investigation concludes.

Her phone rings. Peaceful moments in her line of work are always fleeting. She reaches into her pocket and finds the Deputy Director of Operations on the caller ID. Her boss is not the type to keep waiting. She answers. "Morning, Mr. Thompson."

Scott "Woody" Thompson's face appears on the FaceTime call. Smart and clean-shaven. Gray hair, not a strand out of place, is neatly parted to match his executive level position at Langley. An American flag pinned to the front of his black suit jacket, and in this, he never deviates. "You set London on fire this morning, Ms. Martinez."

"I think I'll respond with a cliché. Something like, *Just doing my job, sir.*"

Woody chuckles and squints at his screen. "Where are you?"

Martinez reverses the cell phone screen, allowing Woody a view from where she's standing. Before she can reply, he does.

"One World," he says with a certain reverence that reveals what the site means to America's intelligence community.

Martinez nods solemnly. "Yes, sir." She lets the phone swallow up the horizon. "Jen and her team are on their way to London. Andrew should touch down at Langley within the hour."

"New Scotland Yard is expecting Jen, and they're eager to work with her."

"How are things looking across the pond, sir?"

"Already a knife fight. The British intelligence apparatus recognizes the threat, but they're stuck. Gombe Wireless is a licensed entity, and until this point, it's been operating legally on their shores. MI6 and the GCHQ want it gone immediately. MI5 and the Crown's prosecutor have something else in mind."

This is what happens when you take your eyes off a threat. It got too far, and now there are serious road blocks. "We can't wait on this, Deputy Director."

"MI5 is adamant about their approach, Ms. Martinez. Frankly, so am I. Until we find irrefutable evidence that Gombe has broken British law, we cannot take it offline. What we've learned about their behavior in the U.S. and other European countries only gives us grounds to initiate surveillance on the company and its executives."

"It could be weeks, months, a year before they cross that line, sir," Martinez replies. "My fear is that when they do, it could be devastating."

Woody leans back in his chair and throws up his hands. "There's a consensus around what you just said. Trust me. But there's a second worst-case scenario: we take down Gombe's PoP in London with shaky evidence, and they beat the British government in the courts. They'll get back online with a level of impunity I won't be able to tolerate."

Martinez submits reluctantly. When Woody's right, there's no arguing. But it's still not what she wants to hear. "I'll let Jen know the situation."

"Meantime, the NCSC is monitoring Gombe's digital actions within London's borders. SO15 and JTAC are working to set up surveillance on the ground level. I expect they'll want to plug Jen and her team in there."

Martinez nods. The National Cyber Security Center, or NCSC, is Britain's defensive arm against cyber warfare and crime. SO15 is New Scotland Yard's Counter Terrorism Command. They're the sharp end of the spear, while the Joint Terrorism Analysis Center based at MI5 feeds them all the information they need to stay busy.

Woody adds, "We also have a Five Eyes problem, and I need your insight."

Martinez nods. "Sir."

"As of oh-six-thirty, we've terminated the exchange of TS/SCI level of intelligence with the British government. Bad timing with something brewing on Ukraine's border. Do you believe that these Founders are acting on behalf of the Russian government?"

Martinez gnaws on the question. One she's asked herself many times. And it's growing more important by the hour. Russia's president is amassing tanks on Ukraine's border, and America's most powerful European ally is compromised. "To date, we have no evidence connecting the Founders directly to the Russian government. Although we believe that members of the organization were members of the Russian military—Spetsnaz or intelligence types, sir."

"A lot of that type of thing over there."

"Russia's blurry lines, sir," Martinez replies. Woody slips into thought and drops his pen on his pad. A sign that the conversation is over. "Will that be all, Mr. Thompson?"

Woody nods. "I'll pass word to the British."

"Thank you, sir. And thank you again for cutting the red tape on my request."

"We need answers about who we're dealing with, Ms. Martinez. The man you're going to meet might have them. But don't take too long in Wyoming. You're needed elsewhere."

Martinez nods. "Sir."

"Ma'am," Woody replies before terminating the call.

"Wish I could see it through your eyes."

Martinez finds Sam Herbert standing by her side. He's the one who got her past security and onto the top floor before the tourists poured in. "You've got the important job, Sam. Lot of decent people down there, and they need help *now*."

"That's what I'm worried about," Herbert says. "The Likas were building machine guns several blocks from a playground. When you're finished with whatever you've got going on, I want what you have on the Lika Syndicate."

"We'll consider it a thank-you for all those extra overtime hours you put in," Martinez says, extending her hand. They shake, and before she starts toward the elevator, she gives him a smirk. "May not be much left though."

Seventeen

During Andrew's short flight between New York and Langley, his mind was on one thing: Void—what it is, and what its potential connection to Gombe Wireless may be. Only several hours have passed since Gombe's servers went online in London, but a pattern is already emerging.

He's flying solo in the Technical Access Group's suite buried in the Agency's basement: the Compartmentalized Operations Section. It comprises multiple offices, a conference room, and storage for equipment. His desk is in the center of the space, where intelligence-gathering operations take place. It's flanked by several other computer stations with a center screen dominating the front of the room.

Andrew's desk is the neatest. Papers are stacked and organized. Computer cables zip-tied and tucked away. A DNA double helix flanks his monitor, only the genes are replaced with green binary code: *00. 01. 10. 11.* Four combinations capable of infinite possibilities.

Langley is the end of a long journey for him. Life before the Agency had an entirely different purpose. He'd been a professor at the Massachusetts Institute of Technology and the head engineer on the school's

Advanced NeuroNet Engine project. He wrote the code for the world's first successful quantum computer.

Success like that doesn't go unnoticed.

China's Ministry of State Security took an interest, and when tensions ratcheted up between Washington and Beijing, Andrew was "repatriated." Kidnapped, with the added "honor" of returning to the homeland for mandatory government service.

Torture and detention changed Andrew. As a professor at MIT, he was shy and reserved. Buried himself in work and only appeared when students needed his help. In that sense, free time didn't exist. Evenings were often spent fertilizing supple minds. Challenging concepts were no match for his patience and intellect, and students never left without the answers they needed to succeed.

Jen and the Group saved him from Beijing. But the shy professor was gone. China's secret police introduced him to tyranny, and he swore to stand against it until his final day. He became a soldier, no longer shy or even fearful.

"Traffic is shifting away from TOR, Andrew."

Andrew listens as Anne, the Advanced NeuroNet Engine, uses the room's surround sound speakers to explain further.

"I'm also detecting a lot of chatter on Crane. Interest in a TOR alternative is building."

TOR is the dark web. A version of the internet hidden away from mainstream users. Its traffic is encrypted and difficult to track, but that has changed with Anne and a Top-Secret/SCI program known as Bitter Vigilante.

A joint task force of federal law enforcement and intelligence agencies founded Bitter Vigilante, and they've used the quantum computer to decrypt and monitor illicit activity on the dark web. Bitcoin's blockchain was cracked, and the identities hidden behind obscure crypto wallets were exposed. Hundreds of narcotics and weapons traffickers have been apprehended with Anne's assistance.

But that set off a race to replace TOR's dark web marketplace, and he's wondering if that's the reason behind TOR's mass exodus.

"Show me what people are talking about on Crane," Andrew orders.

"One moment."

A chat forum known as Crane appears on the center screen. It's the dark web's largest social gathering point, but it's also a virtual bazaar. Everything from fentanyl to ransomware to hand grenades can be purchased on this forum—that is, until Bitter Vigilante arrived.

The chat forum is buzzing. Full of references to a new dark web called Void. Quantum-resistant encryptions are being advertised, along with the ability to hide from America's intelligence agencies. Only one tool in the world can offer services like that: another quantum computer.

"How many unique posts mention Void, Anne?"

"Two thousand seven hundred posts, Andrew. About a hundred were made in the last twenty minutes."

Makes sense, considering a powerful computer network just came online in London. But it also appears a marketing campaign has been building buzz around Void for months. People were waiting, watching, and talking. All hoping Void would deliver as advertised.

"Have you been able to find a download link for Void's browser?" Andrew asks.

"No. It appears the download link is shared via invite only."

Andrew smirks at the challenge. Trust is scarce on the dark web. Merchants and hackers spend serious time and resources building relationships in this medium. Meetings are never face-to-face, but if a client has completed dozens of transactions, bonds form. Avatars become the equivalent of human faces.

Andrew has developed a relationship or two while moonlighting for Bitter Vigilante. Sometimes, certain items become available when they shouldn't be. Explosives. Chemical or biological agents. He has purchased them from the world's worst, and his dark web ID has some notoriety.

He searches his contact list on Crane, many of which are online. He crafts multiple messages, each asking for an invite into Void.

A contact replies with a brief message: *Here's the download link. Send us a message when you've got a verified account set up.*

Andrew clicks a link and downloads Void's software. He sets it up on a virtual machine—an artificial environment that will allow it to run without being installed directly on Langley's computer network. If it is malicious software, it can't be allowed to compromise the Agency's internal networks.

Void opens automatically after the install. Like TOR, it's essentially an internet browser, just extremely well encrypted. But it's sleek. The user interface is black, flowing, and functional. Void is a dark place with a vibe to match.

After familiarizing himself with basic functions, he surfs this new dark web. It's obvious that Void's engineers worked with a single purpose in mind: facilitate commerce.

There's already an active forum that reminds Andrew of TOR's heyday. Sellers are looking to offload the types of items that would shock the average person. Drugs. Machine guns. Sophisticated weapons and advanced hacking tools. Sex always sells, and he finds it before too long.

Lust.

When he tries to open the link, a message pops up. *Verified Account Required*. At the bottom a small icon invites him to create one. A challenge, no doubt. He clicks the link, eager to find out what it'll take to gain access to the escort service connected to American's FCC, the Lika Syndicate, and Gombe Wireless. Each a big deal in and of itself, but Andrew can't shake a simple word out of his imagination: *Remove.*

Fitting way to describe what he's going to do to Void.

EIGHTEEN

CENO LIKA'S BLACK LINCOLN TOWN CAR IS SHELTERED beneath a subway train's overpass. Offers nice concealment. Same with the barbed-wire fencing and trash heaps along the overpass's embankments.

Snow is still falling. Temperatures have reached minus ten degrees, and fog rolls across the windshield as the car's defrosters work overtime.

The Lincoln is old. Close to a hundred ninety thousand miles on the odometer. Built right, it's wide as a city bus and sturdier than a tank. Black leather seats are fully occupied. Ceno sits behind the wheel while three of his most capable enforcers ride shotgun. Each one is a carbon copy of the next. Large men, borne of old country stock, bred for violence.

Their emotions about the day's murders range from shock and sadness to rage. All these men are related in some way or another. Could be distant, but blood is blood. Assaults on their kin do not go unanswered. Watching drifts of snow float by, they want violence by day's end.

A Crown Vic climbs a curb and glides toward the Town Car. Police sirens bulge in the windshield. A silver flashlight protrudes from the driver's-side window. But there are no squad car markings.

Both vehicles' driver-side windows align. Typical cop style. Allows officers to watch a full three hundred sixty degrees around their vehicles.

Ceno rolls down his window and regrets it. A blast of body odor and vodka wafts from the Crown Vic. He sizes up the detective inside. Older man. Early sixties with blotchy red skin, hanging jowls. Couple of years away from the retirement of his dreams. Ready to leave this city with a lingering question: What will it do without him?

"Got what you're looking for," the detective says, handing over a manila envelope.

Ceno unwinds the red twine and slides out several rap sheets. Doesn't recognize the faces, but the last names are very, very familiar: Dibra. They're twin brothers named Arben and Tirana. The brothers are in their early twenties with wiry frames and stone-dead eyes. Recent addresses are also listed, along with employment statuses—of which they have none. "How long have they been in the city?"

"The brothers got here around twelve months ago. Been sneaking more in ever since."

Ceno leans closer to the detective. "You tell me this now?"

The detective squeezes the steering wheel and looks down to his crotch. Danger. "I didn't realize it was important, sir."

"Money," Ceno demands as he looks to the man on his right. Halit Voka. Two hundred eighty pounds. Wears a track suit in the middle of the winter because normal coats overheat him. A thick envelope lands in his palm, and Ceno passes it between the vehicles. "Get back to your desk. Keep looking for anyone associated with these men."

Ceno rolls up the window and puts the Lincoln in drive. Halit has the apartment's address entered into the GPS before the car hits the street. Less than twenty minutes away, and that's if the traffic is bad.

————

Street parking in the projects is always a bear. Ceno steps out of the Lincoln after double-parking and pops the trunk. The interior looks like a local hardware store. He reaches in and dispenses the items.

Sledgehammer goes to Halit. Project doors are made of steel, and they're often reinforced with multiple deadbolts. Getting inside the apartment will be his job.

Mirsad Qosja puts his fist through several rolls of duct tape and grabs a blowtorch—handy in the event a clothes iron can't be found in the apartment. Steam rises from the top of his bald head and dissipates into drifts of snow. Like Halit, he married into the Lika family through one of Ceno's cousins in the old country.

A drill with extra bits gets passed off to Olsi Kurti—the last living link to the Cro-Magnon man. Olsi's hairline stretches so far down his forehead, it threatens to combine with his eyebrows. But it's a blessing because it keeps his few remaining brain cells warm. The Neanderthal likes to hum when he walks—soothing, he says—and he rarely speaks.

Olsi stows the bits in his black leather jacket and palms a backup battery. He gives the drill's trigger a squeeze. One hundred twenty volts, ready and able to twist a chunk of metal into someone's femur. He grins, and the ruts in his face tighten.

Ceno slams the trunk shut and leads the charge toward Tower Three. The courtyard is busy, despite the weather. Young kids roll up snowmen or sling snowballs at each other. Fiends drift between the brick towers, searching for dealers willing to front them a fix. Honest men and women trudge along sidewalks as they prepare to brave mass transit and harsh weather for a day's pay.

They step into the tower lobby. The concrete jungle's hierarchy becomes visible. Top of the food chain, clustered in warm hallways, while the lookouts and bag men shuffle between the towers. Blunt smoke curls against broken ceiling tiles and flickering fluorescent lights. Graffiti everywhere, paying homage to the fallen or finalizing territorial disputes. Someone kills the radio. The lobby's occupants stop and stare.

But no one says a word to the four Albanians crossing to the elevators. Close to a dozen armed gangbangers would rather keep their mouths shut than risk a conflict with the Lika Syndicate.

Ceno presses the elevator call button. Doesn't even throw the gangbangers a sideways glance. They're nothing to him, to his family—a unit built on absolute loyalty. Something they'd never understand. The empty carriage presents itself, and he steps aboard. Twenty-seventh floor.

They step off the elevator, find young kids playing in the waiting area. Two- and three-year-olds, tossing balls around or grooming Barbie dolls. A piercing whistle fills the air. Nervous mothers bolt from their apartments and grab their kids. Half a dozen doors slap shut.

Ceno walks to Apartment 2773, and every door he passes makes a sound: shooting deadbolts, chains sliding into tracks. But the unit he's interested in hasn't caught on. He puts his ear to the door and hears a familiar Albanian radio program.

The Dibras are home.

Halit orients to the door like a batter on home plate. Grinning, he nods to Ceno. "I go in first," he grumbles in broken English.

Ceno shrugs. "Then go in first."

Halit swings and the door folds like a soda can. He storms the apartment. Size doesn't stop him from moving fast. Nor does it stop him from engaging a man armed with a shotgun just feet away. He hurls the sledgehammer like a battle axe, and it crashes into the victim's chest. The sledge drops, and the victim follows close behind.

Mirsad trails Halit through the door and ducks into the kitchen. A man had been standing by the oven, cooking up breakfast. Bacon grease slings across Mirsad's chest and neck, but his arms stop the boiling liquid from hitting his face.

Instead of dodging an incoming skillet, Mirsad grabs the edges, smiles at the man while his flesh burns. He wrenches the skillet out of the aggressor's hands, grabs the man by the neck, and pushes his face onto the burner. Screams fill the apartment. When they finally stop, Mirsad lifts the man's smoldering face off the burner and hurls him into the refrigerator.

Ceno finds the men he'd been looking for. The twin brothers. Side by side on a dingy living room couch. At least they were until he rounded the corner. One lunges for a pistol while the other goes wide to seize a sawed-off twelve-gauge.

Ceno dives across the living room, tackles both men before they get too far apart, and traps them in a bear hug. Halit and Olsi aren't far behind. To call it a scuffle would imply an even match up. That isn't the case.

Ceno buries a knee into Arben's gut while taking control of the

Beretta in his hand. A round of vicious elbows to the cheek and jaw knock the fight out of his eyes.

Tirana's treatment is worse. Halit and Olsi each take an arm. Twisting and pulling and breaking, all while they levitate him off the ground. By the time they sit him in a nearby chair, he looks like Gumby. Duct tape chases around his chest and arms, binding him to the chair.

Ceno lifts a still dazed Arben off the couch, dumps him into another wooden chair, and waits while Mirsad braces him. "Grab the other two."

Halit and Mirsad disappear before returning with the remaining men. The cook's face is bright red and glistening. He's barely conscious, struggling to process the pain. He's locked into position with duct tape.

The man who caught the sledge is wheezing. Spitting up blood. Sternum shattered, his chest is bouncing up and down violently. He just sits, gulps up air, body on autopilot as it tries to stay alive.

Ceno circles the apartment. Finds nothing but problems. He tries to keep his temper in a box, but it's tough. These men are—*were*—a cancer that festered too long.

Rubber-banded cash is piled on the table. Crinkled and dirty. Street money. Half a dozen burner cells lie amongst the cash, along with a list of names and numbers. All women. These guys are running hookers, a market his family has worked hard to corner since arriving in the Bronx decades ago. Their dominance is unchallenged—until now.

He pockets the cash and the numbers because he'll take over the girls.

Baggies of marijuana are also on the table. Pipes full of ash lie on their sides. Personal use. Doesn't look like they were dealing. Smart enough. Save the serious jail time for the gangbangers.

Ceno steps toward a nearby bedroom and peers through the cracked door. Someone is lying on the bed, covered by a sheet. The commotion hasn't disturbed the person—a bad sign. He pushes open the door.

A naked woman is lying unconscious between the sheets. Needle and a spoon waiting on the nightstand. Dirtbags in the living room are keeping her loaded, taking turns. Ceno nods. Recognizes it for what it is: they're cold, hard men. The type that can fit into his world, all while surviving and earning respect. *The old country.*

Ceno is worse.

He flips the mattress. The woman tumbles into the project's cinder-block wall, and he doesn't give her a second glance. He's looking for the money that would have been in Sandro's safe. More of the documents. Tough luck she's in the way.

When he doesn't find anything, he wonders: *Was Sandro that lucky? Was the safe truly empty when they found it? Did he have time to shred them all?* Maybe, but he can't rest until he's sure. If the Dibras found that type of leverage . . .

Carefully, he creeps into the second bedroom. He finds a giant mound of cash on the dresser. The bills appear to be uncirculated, but it's only twenty-thousand. Sandro had hundreds in the safe. *Where is the rest of it?*

He pockets the cash, shuts the door, and returns to the men taped to the chairs.

"Look at this."

Ceno takes a stack of business cards, Polaroid pictures, and match-books from Halit. The matchbooks are from his local brothels. The Polaroids show the outside of his deli. *His deli.* Finally, the business card is from the brake shop. This is the truth he came to find.

Rage is near blinding. Ceno steps to Arben and backhands him in the face. Once, twice, then a third time. Gashes open on the twin's cheek, and Ceno waits for the lights to blink back on in his eyes before waving the evidence in his face. "You killed my uncle."

Arben laughs and his eyes sparkle. After spitting blood at Ceno's feet, he says, "Your family is *mutt. If* Sandro is dead, I'm sure he went out like a bitch. Just like you will."

Ceno places the evidence in his jacket pocket. He pulls out the CZ and aligns the sights on Arben's trachea. *This is tradition.* A .32 caliber bullet bounces between his spine and Adam's apple before finally settling against a vertebra.

Arben struggles against the chair as his lungs fill with blood. Watching the struggle fills Ceno with something primal. This is *hakmarrja*—revenge. A divine right bestowed on him by the Kanun. Blood is flowing, and he wants more.

Tirana's attitude deteriorates. He screams and curses Ceno, overcome with rage as he watches his brother die. He kicks against the ground and his chair tips back. His head bounces hard on the linoleum tiles.

Ceno recognizes the futility in asking questions. The man just witnessed his brother's execution. Getting answers from this point forward will be challenging, but that will sweeten his revenge. "Where is the rest of my money?"

Tirana wails as Halit presses his entire two-hundred-eighty-pound frame against his broken elbow. It's an odd skill to possess, but Halit steps back moments before his victim passes out.

"Where?" Ceno repeats.

"We don't have a lot of cash here!" Tirana screams. "But there's a storage locker. The keys are on top of the refrigerator."

Ceno doesn't reply, only because he believes Tirana. Men reach a point where they'll do anything to stop the pain. But his suffering won't end until it absolutely must. Ceno draws closer and fires the CZ. Hitting Tirana's stomach is easy from point-blank range. Seven bullets puncture his abdomen, and the pistol's slide locks open.

He'll die on his back, drowning in his own blood and shit like his brother.

Ceno doesn't recognize the other two. Won't give them the honor of dying by his family's pistol. While he reloads the CZ, he allows his men to finish them. The drill spins up, and for a brief, magical moment, the Neanderthal smiles. When the bit stops moving, the apartment is dripping red.

———

Ceno's Nikes stick and crackle as he steps off the elevator on the ground floor. Boom boxes are off, and the lobby's gangbangers stare after him, shocked at the bloody footprints he leaves on his way to the exit. His men walk at his flank, tools slung over their shoulders like proud laborers. Remorse is for the weak, and real criminals balk at prison time. Today's message isn't just for the Dibras; it's for the entire neighborhood.

The Lika Syndicate is untouchable. Period.

The Lincoln is still double-parked. Thirty minutes was all it took for Ceno to get the answers he needed about his uncle's murder. His adrenaline is surging, and the chilled air doesn't faze him. After checking on the storage locker, he'll return home and pack a bag. London is his next stop. Sandro's too. His family will wait on them both to begin the forty-day mourning period, and there won't be any more delays.

NINETEEN

ZOOM. ZOOM. *AH, THE PERFECT CLOSE-UP.*

Jen chuckles and snaps a photograph of Sloane as she dozes in the Gulfstream's seat. Her mouth is open, and a string of drool has settled on her shoulder. Relentless, Jen cues up a group chat on her cell and attaches the image. Send.

The phone in front of Sloane buzzes. Hardwired, she lunges for it. By the time she reads the text, Hastings and the others are chuckling in nearby seats. Terrance chimes in with a quick text: *ew.*

"You know, that's probably going to end up as his lock screen," Sloane remarks.

"What? You aren't glad to hear from Terrance?" Jen asks.

Sloane tosses her phone on the table and rolls her eyes. She unbuckles and starts to the front of the cabin for refreshments.

Jen doesn't laugh. No reason to rub it in. But she questions why Sloane would be foolish enough to fall asleep in front of her. After she photographed Jen in Brooklyn, the battle lines were drawn. And on long flights like these, there's plenty of time to plot revenge.

Mission complete, she looks across the cabin to her other teammates. The Technical Access Group has grown exponentially since Mexico City, and the additions are welcomed.

Hastings is reading an NSA–generated textbook on computer espionage. He'd been a troop sergeant in Delta, which made him top of the heap, and he's kept the trend going since joining the Technical Access Group. He's spent hours studying the craft, trying to be helpful to Jen and the others wherever he can. Watching him work, Jen's amused; the crazy bastard may be running around with a mind to rival Terrance or Andrew.

Part of Animal's growth is correlated with his food consumption, and in Mexico City, when he'd joked about wine—well, he wasn't joking. He's a chef, and when he couldn't maintain the physique he wanted from Big Macs and Mexican pizzas from Taco Bell, he went all-in on teaching himself the fine art of cuisine.

Coco. Sniper. Gun nut. Entranced by the Group's virtually unlimited budget. He's studying a Knight's Armament catalogue, filled with wonder. When she ordered Staccato 2011s for the team, he was the first man to arrive on the range—tough feat inside the ultra-competitive world of tier-one special operations. He was busy trying to choose the tightest pistols until Hastings arrived, and a fistfight threatened to break out.

Gray, the picture-perfect Californian, is studying medicine. Special forces medics, like doctors, continually polish their craft. And in this sense, he is the Group's doctor. He carries around charts for individual Group members, and when headaches, backaches, bumps, or bruises emerge, he's Johnny-on-the-spot with a pharmacy full of goodies.

These men became acquainted with evil they hadn't witnessed before in Mexico City. Tough feat, given their level of experience in the world's most hostile environments. But Jen knows the other reason they joined the dark side; they enjoyed working with her and the Technical Access Group. They were doing serious work in the Unit, but this . . . ? It took them to another level.

Sloane returns and drops back into the seat across from Jen. They exchange glances and laugh together. They've known each other since South Korea, and Jen's prank is a welcome addition to a long-running memory.

Jen's phone buzzes again. She reads a message from Martinez and unfastens her seatbelt. "We've got something."

Sloane grabs her laptop and stands. "Watch that."

"What?" Jen asks, but it's too late. Her laptop charger is tied to the table's leg. It nearly rips the computer out of her hand as she tries to stand. *Oh, the timing.* Now it's Sloane's turn to laugh while she hustles down the aisle.

Jen untangles her cord and starts for the back of the jet. "Al, come on, and bring your laptop."

Hastings grabs his gear and hustles up behind them.

Jen reaches a secure door and punches a code into the cipher lock. It opens into a SCIF, which will be used for the briefing Martinez has on tap. Half a dozen pilot chairs face a television screen on the back wall. Links back to Langley are secure, and the space is soundproof.

Jen drops into a seat and brings her laptop online. The others follow, and she begins a conference call. Martinez joins, followed by Andrew. Faces are clear, and voice quality is superb. "What's going on in London, Gabby?"

"We're making solid progress. The Brits have launched a Major Covert Terrorism Investigation into Gombe Wireless, and I've been added to the investigation's executive liaison board. We've got sway in the decision-making process now."

This was the progress Jen was hoping to hear. MCTIs are the most potent investigative tools in the British government's arsenal. It will give law enforcement and intelligence agencies tremendous latitude in how they observe and collect intelligence on Gombe Wireless. "COA?"

"No course of action yet. We're hung up on British law," Martinez replies.

"So, we can stare all we like," Sloane adds.

"But we can't get hands on," Hastings finishes.

"That brings us to the reason I called the meeting. We have info on Void, as well as a possible solution," Martinez states. "Mr. Xiao."

"Void is a new dark web browser coupled with a marketplace," Andrew explains before diving into the quantum-resistant encryption standards. "I've conducted a soft probe against Void's firewalls . . . I think the encryptions they're advertising are real."

Sloane puts an elbow on her desk and rubs her brow. "Jesus."

Jen feels the pain, just like Sloane. This goes back to Mexico City. Peru. *Couldn't have done it without you, Ms. Yates.* Her blood gets a little hotter, and she'd love to send a firm reply to whoever wrote that message.

"It's already exploding in popularity, and there are some serious dollar signs involved," Andrew continues. "Void's administrators are charging ten percent fees on transactions that occur in their network."

"Previous dark web markets made *billions* with the same strategy. This could easily top it," Martinez observes.

"Have you been able to estimate the user base?" Jen asks.

"I've only been able to read through product listings and requests," Andrew replies. "When a listing disappears or product availability numbers change, we can see it. Based on that activity alone, we're estimating over five thousand active users, and it's climbing rapidly."

"Only a matter of time before CBRN threats emerge on that thing," Hastings notes. He spent a decade hunting terrorists in the Middle East, and he'll never be able to stop viewing the world through that lens.

Andrew nods. "We're trending in that direction. Arms bazaars that could rival the Middle East and Africa are popping up on Void. Fentanyl is available by the drum—tack on air freight for a nominal fee." Andrew looks to Martinez. "I went over Void's house rules. They only have one, and we've seen it before in previous dark web markets: no transactions in Russia."

Martinez frowns. That goes back to the question Woody asked her only hours ago. "So the Russian government could be involved here?"

"It's possible, which is why I wanted to bring it to your attention," Andrew replies. "But we can say with certainty that the people responsible for this thing are interested in staying off the FSB's radar."

Jen is tapping a pen against her laptop while she listens. These discoveries have serious consequences, but she's still missing an important piece of information. "How did you link Gombe Wireless to Void, Andrew?"

"Timing," Andrew states. "Gombe came online at 11:28 a.m. in London. Not five minutes later, Void blinked to life."

"That's not a coincidence," Martinez confirms.

"Neither is my inability to find it, ma'am," Andrew says with a sigh. He forwards a digital map of London to their laptops, and it's filled with GPS pins. They correspond both to internet servers being used by Gombe and routers belonging to individual customers. "They simultaneously launched Void along with thousands of other pieces of equipment across London. It's a freaking brilliant form of camouflage."

Sloane studies the map. "And they'll have hidden Void's servers behind proxy chains or a solid VPN."

"Which means there's a strong chance Void's server isn't even shown on the map," Andrew states. "I'd bet my last buck that Gombe is providing Void with an internet source, but I can't link them—at least, not with their quantum-resistant encryptions."

Jen's buzzing. She knows a way to make the connection. She recalls the photographs she found in Liev Frankel's Brooklyn apartment. *Remove.* "Did you find Lust's page on Void, Andrew?"

"I did, ma'am. Their services are available in New York and London."

Jen nods. When Anne tried to access the website on Lust's business card, they got a 404 error. Website down. That's because it was moving to Void, and Frankel was helping. "Tell me about the barriers to entry. Can I just hop on Void's browser, punch in Lust's dark website, and book a girl? Do I need an account?"

"You need an ID-verified account to transact anywhere on Void. That includes Lust."

"Where are you going with this, Jen?" Martinez asks.

"I think the Founders are using the Lika Syndicate in the same way they used Alex Varga's cartel."

"Front men," Sloane observes.

"More like business partners. The Likas are using the Founders' technology to run girls and sell drugs. There's a chance that people inside that organization have information on Void—server locations, information about engineers . . ."

"Varga's cartel protected Founders technology in Mexico City," Martinez adds. "Which might be why Void was set up in London—a Lika stronghold."

"You got it." Jen's grin is a mile wide. She's got vivid memories. Base stations. Cartel thugs basking in Mexico City's mellow sunshine as they bled out in the sand. Shame it's cold in London, but that's the temperature her new Albanian friends will end up having anyway. "We need an account on Void, Andrew. It's the best avenue we have into this network."

"Already working in that direction, ma'am. Anne and I are mapping out the account's identity verification requirements now. Once I'm confident, I'll create it."

"That's your priority, Mr. Xiao," Martinez orders as she pecks out information on her laptop. "Jen, I want your team to keep brainstorming this. If we can link Gombe Wireless to high-level criminal activity, we'll have everything we need to take their servers offline in London."

Jen takes notes of her own. The British can't risk a legal battle with Gombe Wireless. While she hates letting the internet service provider continue to function, it's a valid argument. Tying Gombe to Void will give the British everything they need to win this fight.

"I'm going to brief the board," Martinez continues. "By the time you land in London, you'll be able to get straight to work."

"We'll be prepared."

TWENTY

FASTEN-SEATBELTS LIGHTS DIM, AND JEN HOPS OUT OF HER seat inside the SCIF. They used every bit of the two hours remaining in the flight to game out a series of actions to run against Void. She keys out of the suite and returns to her seat in the cabin. The portside window gives her a clear view of the hangar as the jet settles into position.

Two armed-response vehicles belonging to London's Metro Police Service—or New Scotland Yard—speed into the hangar. The undercover vehicles have tinted windows and sirens concealed in their windshields. They swoop around and park parallel with the jet as its turbines power down.

While Jen rolls up her laptop charger, her phone buzzes. Reaching down, she finds a message from Sam Herbert, the NYPD detective, and reads it off to Sloane. "Four dead in the Bronx. All of them Dibras."

Sloane stops packing and smiles at Jen. "The Likas believe in fairy tales."

Jen nods. She misled the Lika Syndicate, and now they're doing the Lord's work. More important, they're clueless that law enforcement is closing in.

Satisfied with the news, Jen throws her messenger bag over her shoulder and leads her team off the jet. A New Scotland Yard officer approaches her as she crosses the hangar. Bald, but with a five o'clock shadow. Appears no-nonsense in a camel trench coat. "Jen Yates, National Clandestine Service," she says, shaking his hand.

"Detective Sergeant Ray Toliver, SO15," he replies. "NCS . . . thought you lot were with Special Activities."

Jen smirks at Toliver. *SO15.* New Scotland Yard's Counter Terrorism Command. A specialized branch inside the British Police. It handles the worst domestic terror threats facing Great Britain. Toliver's rough exterior matches his position in the world. "I'm so far off in the weeds these days, I tend to forget where I work."

Toliver nods, hitches his hands to his belt. Near fifty, he's in better shape than men half his age. "Either way, I've heard a lot about you, Ms. Yates. Sorry we're meeting under these circumstances."

"Just Jen," she replies, registering his disappointment. Events like these are intelligence failures, and good officers hold themselves accountable. She's no exception to the rule. "We'll get this mess straightened out."

"Yes, ma'am," Toliver says before giving Al Hastings a nod. "Heard you lads were with Major Bingham. While I was with the Special Air Service, I did some work with him in Iraq. Think it was around twenty-ten."

Hastings and the other operators perk up. With those words, Toliver has instantly joined their brotherhood. "Best man I ever served with," Hastings says as the two operators shake hands.

After brief introductions between Toliver and the other members of the team, he turns his attention back to Jen. "Haven't got much of a speech prepared. Brass told me to give you whatever you need, let you get on your way."

"I need a vehicle and a safe house in London. We're looking to recruit an asset in the city. Once we make the detention, we'll need a place to properly vet the candidate."

"We're finalizing all of that right now," Toliver replies. "I got word that a few of yours would be working with me at the Joint Terrorism Analysis Center?"

Jen directs a thumb toward Sloane, Gray, and Coco. "They're ready to assist with whatever you need."

Coco's face sinks. The Group ordered new toys from Knights Armament, but he won't be putting them to use. "I want to go home," he mutters.

"Me too, man," Gray adds.

Jen is not happy about the two operators complaining. They want to be with her, where the action is. The reason Hastings and Animal are beaming. They'll be raising hell on London's streets. Her look changes their attitudes.

Coco smiles and gives Jen two thumbs-up. "I love London this time of year."

"Running around in the cold is just great for my joints," Gray shouts as he zips up his jacket and folds his arms over his chest.

"The short straw. I remember those days," Toliver replies, laughing.

Jen is relieved that he's not taking it personally, but she's still eager to get off the subject. They're guests in London, after all. "I've been told that you'll be attaching a liaison officer to my team. Wouldn't be you, by chance, would it?"

"Sorry, Jen. I'm middle management these days," Toliver replies, sensing her apprehension. "I know it's an inconvenience, but this investigation falls under oh-five's Terror Act. That gives you a lot of leeway, but we need one of ours making sure you don't exceed any legal boundaries."

Jen sourly looks around the hangar. Doesn't see a candidate that would even come close to fitting the type of individual she'll need. "We're missing someone then."

"He's late. Had him running a few last-minute errands before you lot arrived."

Before Toliver can explain further, a high-powered engine speeds toward the hangar. A black BMW 750li screeches to a stop by the other vehicles. It has tinted windows and gangster rims.

Jen nearly cringes as the driver exits. He's wearing a black leather jacket, and the sides of his head are shaved. But that's not the actual issue; he doesn't look a day older than twenty-five, and he's full of bravado.

Toliver leans closer to Jen, whispers. "Both of his parents are immigrants from Albania. He speaks the language fluently. Graduated from Oxford Law. This is his second year with Special Branch, and he's an expert on Eastern European organized crime."

Jen gets it. Having a natural speaker on the team is vital. Plus, he's versed on the criminals they'll be targeting. New Scotland Yard takes great pains to recruit officers like him. England is changing. Kids like him are part of the future, and pivotal to keeping the country safe. But *kid* is the operative word, right alongside *inexperienced*.

As the young man closes in, she finds him baby-faced, despite the black stubble on his cheeks. He's cocky. As she replays what she just heard from Toliver, she gets stuck on a single word: lawyer.

Dear God . . .

"Kabir Broja," Toliver says as he points out Jen for an introduction. "This is Ms. Yates. Sure you've heard of her by now."

"Nice to meet you, Jen!"

Jen contemplates taking a personal moment to count to ten. All the self-help books recommend it for anger. "Nice to meet you, Mr. Broja," she replies dryly as he vigorously pumps her hand.

"Thanks for having me onboard. This is my first assignment in cover, and I'm looking forward to the experience," Kabir says, slapping Jen on the shoulder. He approaches Hastings and Animal, shakes their hands. "Good to meet you lads."

"Yeah."

"Cool."

"Right, then!" Toliver snaps. "You'll enjoy working with him." He leans closer and adds sternly, "Take care of him, Jen."

Before Jen can reply, Toliver executes an about-face and rushes toward the convoy of vehicles. Sloane, Coco, and Gray snicker as they speed behind him.

Kabir is oblivious. He hitches his hands to his overpriced jeans as the convoy tears off, leaving his BMW alone by the entrance. He glows at Jen. "Where to first?"

Jen is still hanging on Toliver's last statement. *Take care of him.* This kid is now her responsibility, and it's the last thing she needs. "Let's start with our safe house."

TWENTY-ONE

ALL THE APARTMENT WINDOWS ARE OPEN, AND SNOWDRIFTS spin like tops on the hardwood floor. Still, Victor Orlov needs his gas mask to work in the environment.

He has occupied the central London flat for several months. Plenty of time for him to soil it with strands of hair, fingerprints, and other types of bodily fluids. Like any model tenant, he's giving the apartment a thorough cleaning before he terminates his lease.

Ammonia-based cleaning solution has the white walls glistening. Pools of it are collecting in the floorboards. The kitchen sink is plugged, and the basins are full of it. Anything he may have touched in the apartment, like kitchen knives and forks, is soaking in the substance. It's leaching body oils away, but that's not all. It's damaging remaining DNA on a microscopic level. An important reason why he chose ammonia over bleach.

As he finishes the cleaning process, he swears he's never occupied a space so tidy in his entire life. While he was enduring Spetsnaz selection, the training cadre were merciless about the hygiene in their barracks. Students learned to love scrubbing toilets about as much as running. This place would please even the most hardened instructor.

Shame he's going to dirty it up again.

Wearing a hairnet, booties, and latex gloves, he walks from room to room, spreading bits of hair wherever he walks. He's got a plastic bag full of it. Black, brown, blonde, red—even green and blue—collected from local hair salons and barber shops.

Returning to the kitchen, he tears open a bag of trash. This one was taken from a Chinese restaurant across town. As he dumps the trash into his bin, he notices used utensils, receipts, and half-eaten cartons of General Tso's chicken.

Dirty enough. *If* authorities find this location, they'll discover enough DNA evidence to suggest half of London occupied the flat at one point or another. *If* they find his DNA, it'll be corroded by ammonia and disregarded in the milieu.

Back in the living room, he is set to finish his last task. A surprise for New Scotland Yard, *if* they're lucky enough to find it. A motion detector is mounted in a corner, directly across from the main door. Exposed wires snake along the wall before terminating at a small end table. Opening a set of terminals, he plugs the wires into a large battery.

He smiles like a gypsy fortune teller as the motion detector's face glows red.

Another set of wires connects to a circuit board. A digital cooking timer clicks on, and he sets it for five minutes—ample time to get out of the flat. Once that screen flashes zero, his device will be armed.

He's gone far in London. To protect himself, to protect his organization—the zakonny vladelets. The Founders. But far is all he knows. It's a hard lesson he learned as a young boy.

In 1996, the Soviet Union wasn't just collapsing; it was being looted by a cabal of political and business elites. Victor's family was not amongst the privileged class. His father had been an uneducated laborer. He was common, and that was okay.

But he'd been an alcoholic. In the newborn Russian Federation, alcoholism wasn't just tolerated, it was encouraged. Vodka was the only thing the country seemed to have an excess of. Cheap salve to numb the masses, and the masses had an unquenchable thirst.

Victor's father was prone to extremes. In alcoholism, in depression, in domestic violence. The reason Victor and Anastasia—inseparable in those days—spent so little time at home. Also the reason why their mother shrank to a shadow of herself. When their father was home, her voice would barely rise above a whisper. Like the twins, she'd tiptoe through the house, all in an effort to leave the drunk undisturbed.

In the mid-nineties, quality food was scarce. And if someone could find food, the price was heavily inflated. Citizens were provided rations, usually cheap tinned meats and bread. Victor's father had been on a bender. Alcohol got the better of his spirit, and his stomach got the better of the family's food ration.

At twelve, he was half his father's size. Victor knew he couldn't fight the man when he'd found him passed out amongst the empty wrappers, but he'd given it serious thought. He and Anastasia endured an entire day at school, hands shaking, stomachs growling, starving. He knew what he needed to do, and he spent the day hashing out his plan.

When the dismissal bell rang, he slipped away from Anastasia and snuck into the local black market. He hadn't told her what he was going to do, and he knew that she'd worry. But he was going to fix things for them both.

Smugglers reigned in those days. People who could import goods made fortunes, and they exported their earnings to financial safe havens. Victor's stomach was clawing at him when he reached the black market's grocery section. Fresh food, and man, it smelled good. That only weakened his legs, and he worried as he waited for the opportunity he so desperately needed. Would they carry him to safety, or would his strength give out?

Victor found his answer when a deli owner turned his back on his counter. Moving as quickly as he could, Victor snatched up an entire ham, a roll of cheese, and a package of crackers. Always weary of theft, the deli owner spun around and hollered for the boy as he ran.

"Thief! Thief!" he shouted as he pointed Victor out to nearby police officers.

The cops' whistles and shouts weren't what Victor worried about as he ran. It was rubber truncheons. Cheap, like the vodka his father drank, and made from recycled tires. Suddenly, his legs gained strength as he weaved through the crowd and into the streets.

Outside, he sprinted for the first thing he saw: steam bellows connected to a nearby plant. They were everywhere, powered by coal from a nearby mine. As he drew closer, he realized what a fool he'd been; he panicked and abandoned his escape plan. Everyone knew not to get close to the bellows. If a person survived the encounter, they'd be scalded, blistered, marked for life.

The police officers slowed behind him. At first he thought they were out of energy. Vodka and cigarettes, like dear old dad. But he realized they were laughing. Mocking him. Encouraging him on.

"Yes! Enjoy your dinner, boy!"

"Why not leave us some? It's going to go to waste!"

The earth around the bellows was black. Tearing off a mitten, he opened a service grate. His skin hissed, but he threw it open anyway. When he looked back at the two policemen, they were still laughing. Unfazed that a twelve-year-old boy was about to die for a meal.

In that moment he hated them, and that's what propelled him into the tunnel.

Victor's heavy winter coat protected the food while he ran, and as he descended farther into the tunnel, it protected his skin too. The tunnel was for service and inspection of steam lines. Daylight was already scarce, but he saw warning signs not to progress farther. Steam was rippling along the ceiling. Temperatures rose, and it became hard to breathe.

Then he saw it. A safe cubby—at least, that's what he thought it was. He came upon valves and gauges in a concrete pocket. It had a little red phone to report back to the same plant his father slaved away in.

Victor peeked out of the cubby and glanced down the long tunnel. He could see the cops, but they couldn't see him. They ventured closer to the grate, wondering if they'd been duped. When they couldn't see Victor, they shrugged their shoulders and wrote him off as dead.

Thirty minutes was all Victor could stand. But he and Anastasia were starving, so he stayed in that cubby for an hour, needing to be certain that the police had left the area. When he finally emerged, he was drenched with sweat. He wasn't burned, but his skin was deep red.

Running hard, he dropped into a pile of fresh snow and shoveled it into his mouth. A mistake he paid for when he finally returned to Anastasia. He was frozen and shivering—suffering cramps from the snow he ate. Victor's arms were locked up, and she struggled to remove his jacket, but when she did, she saw what he'd done.

Together, they wept and ate, fighting to stay warm. That day Victor had dared to go further, where others wouldn't, and he was rewarded with sustenance. When the next round of rations came, their hands weren't shaking or needy.

Just like that day, London's temperatures outside are hovering around zero degrees centigrade. But the chill driving Victor forward is decades old. Now he's ice, and pitiless, and brutal. Exactly how he needs to be. In less than an hour, he's going to execute multiple members of the Dibra crime family.

Ceno Lika is coming to London to mourn. And seek revenge. All he'll find are bodies. The Lika Syndicate is responsible for maintaining Void's servers, and Victor won't let London turn into a warzone. The murders will be a final act, completing his masterwork in London. And by this time tomorrow, he'll be headed for St. Petersburg.

TWENTY-TWO

THE RIDE FROM HEATHROW TO THE SAFE HOUSE HAS BEEN nightmarish. Behind the wheel, Kabir keeps yammering, barely pausing to breathe. Jen is next to him in the passenger seat, studying him as he navigates London.

Both of his hands are shaking; it's most noticeable when he tries to operate the blinker. Tension in his throat is forcing him to constantly clear it. His speech is rushed. He lacks confidence with her Group, and he's overcompensating for it.

Jen wonders if she was this way when she disappeared into Montana's backwoods. She was young then too. And just like Kabir, she wasn't prepared to handle the consequences of her actions. She learned her lessons the hard way, and her gut is telling her that Kabir will endure the same style of education.

The vehicle stops at a red light, and Kabir points at a high-rise on the corner. "Crispe House. The Hellbianz control it. They're the Lika Syndicate's foot soldiers, selling drugs and eating the charges that come along with it."

Silence.

"Close to three hundred of 'em. They record gang ballads—little music videos—and put them on the internet. Crazy, right?"

More silence, save Kabir's awkward laughter.

"Yeah," he says, picking the conversation back up for himself. "The Albanian gangs are the country's worst. They make up one percent of the organized crime population, but ten percent of the prison population."

Jen rolls her eyes. More lawyer than a cop, and she wonders how long it'll take for him to start quoting New Scotland Yard's rulebook once their work begins.

"I have a question," Animal says, his tone overly gruff.

Kabir looks in the rearview. "Shoot, mate."

"This your piece of shit car?"

Kabir laughs again. "Picked it up from the motor pool before I went to the airport. Good cover in an area like this."

Jen's eyebrow arches. The rookie missed Animal's dig. It was a soft gut check, and she has the feeling more are on the way. "Where are we exactly, Mr. Broja?"

"Barking, Jen. This neighborhood is a Lika Syndicate stronghold."

It looks like London from the picture books. Narrow streets. Charming one- or two-story shops. Hard to believe that some of the country's most ruthless criminals have laid claim to it.

Kabir flips on the blinker and turns into one of the neighborhood's side streets. The homes are made of stone, and they'd be better described as cottages. He slings the car into a driveway but doesn't kill the engine. Instead, he raps on the steering wheel like a drum.

Jen tunes out the noise as she checks out the exterior. The safe house is rundown. Looks like a bunch of party animals lived here before the authorities tossed them out. A beer can is tangled up in a bush. Tie-dyed bed sheets hang over the upstairs windows.

She has stayed in a decent cross section of safe houses during her career, and alarm bells are sounding . . . This won't be fun. But if a good time is what she was after, she'd be in Texas, riding horses on her parents' ranch.

On the upside, the team will only be stationed here for forty-eight hours, max. Their immediate goal is to recruit an asset. The residence will give them a place to make contact without leading Lika Syndicate members back to MI5's Joint Terrorism Analysis Center on the Thames.

Kabir still hasn't moved, and the BMW's Xenon lamps remain striped across the garage door. Jen gives him a nod from the passenger seat. "What are you waiting for?"

"Sorry, Jen," Kabir replies. "Think you'll need to give it a nudge."

Jen holds back her irritation. Forget ma'am, there wasn't even a please or thank-you. As she steps out of the car, Animal and Hastings are staring daggers at Kabir. While she's not the type to haze a new team-mate, that's what's coming. And for good reason, unfortunately.

She rips open the garage door and stands aside. While Kabir parks, she pays close attention. Time to get a feel for what their new partner is made of—and set some boundaries in the process.

Hastings is sitting on the driver's side, behind Kabir. With timing that's a little too perfect, he throws open the door as Kabir exits and approaches the trunk. Nut shot, but Hastings doesn't apologize or even acknowledge it. He steps out of the car, stretches, and looks around the dingy garage. "Hope it's got heat."

Jen pretends to be oblivious as she pops the trunk and extracts her gear. Kabir is trying to stand upright, get some air back in his lungs. "I'll settle for running water," she says.

"Just have faith," Kabir replies as he props himself up on the side of the car. "Outside's rough, but the inside? Five stars."

Jen ignores him and mouths a silent prayer that Animal and Hastings agree. She checks her phone while the team grabs their gear. Snowflakes are settling on her shoulders, but it doesn't stop Anne from delivering an update on the weather—in Tahiti. An image of crystal-clear blue water pops up next.

Freaking computer. Like the rest of the team, it has a penchant for jokes. Rather than reply, she follows the team through the garage and into the kitchen.

Roaches scatter. Black mold clings to the ceiling tiles. The door leading to the backyard is nailed shut with two-by-fours. Someone kicked it in, and wood splinters are still scattered on the linoleum tile, along with muddy boot prints. As Jen thinks that it couldn't get worse, a rat scurries across a kitchen counter.

Yeah, it always gets worse.

Animal is standing behind Kabir. He cocks back his fist, delivers a hard right-hand into Kabir's shoulder. "Five fucking stars my ass."

The kid lurches forward, clutching the impact zone. "Mate . . ."

"You must like living in shit like this," Hastings adds as he walks to the back door and tests its strength.

Jen watches Kabir as the operators continue inspecting the kitchen. Winning a fight against Animal has worse odds than the mega millions lottery, but that wouldn't stop a hardened shooter from trying after an insult like that.

He's not a fighter. It's the first conclusion she jumps to, and it's a big problem for a team like this. They're planning to engage with violent men, and she needs to have someone not only capable but willing to defend himself.

If there's an upside, it's that she's finding this out before things get serious. She snaps, "Show us our rooms."

Kabir unlocks his jaw. "Yes, ma'am."

Ma'am. That's progress. She catches the look in his eyes. He's furious, insulted. Possibly on the verge of tears. She lands on another possibility: he's respectful, only he's ditched his manners in favor of passing the bro-test. Young, college-educated. Traditional, religious parents. Positive traits, and she considers them as the tour starts.

The living room has furniture moldier than the ceiling tiles. A sofa is still overturned from when the home was assaulted by gang members, or maybe New Scotland Yard. They stop at a first-floor office that's been converted to a bedroom.

Kabir flips on the light. "Previous occupants slept here." He nods Jen into the room. "It's the best one. You should take it."

Jen labels it a complete disaster. Yellowed Grateful Dead and Phish posters on the walls. Marijuana roaches in the corner, corresponding burn marks in the carpet. If this is the nice one, she's going to have it rough—there's no way she's putting herself over her team. "Al, this is you. I want you close to the front door. Pin a camera to the window once you're settled."

"Got it, Z," Hastings responds. He marches into the space and tosses his bag onto the soiled mattress without a second thought. May be the most heroic thing Jen has ever seen him do.

The three others climb a narrow staircase to the second story. A dark hallway leads to three more bedrooms and a single bathroom. The carpet is completely brown, and it wasn't manufactured that way. It's caked with enough fertilizer to sprout a mushroom cloud over London.

Jen kicks at the plastic tubing running along the side of the hall. "How the hell'd you find this place, Kabir?"

"Civil forfeiture. Previous owners were using it to grow pot."

That explains a lot.

She follows the plastic tubing into the first bedroom and flicks on the light. This was a grow room. Mold on the ceiling; fertilizer on the ground. The tie-dye sheet she noticed in the driveway was being used to hide grow lights. But she spots a fresh mattress wedged between unused flower pots. "Hey! Things are looking up!"

"Slumlord with a heart of gold," Kabir jokes. "Had to get the place ready while you guys were in the air."

"Animal, take whichever room you want," Jen orders. "Plant a camera once you're settled."

"Sure thing, Z."

Jen beckons Kabir into her room before he can stalk out after Animal. She closes the door, trapping him in a private one-on-one. "Figured we'd do some tech familiarization."

"Yes, ma'am," Kabir replies as he takes up a position in the far corner.

Jen throws her kit on the bed, takes her time unpacking, and doesn't say a word. She wants to see if he'll complain about Animal or Hastings. This is the chance to do it. But he stays quiet. *Good.* He's not a whiner, and the position he's taken in the room is a sign of respect.

Jen's mind is made up. Regardless of what New Scotland Yard wanted, the decision to let Kabir operate with the team is hers alone. Their safety is her responsibility, and she won't jeopardize it for anyone, including superior officers. Kabir wouldn't be her first choice, but he'll stay. He's learned his place, and if he becomes difficult, he can be managed.

"I can't teach you anything if you're standing all the way over there," Jen says.

Kabir advances to the side of the bed with an awkward laugh. "What am I thinking?"

Jen knows what he's thinking, which is why she removes a bottle of aspirin from her backpack. She tries not to chuckle as he ladles out three tablets and chokes them down. Animal's knuckles probably left divots in the poor kid's arm. Next, she gives him an iPhone. "Agency special, and it's fully synced with Anne. The operating system is unique, but the home screen and applications are identical matches to Apple's."

"The Advanced NeuroNet Engine," he says, captivated by the device as it powers up. "I've heard so much about it."

"GCHQ will have its own soon," she replies, referring to a joint technology venture budding between their two governments. "Your phone will stay connected with Anne via satellite, Wi-Fi, or cellular signals. If, by chance, you lose connectivity, local devices can still be controlled via Bluetooth."

Kabir struggles to unlock the device. "Don't think Anne likes me too much."

"All she needs is a handshake," Jen says. "Anne, confirm Mr. Broja's biometrics, and grant him control of this device."

Anne responds through the cell's speakers. "Absolutely, Ms. Yates."

Kabir almost jumps as the phone starts talking. He follows the prompts on the screen and allows Anne to take pictures and video of his face. Samples of his voice. Sets of fingerprints.

Kids these days. Technology natives. So easy for them, and Jen is pleased to see that as the setup process finishes. "Anne, sync with friendly devices in our vicinity."

Kabir smiles again as the phone shows him the other pieces of quantum-powered technology the Group is using. Cell phones. Cameras that Hastings and Animal are placing around the safe house. Laptops and drones. "This is unreal."

Jen hands him a small protective case. "Your personal Whisper. It's a bone-mic. Just put it behind your ear. Anne will automatically pick up what you say through your cell and relay messages to the team."

"Thanks."

One simple word, and it's genuine too. "Don't mention it."

Kabir stows the tech in his jacket pocket and offers Jen a boyish smile. It's a genuine match to the kid she saw in the hangar. No more bravado or false confidence, just honesty.

"Why do they call you Z?" he asks.

"Zero—short for Zero Day. It was the first call sign I used during an assignment in Venezuela. Stuck with me, I guess." She plucks her laptop out of her backpack and sits on the mattress. "All right . . . I've gotta make sure our network is concealed."

"Guess I'll go get settled."

Before Kabir can open the door, she says, "You'll be a solid addition to the team. Look forward to working with you."

Kabir pauses but doesn't reply. He just absorbs the compliment, and Jen senses a leap in confidence. Before the door shuts, she's pecking out a text message to Hastings and Animal: *Go easy on Kabir, I've got him figured out.*

TWENTY-THREE

HOUSEKEEPING IS NONEXISTENT, AND THE CIGARETTE Victor—still dressed as Howard Hamlin—is smoking is to keep the hotel room's stench from activating his gag reflex. Just moments ago, he checked into the Chesterfield Inn. Owned and operated by the Dibras, it's dedicated to all sorts of criminal activity, but its primary source of income is prostitution.

The check-in counter had a jar full of condoms with enough flavor combinations to make a bag of Skittles jealous. At the insistence of the Filipino clerk, he settled for the hourly rate. Sixty minutes, and finishing early is always preferred.

Cigarette half burnt, he scrutinizes the room, wondering how anyone could screw in a place like this. Stains on the bedspread. Discarded glass pipes burned black from cooking crack cocaine. There's a dresser, but the television on top of it is fake. Didn't stop someone from trying to steal it.

The people in this hotel don't care about themselves or others. Personal traits that are typically undesirable. But tonight Victor considers them a bonus. They won't interfere with the execution he's about to commit, nor will they assist law enforcement with their investigation. Hell, he's doubting that they'll even call the cops.

Cigarette wedged in his mouth, he reaches for the suppressed Glock 35 next to him on the bed. It was his sidearm during his Spetsnaz stint. And given his unique discharge circumstances, he was able to keep it. This gun's been his companion in some very dark corners of the world, including Mexico City.

The pistol's slide has been milled for red dot sight, and after checking its brightness, he flexes his hand on the custom grip stippling. Latex gloves give him an extra degree of purchase. Twisting the suppressor, he finds it snug. Finally, he press checks the weapon, and a shiny brass shell casing peeks out of the chamber.

To the bathroom. Hookers have written their numbers on the mirror. Hearts with arrows and "time of your life" offerings. The temptation is almost impossible to resist. Instead, he tosses the cigarette in the toilet and flushes it. Next time, maybe.

The glass door to the balcony pops and sheds a glaze of ice. Good sign. The other balconies between him and his target will probably be unused. He leans over the frigid rail and looks down several stories. The alley below is vacant. Who wants to bang in the cold?

He finds the railing solid as he lifts his leg over. The next balcony is four feet away. Not far, but the slippery conditions force him to take it slow. With his left hand stretched out, he leaps, gets a foothold, and latches onto the railing.

On the new balcony, he peeks into the hotel room. Dark. Unoccupied. Same result on the balcony next to that. He's gaining momentum as he nears the hotel's corner suite. Up close, he can see the cracked balcony door. Cigarette smoke is seeping out of the opening. A crummy action movie is blasting on the television. Must be the presidential suite if it has a TV and cable.

With both legs over the railing, he jumps to the final balcony.

Could be the blood pulsing in his ears, but the metal seems to strain a little louder under his weight. He pulls the pistol from under his jacket and raises it toward the door. He waits for a response.

"They call you stainless steel on the streets."

Chuck Norris's voice follows. Canned sounds from the television's crappy speakers. But Vehbi Dibra's hoarse laughter is not part of the script. It's vivid and clear and strains the metal bedframe.

Victor considers it safe to move and throws a leg over the rail. His boots crunch the snow as he pies off the balcony, weapon raised. The red dot sight stays fixed on the gap in the door.

Bare feet hang off the hotel bed. Black jeans start at the ankle, and Victor keeps moving to find them torn at the knees. Thick, black chest hair blooming out from a wife-beater T-shirt. An ashtray bobs up and down on Vehbi's chest, and a cigarette smolders on his lip. He's smiling at *Code of Silence*, oblivious to the threat ten feet away.

Victor settles the red dot on his right temple. He uses his left thumb to apply pressure to the rear of the Glock's slide to prevent the weapon from cycling. He won't leave shell casings behind, but more important, the gunshot will be quieter. He rushes through the trigger's take-up, stops at the breaking point. Applied pressure . . .

A puff of air escapes the suppressor. A wet thud echoes in the room as the bullet smacks the side of Vehbi's head. Low impact, boring into his brain stem. Vehbi starts, jackknifes on the bed, and stares at the television like a confused toddler.

Victor has seen it before. In Syria. Bullets that should stop a man cold somehow doing the opposite. At times the human body behaves like it can defy physics. But Vehbi is one hundred percent dead. His body just hasn't caught on.

Heaving open the balcony door, Victor rushes into the room and finds an empty chair in the corner. He breezes past Vehbi, who is wheezing on the bed, and enters the bathroom. Clear.

He approaches the peephole and looks out into the hallway. Earlier, he'd marked two guards standing by the entrance, and they're still there, oblivious that their boss has been executed.

Victor manually cycles the pistol and plucks the spent casing out of the air as he returns to the bed. Vehbi's eyes follow him lamely as he squares up and angles the pistol toward his forehead. Zero recognition. Vehbi doesn't flinch or attempt to shield himself before a single gunshot evacuates his brain.

Victor checks for a pulse and finds nothing. No way for him to survive, but it pays to be thorough. This jaunt through London is one way, and there won't be any do-overs. He frisks Vehbi and snatches the cell phone out of his pocket. Last item he needed.

Shell casings in his pocket, Victor retraces his steps out of the room and prepares to traverse the balcony back to his own. He'll be looking at the Chesterfield Inn from his rearview in under five minutes, which is the time he needs to reach his next target.

Twenty-Four

ANDREW'S PHONE IS BUZZING, BUT NOW ISN'T THE TIME FOR distractions. He's making the final preparations for his user account on the Void network. Yes, he got access to Void's browser, but he needs to conduct business, and the software's engineers didn't make that easy.

Void requires a verified identity to create the account. Helps filter out law enforcement and rival criminals. It's using what's called a Zero Knowledge Proof to verify Andrew's existence. The verification program acts like a middleman, conducting a search on the applicant, all while keeping his identity secret from Void's administrators. All they'll see is that he's a real person, and nothing more.

Anonymity is critical to cybercrime, and the engineers who designed Void honored that maxim. But he won't trust criminals with his life, or those of his Group.

He's using deepfake technology to render a fake identity and create the account. The person Void will see is computer-generated. Using a face or name that resembles a living human being is out of the question. The people responsible for Void are dangerous, vindictive.

Anne has generated the identity along with multiple layers of verifiable information. Surface-level stuff, like Instagram accounts with posts dating back several years. Same with LinkedIn and Facebook. Then the mid-layer essentials, like medical, criminal, and employment records. Finally, the deep stuff: a Social Security number and corresponding birth records.

He has no idea how far Void can probe, so he's been thorough. He also doesn't know what Void will do if the identity doesn't check out. Ban him from the browser? Forbid him from trying again? There's no time to work around those issues. This will be his only chance.

He starts making the account on his cell phone. Basics first, like his name and birthday. *Deepfake to the rescue.* They go deeper—request information for an active cryptocurrency wallet and his Social Security number. *Check and check.*

He clicks Next and finds the first real challenge. Void wants finger-prints—likely the reason they required a touch-screen device to register the account. He planned for the contingency, and he'll need to use a hacking technique to enter his computer-generated prints. Uncertainty rises. Will Void detect it?

Andrew opens a program on the phone and begins using a hacking technique called Synthetic Touch. The program will trick the iPhone's sensors into thinking that it's being pressed by a finger or thumb. The Advanced NeuroNet Engine has already designed phony prints, and they'll be the ones uploaded to Void's system.

Andrew initiates the process. Void asks for a right-hand thumbprint. He cues up his program, and tiny green lines crawl across the screen's face. *Thank you. Right index finger, please.*

Andrew satisfies the request, thinking that the hack is going according to plan. After two more entries, the phone vibrates, and a message flashes: *Verifying identity.*

He gulps. Isn't that what the *Thank-yous* were for?

A line traverses the edges of a hollow circle. *Processing.*

Another vibration. *Identity verified.*

Andrew takes a gulp of air and allows his pulse to cool off. Felt closer than it should have, or maybe he just worked himself up.

With his account created, he proceeds to Lust's page. A ten-thou-sand-dollar Bitcoin deposit is required to book a girl. Void needed the crypto wallet for a reason, but he wonders why the sum is so high.

Remove. He realizes that many of these women don't come back from their dates, and the Likas are looking for proper compensation.

Andrew's stomach flips. Trading in human lives is gut-wrenching, and he's been on the receiving end of it before. Beijing's ghosts would never let him forget. But he forces himself to continue.

After depositing the money in an escrow wallet, he takes a deeper dive into the webpage.

Classy joint. Nudity is off limits, at least on the girl's individual pages. Leaves something to the imagination. Every girl on the page is exquisite, and so are the asking prices. Ten thousand won't get a man far in Void's world.

He scrolls, scrolls, scrolls. Dozens, maybe a hundred girls are listed on the site. Working in London or New York. The Lika Syndicate's turf. Now it's time to find what he needs.

"Anne, I need you to scrape Lust's web page."

The quantum computer is always ready. "Any specific parameters, Andrew?"

Thorough is the name of the game. "Spend between three and four minutes viewing each page. Use sporadic scrolling. We need to make it look like their newest customer is window-shopping."

"Beginning."

Anne clicks the first listing. Slowly, she scrolls over the girl's photographs. Prices. Home city. The computer stops on a picture, then scrolls back up to another for comparison. "Perfect, Anne. Run simultaneous biometric scans and corresponding background checks. Flag anyone with a known criminal history; same goes for missing persons, or anyone under the age of twenty-one."

Andrew hops up from his desk and pads toward the Group's individual offices. Anne won't be finished for hours, and he's desperate for some shut-eye. Home would be nice, but he's going to settle for a sofa instead.

TWENTY-FIVE

THE JAZZ IS GOOD.

The musicians are locals, but their covers could rival the originals like Al Green and Ray Charles. Lights are low, and the mood is electric. There are forty, maybe fifty people sitting around the jazz club called Lead Belly's, enjoying live music, romantic dates, and potent cocktails.

Victor is sitting in a booth by himself. Back of the bar. Alcohol was too hard to pass up, but he sips slowly. The night isn't over. Steady hands and a clear mind will see him through. Could be thirty seconds; could be thirty minutes. But he'll need to kill somebody soon. Maybe a lot of somebodies. So he sips in the relative dark, the Glock 35 nestled beneath his jacket, suppressor removed.

Redding's "Dock of the Bay" kicks off. Like Otis, Victor is riding the tide. Energy is flowing to the musicians at the center of the room, but he's marking the big-boned, thick fuckers sitting in the corners. They're not paying him any mind—yet.

This club belongs to Isuf Dibra—Vehbi's father—and he's guzzling cocktails in a private second-story lounge that doubles as a meeting area. Getting up there is impossible, but Victor's got a solution in mind.

All good things come in time.

A waitress passes Victor and gives him a sweet smile. Raises his already-elevated spirits. Even with a shock of gray hair, he can pull as much ass as he wants. Blessings be to handsome looks, but more important, to swagger.

Commotion erupts at the front door. Local muscle from the Chesterfield Inn—just the ones Victor was waiting for. They've come to deliver news that no father should hear over the phone. That's discipline. That's respect.

Victor is going to waste them for it.

As the local thug rushes across the club's floor, Victor flags down the passing waitress. She finishes with a table, and Victor manipulates the cell phone in his lap. It belonged to Vehbi. He activates the Share My Location feature and sends it to his father, Isuf. Then he wraps it in his cloth napkin.

The waitress arrives, eager, with a smile. "What can I get you?"

Victor matches her smile. It's not for her, but for the bar tab that'll go unpaid. "Hibiki with a big rock."

"Good choice," she replies and scoops Victor's empty glass. "Back in a few."

Before she turns away, Victor raises the napkin. "Oh!" He leans over and places the napkin on her tray. Stops her from feeling the weight of what's hidden inside. "Thanks."

Like an earthquake, things are shifting beneath the club's surface. Thugs squeeze out of booths and bound up the stairs. Several more rush to the front and back doors, no doubt moving to arrange transportation to the hotel. By now the waitress has retreated behind the bar and is clearing her tray, waiting for drink orders to be filled.

Isuf steps to the second-story railing, cell phone in hand. Albanian genetics are on display; he's got some size, along with thick gray hair. Taste is also in his blood, and he's wearing a handsome plaid blazer to prove it. He stares down in the waitress's direction, anguished, and sees only the ghost of his son.

The crowd is grooving. Redding is climaxing.

Isuf allows his phone to guide him down the stairs, flanked by three men. He's transfixed on the bar, the waitress—who is equally confused. She just picked up Victor's napkin and is unwrapping it.

Isuf and his men surround the bar. They're staring at the confused waitress as she cradles the phone in her hand. She looks up, realizing she's been flanked by a pack of wolves. Confusion turns to terror.

"Where did you get that?" Isuf shouts.

She looks at Victor's table but doesn't find the charming gentlemen from moments ago. He's gone. Dine and dash with a unique twist.

But Victor hasn't gone far. He's obtained a deadly advantage. He stands behind Isuf and his men. They should have cut the lights and killed the music when they heard the news, but instead a .40 caliber pistol will do it for them. He raises his pistol and the red dot centers on the back of Isuf's head. A single bullet obliterates his skull.

There's a theory about starting gunfights with your back turned to your opponent. Been tested worldwide with a robust cross-section of subjects. Generally, the practice doesn't end well. Isuf's men prove it. Victor guns them down with double taps to backs, sides, and finally, their chests. It's rapid, efficient, and in Victor's skilled hands, the pistol sounds almost like a machine gun.

Instruments drop; microphones screech. Screams lead to panic, and a stampede ensues. The bursts of gunfire happened too fast for the crowd to process. People are confused, unsure of where it originated.

Victor stows his pistol and drops low, protecting his head from potential return fire as he blends with the crowd. Dozens of people swallow him as they surge toward the front exit. It takes all his strength to remain upright and not get trampled.

Caught in the flurry, he scans his surroundings. Men are tending to Isuf, who is completely unresponsive. None of them look in his direction. But one of the bouncers working the door witnessed the shooting and has his eyes on Victor.

The bouncer is shouting for help as the crowd brings Victor closer to him. But amid the noise and confusion, he can't get the attention he needs. Then Victor spots a flashlight in his hands. Classic trick to mark troublemakers in a darkened environment. If that light shines on Victor, he could be in trouble.

Victor buries an elbow into a woman's back and drives forward. People are funneling through the exit, and pressure is building. The surge pins the bouncer into the side wall.

A folding knife is in Victor's hand as he comes within reach. The crowd doesn't allow him to stop and address the threat properly. He keeps the blade low to avoid another scare and is afforded just enough time to sink the blade twice into the bouncer's abdomen.

He hears a thud behind him, but he doesn't look back to survey the damage. The crowd pulls him onto the sidewalk. Flashing blue lights skate along icy streets, and they're coming closer. Continuing to use the crowd, he runs down the sidewalk and veers into an alleyway. The van is a block away, and the man he came to kill is dead. Time to get the hell out of London for good.

Twenty-Six

Sunrise. Orange and pink hues ricochet against rocky mountain peaks and settle in the clouds above.

Martinez is behind the wheel of a rental SUV, thanking the heavens for the chains on her tires. Guardrails are noticeably absent on the windy mountain road she's traversing. It's snowed over, and the SUV's tail slides out at random, along with her composure.

She wishes she could have brought a driver so she could focus on the talking points, but coming alone was the meeting's central condition. There's an upside: if she arrives in one piece, she'll have an entire afternoon to spend with a unique man.

To date, Colonel Ilzat Karavayev is the highest-ranking defector from GRU, Russia's premier intelligence service. His storied departure occurred just over six years ago. The colonel had crossed the wrong people, and the Russian government placed a target on his head. Through sheer luck, he survived an assassination attempt and opted against giving his enemies a second opportunity.

After a harrowing trek across Russia's porous border into Ukraine, he appeared in the U.S. embassy's lobby, pleading for asylum. Not long after it was granted, information about his career began flowing.

Martinez has traveled to Wyoming, hoping he'll have data stashed in his records about the Founders. Alex Varga's dossier was illuminating, but the information is too general. The *rightful owners* grew in communism's shadow and remained hidden there for decades. If she wants to catch Victor Orlov and the people controlling him, she has to get smarter.

The colonel's debrief records don't mention the Founders by name, but after almost thirty years in Russian intelligence, she considers it likely that he's heard whispers.

57222.

Martinez hits the brakes and skids past the colonel's mailbox. After regaining control, she reverses and starts up the driveway. Snow hasn't been shoveled off the road. Pine trees loom over the trail with heavily laden branches. She peers into the surrounding wilderness and notices snowmobile tracks.

Seems like she chose the incorrect vehicle. Or she's late for an unplanned meeting.

The colonel is paranoid for good reason. She had to make special inquiries to access him. Leaks happen, and she gets nervous. Reaching for the 2011 hidden in the center console, she props it on her leg, index finger resting against the trigger guard.

Karavayev's cabin comes into view. A sleek, black snowmobile is parked in front. Hasn't been there long. No snow on the seat, and the tracks behind it are fresh. When she's fifty yards away, she decides it's close enough. She places the SUV in park and steps into the snow.

She studies the cabin, no doubt constructed by one of Wyoming's overpaid builders. It's a true log cabin, built with unprocessed sticks of timber. Sloping roofs prevent snow from piling up top. Giant windows offer picturesque views of the countryside. If Martinez wasn't afraid for her life, she would stop to stare at the surrounding peaks.

The cabin's lights are off, and she can't detect any movement. Bad sign. Cameras and motion detectors affixed to the cabin should have given her presence away. The colonel is expecting her, and she's right on time.

Despite her better judgment, she presses forward. If this is a murder scene, she needs to investigate and report it. If a killer is still in the area, she'd like to ask him some questions before taking a shot at him herself.

Martinez steps into the no-man's-land between the cabin and the tree line. Just a field of pristine snow, and she forges through the knee-high powder, heart flailing.

She's halfway to the door when something snaps behind her. Before she can turn to look, a M67 fragmentation grenade falls between her legs. Without a second's hesitation, she dives into the snow. She sinks in, praying that it'll protect her from the blast.

Three seconds.

Five, then ten.

The explosion doesn't come.

She struggles to push herself upright and search for whoever threw the frag. A camouflaged man appears only five feet away, pointing a rifle at her head. He's wearing snow shoes, which allowed him to close on her so quickly.

"Drop the gun. Stand up, slowly."

Martinez follows the command but struggles to identify the man, whose face is covered by a white balaclava.

"Did you bring identification?"

"In my jacket," Martinez replies.

"Reach for it, but take your time. We have all day."

Russian accent. Wrinkles under his eyes. Martinez realizes she has found Colonel Ilzat Karavayev. The colonel's fearsome reputation was earned long ago, but he's reinforcing it today. She raises a black wallet in the air.

"Open it. Show it to me."

Martinez complies, trying not to roll her eyes. The paranoid asshole is reading her ID through his magnified rifle scope. "That's a first."

"Make do with what you've got, Ms. Martinez. Why the gun?" he asks, lowering his rifle and removing his balaclava.

"Funny feeling."

The colonel nods. "I've had plenty of those over the course of my career. Listened to every one of them. That's why I'm still alive."

"Can I retrieve my pistol?"

"You may not. I'll return it to you once our meeting is over." The colonel walks over and retrieves his grenade. He grunts and stands back up. "That crack you heard wasn't a branch. It was my shoulder. Youth and I parted ways a long time ago."

"Just pop a few aspirin and let's get on with it," Martinez replies, unable to hide her annoyance. She's freezing, and her clothes are getting soaked with melting snow.

The colonel laughs and tosses her the frag. "They sell them at the local gun shop."

Martinez turns the hunk of green metal over and finds a hole drilled in the bottom. "A dummy grenade?"

"Dummy." He snorts out a laugh. "Good word for it." He grabs her 2011 and brushes some snow off her shoulders. "C'mon. I've got some of those aspirin in the house. Looks like you could use them more than me."

Twenty-Seven

THE RAP SHEET WOULD BE A MILE LONG IF IT WEREN'T digitized. Sloane is in the passenger seat of a New Scotland Yard BMW X5, reviewing information on a potential witness to last night's shooting at the Chesterfield Inn. Judging by his criminal record and employment history, securing his cooperation will be a challenge.

Last night's violence is connected to Jen's work in the Bronx. More of the Lord's work. If she can pin the homicides to a member of the Lika Syndicate, she may be able to turn him. Use him as a witness. Crack open Lust and, by extension, Void.

If she fails to turn the shooter, she'll still have a useful ally in the Crown's prosecutor. The Lika's have businesses speckled around London, and search warrants would follow the murderer's arrest. Searches like that could yield some interesting pieces of technology.

"Hello," she says, eyes bulging at Leelee Paragno's most recent mugshot. Wasn't his best night. The five-foot-six-inch Filipino man was wearing his finest black dress when he was arrested for solicitation. During an altercation with MPS's Narcotics Division, his lipstick was smudged and his hair was disheveled.

"That was in June . . . twenty-twenty. After his most recent arrest, he picked up steady work as the night clerk at Chesterfield Inn," Toliver notes as he focuses on the road ahead. The Bimmer's blue siren is doing its best to part traffic, but during morning rush hour, motorists have plans of their own. "Detectives told me that he can put up a real fight, and he likes a blade."

"Got it," Sloane replies, still focused on the mugshot. Leelee is in his early forties, which makes him a career criminal. Got a taste for needles and anabolic steroids. He's short, but striated muscles traverse his frame. Not someone to take lightly.

She hops on her radio and relays the news to Gray and Coco, who are following close behind in their own X5. Both operators have spent enough time in faraway lands that driving on the wrong side of the road feels right. Toliver trusted them with a vehicle, and they haven't scratched its glossy black paint—yet.

The operators acknowledge the warning as Leelee's apartment building comes into view. Two stories that wrap around a central parking lot. Type of place that could have been a motel. Or a strip mall with one too many massage parlors. But residential zoning didn't stop the landlord from turning the complex into a haven for illicit behavior. Rent is paid in cash with utilities packaged in from a centralized bill. Helps tenants hide their residences from law enforcement.

"Hang on!" Toliver orders as he jerks the Bimmer into the parking lot. He mashes the brakes and blocks part of the entrance. Gray and Coco pull in and block the remaining half. No vehicles in or out until their work is through.

Sloane adjusts the New Scotland Yard badge affixed to her gun belt before drawing her Staccato P and rushing out of the vehicle. Like Jen's, her pistol has a red dot sight and a weapon-mounted light. With twenty-one rounds in the magazine, she's got steam to fight all day and into the night.

Toliver grabs his Benelli M4 shotgun from the mount in the footwell and exits the vehicle. Gray and Coco have already formed up with their 2011s drawn. "Round back! Probably where the action is going to be!"

Without a word, the two operators sprint toward the rear of the building and disappear around the corner.

Sloane beats Toliver to the stairs, and she takes them in twos.

Leelee's apartment is in the center of the horseshoe, and she zeroes in on it as she walks. Each apartment has a large central window, but they're all barred over.

They slow to a creep so that their footsteps don't alert their subject. Sloane stops at the window's edge, and Toliver crosses to the far side of the door and presses his back into the wall.

She peeks through a gap in the curtains. Leelee is sitting on the sofa, talking, but he doesn't have a phone up to his ear. Someone is seated across from him in the living room, and the conversation appears tense. Most likely the mafia extracting *her* statement. Drove all this way for it too. She makes eye contact with Toliver and holds up two fingers.

Toliver acknowledges and bangs his fist into the door. Hard, violent. "Leelee Paragno! Police! We'd like to talk to you about last night!"

Sloane maintains visual contact with the subject, and like an actor on cue, Leelee jumps at the announcement. Sad so few people have an interest in speaking with the police these days, but Sloane is ready to do some convincing. After a quick exchange, he runs down a hallway leading deeper into the apartment. "He's bolting."

"You have the wrong address!" a second man shouts.

"We'll see about that," Toliver says as he steps in front of the door and drives his wingtip into the wood. Hasn't lost a step since the Mideast, and the door gives on the first blow. He doesn't wait an instant before storming the apartment, shotgun raised.

Sloane follows him into the fight. A large Albanian man is standing just feet from the door, and he doesn't appear fazed by law enforcement officers and their weapons. He's tall, with a tanned, chiseled face. Bulging, enraged eyes. An AK-47 is tattooed on his neck, and he's got a spiderweb on the back of his hand. This only goes one way.

"Get down on the ground!" they order in unison.

Sloane drops her 2011's safety as she scans him for weapons. Nothing visible, but she's not sure that would stop her from squeezing the trigger.

A crash down the hall is followed by breaking glass.

"Go on, Hamilton! I've got this," Toliver says as he stares down his shotgun's sight.

Sloane doesn't question Toliver's ability to manage the situation. She tears off in Leelee's direction, willing to let nature run its course.

Toliver drops out of his shooting position and stands relaxed. He raises the shotgun and settles the barrel on his shoulder. He gives the Albanian a devious grin. "That what you wanted, boy?"

The Albanian's eyes flash and he lunges forward, but Toliver knew the attempted tackle was coming. He jerks the buttstock up and jams it forward. It crashes into the Albanian's nose.

The thug stumbles backward, giving Toliver another opening. He flips the shotgun off his shoulder. Once he's got it positioned in his hands, he drives the muzzle into the Albanian's cheek. A bone snaps, and a half-moon gash marks the barrel's impact point.

Semiconscious, the Albanian falls onto his back. Toliver puts the Benelli's muzzle in his face. The safety clicks off. "Think the stars are bad? Just wait until I show you the fireworks. Turn the fuck over and put your hands behind your back."

———

Mascara, eyeliner, and lip gloss are scattered across the bathroom's tile floor.

Leelee's vanity has been toppled, and it's wedged between the door and the toilet, sealing the room while he tries to break free. He hears banging on the door and figures it's the silly bitch he caught peeking into his window.

People have always judged him by his sexuality, but they're mistaken. He's a fighter. He was getting passed around dance bars in the Philippines before he could read and write, and the West's criminal justice system is little more than an extended trip to his favorite nightclub.

Like any proper felon, he'd like to delay his trip upstate, which is why he's already got one foot out of his bathroom window. It's a tight fit, but that's never stopped him before. He drops his head and eases his torso out of the opening. Straddling the windowsill, he looks down and judges the drop. Ten feet. Lucky there's a car parked in the alley below the window.

With an explosion, the bathroom door nearly splits in half. "Leelee Paragno! Stop right now!"

Only one way to respond. Leelee laughs and kicks his remaining leg through the window. With just the right amount of force, he pushes off the sill and lands on the car's roof.

Leaving a trail of creased metal behind, he leaps off the sedan and runs back toward the parking lot. He ventures a rearward glance at the bathroom window. Same bitch from before, but now she's cost him his security deposit. Jerking up his hand, he flips her the bird.

Amusing, until she smiles back and waves.

Then he feels a baseball bat cross his chest and goes flying. Breathless from the blow, he looks up from his back and finds a very large man standing over him. When he realizes it wasn't a Louisville Slugger but the freaking guy's arm, he's disappointed in himself. *That was too easy.*

The man is flexing blood back into his arm. "Maybe we should pretend it was our first time, Coco."

"Then he could feel like he had a chance."

"Fuck you guys," Leelee responds as he struggles to breathe again.

Gray pulls a set of cuffs out of his pocket and ratchets them open. "C'mon, you sexy beast. Turn over."

"Don't you know you're supposed to buy me a drink first?" Leelee jokes. He licks his lips and blows Coco a kiss. "Give me your number, daddy, and I'll answer *all* your questions."

Twenty-Eight

Specks of mildew have fallen from the ceiling and settled on Jen's laptop screen. An overturned planter next to her bed shifts at random, and she's concerned a rodent has made a den of it. Afraid of what she'll find, she has decided to leave the creature alone. It was here before she arrived, and it'll be here long after too. Besides, there aren't any fresh bite marks on her skin from last night. Call it a favor for a favor.

Andrew's list of potential candidates reached Jen's inbox several hours ago, and she's been working on it ever since. It was generated from Lust's page on Void and is composed of escorts working in London.

When she started, there were seventeen names. After carefully considering each woman, she has narrowed the list down to four. They share a few similarities: young, from Eastern Europe, and have missing person's reports filed in their home countries. Reports like these raise the specter of kidnapping and human trafficking, which will increase the probability that the candidate will want to cooperate with law enforcement and return to her family.

Scrolling through the faces on her laptop, it's hard not to feel guilty. These women have been exploited. In a way, she's going to do the same.

Better me than them. One of the maxims that help her press forward when situations turn bleak.

Today, it's failing to help her find her resolve. Sacrificing *herself* has always been easy. But another human being? That's something she's never been capable of. In a way, it has probably harmed her career, but those fancy window offices come with a price she's not willing to pay.

She slowly scrolls through the photographs, making a silent promise to each. Destroying Gombe Wireless will be for country. Lust and its operators will be for Jen. Whatever sacrifice she asks one or more of these women to make will be rewarded. Before she leaves London, they'll be free.

Jen clicks her laptop shut, feeling like she's found her true north and descends the stairs to the kitchen. Breakfast is on the table, but she hears a pistol's slide working instead of smacking lips. Sounds like her text message to Hastings and Animal was well received.

She enters the kitchen as Hastings shows off his Staccato P to Kabir. The kid's grin is wider than when he met Anne last night. Telltale sign of a gun nut.

"That freaking slide is like butter, mate," Kabir says while racking the slide back and forth.

"Try the trigger," Hastings comments before looking to Jen. "Got you a breakfast burrito, Z. In the bag on the counter."

"Thanks. Got a freaking appetite like no other," Jen lies, setting her laptop down on the counter beside the bag. Hunger vanished when she saw the first girl on her laptop screen, and it hasn't returned since.

The pistol's hammer drops. Kabir laughs and beams at the pistol like a proud uncle. "That trigger pull is around half the weight of my service Glock."

Animal gulps down his burrito and reaches into a paper bag for a second. He gives Jen a nod, eyes gleaming. "Z popped Sandro Lika with hers the other night."

"Add another trophy gun to her collection," Hastings adds.

Kabir eyes Jen's pistol, a thirsty look on his face. "Can I touch it, Z?"

"Hell no!" Jen exclaims, nearly spitting up a mouthful of orange juice. Animal and Hastings are laughing like a couple of drunk teenagers. She's glad to see it. Last night, they'd been hard on the kid.

Most top-tier units don't haze new members, including hers, but it was for good reason. As of this morning, all is forgiven. "But I do need a quick hand."

Kabir returns Hastings' pistol and joins Jen at the counter. "What do you have for me?"

Hastings holsters the 2011 and starts for the kitchen door. "We're going to go work on our kits, Z. Holler if you need anything."

As Animal rumbles past, he adds, "You're about to miss the real fun, kid."

Kabir looks after them, jealous.

"Don't worry, you can go bug them in a few minutes," Jen says, angling the laptop in his direction. "Screen these candidates. Let me know if you see anything that our initial workups might have missed."

Kabir analyzes the photographs. There is no nudity, but the women wear revealing dresses, which is helpful. He stops on his first candidate and hovers the laptop's curser over one of her tattoos. "This girl is from Estonia. She's a mobster's girlfriend."

Jen glances at the computer and recognizes the candidate. Kabir nailed her country of origin based on the photograph alone. Toliver hadn't been kidding about his talent; the kid's a magnificent analyst, just lacking in street smarts. "Why would her family file a missing person's report if she's connected to organized crime?"

"The family isn't in the mafia, and she left without their consent." Kabir takes a hard look at the girl and sighs. "She could have made her boyfriend mad—cheated or something. So he sent her away. There's also a chance he's using her to make money."

Jen can only shake her head at a culture she'll never understand. Whatever the girl's transgression, she doesn't deserve a life of prostitution. "I see."

"She'll be a poor candidate though. Once you're connected to a family, you stay with it," Kabir says as he continues examining the photographs.

Jen lets Kabir continue his analysis.

"Her." Kabir suddenly stops scrolling and twists the laptop to face Jen. "I want to pick her."

Serai Konci. A candidate that had jumped out at Jen too. The girl is nineteen. No tattoos or other unique identifying markings. She's wearing a silk dress and is sitting on the edge of a bed with her legs crossed. She's smiling, but her body is rigid, and the photo appears forced. "What do you see in her?"

"The red-and-white wool bracelet she's wearing. It's called a *verore*. People wear them to celebrate *Dita e Verës*—The Summer Day Festival."

To Jen, the bracelet resembles a candy cane, but it's tattered and dirty. Been through the wringer, yet the girl refuses to let it go. A keepsake with memories of the people she loves attached to it.

"Albanians celebrate the holiday on March first," Kabir continues. "It's a new year celebration that marks the end of winter. Towns across the country put on huge festivals, and people trade verores with their loved ones."

"Have a look at her file," Jen says, her suspicions about the bracelet confirmed. "There's a missing person's report that was filed twelve months ago."

"Knew it," Kabir says as he reads the file prepared by Anne. "She's from Shkodra, one of Albanian's most violent regions. The Lika Syndicate also has deep ties to the area. There's a strong possibility that they brought her to London."

"There aren't any immigration documents linked to her presence in London, which means she came in the hard way."

Kabir's features get heavy. "She'd have seen a lot on her journey."

Jen can't argue. The kid is dead on, and she's getting a good feeling about their candidate. "Let's lock this in . . . and *excellent* work, by the way."

"Thanks." Kabir glows, then changes the subject. "We need to talk about the detention."

A discussion is the last thing she wants, but it appears he is interested in planning the candidate's arrest. His analysis may have been solid, but he's not an experienced operator. Moreover, the people on this team are her responsibility. That includes him. He's technically a *partner*, but she needs to maintain strict control over this element. "I already have a hotel in mind. Someplace nice with a restaurant in the lobby. What do you think about that?"

"Just okay," Kabir replies as he rocks his hand. "If she's traveling with security, extracting her could create a scene and put British civilians in danger. Can we find a crowded venue? A place where we could grab her without anyone noticing?"

"If we go with a venue that's too crowded, we'll have trouble tracking our candidate and marking her handlers. That puts my operators at risk. Hotels have digital security embedded, and their tech is usually high quality. We can tap in and use it as a force multiplier."

Kabir hitches his hands to his pants as he mulls over Jen's idea.

But Jen isn't interested in his rebuttal, so she fills him in on the second half of her plan. Give him something serious to worry about. "I want you to make first contact with the candidate. The hotel restaurant will be ideal for that."

"What?" he stammers, face reddening. "Why am I meeting the candidate?"

"My guys are too intimidating, and they're heavily tattooed. Our girl could get cold feet and bolt. You also speak the language." She can see his nerves tying themselves in knots. Tonight, he'll be squared up with men he's only seen in picture books. Funny how quickly his outlook is changing. "Look, no one will be able to get close to you without us seeing. And once we're in the suite, we have total control—and privacy."

Kabir stares at Serai's picture on the screen. Finally, he sighs. "All right . . . I'm with you on the hotel."

"I'll put it in motion."

Jen returns to her bedroom, needing to focus. She drops onto the mattress, laptop cradled on her lap. Before booking Serai, she brings up her chosen hotel's website. The Trafalgar in central London. Rooms are available, and she reserves a two-bedroom suite. Expensive but perfect.

On to the tough part. Void. A number of digital tripwires are built into the dark web platform, and activating one could mean failure.

Grabbing her cell phone, she says, "Anne, I'm preparing to log into Void."

"I'm here to assist, Ms. Yates. How would you like to proceed?"

"Block outside access attempts to my camera. Also, I'd like you to spoof my GPS location. Put me at the Trafalgar."

"Your camera has been disabled. Your GPS location has also been augmented."

"All right, let's see what we have," she whispers.

Jen opens the Void browser on her cell phone and navigates to the login page. Basic credentials are required, and she enters them based on the account data Andrew forwarded to her. A two-factor authentication request appears. Void wants a thumbprint—the first real hurdle.

Jen opens her phone's Synthetic Touch tool and enters the corresponding fingerprint. After what feels like an eternity, the login succeeds. Whoever engineered Void put some serious tech behind the platform, and she can't help but be impressed.

She navigates to Lust and books her candidate for the night. A nonrefundable deposit is extracted from the crypto wallet Andrew set up, and a message pops up on the screen:

Do not deviate from our instructions.

1. Bring your phone to the date.

2. Do not be late.

A countdown clock appears at the bottom of the screen. Matches the date's intended start time. A map pops up moments later with a GPS pin centered on the Trafalgar. Void took it from her phone. Had she been less careful, she'd have exposed her safe house.

Precautions have earned her another advantage. She now knows Void will attempt to track her device, and there's no telling what else it will do. She's going to treat this phone like it's radiated, at least until she has her candidate in custody.

TWENTY-NINE

While Martinez's introduction to Colonel Karavayev was a little rough, she's finding him to be an inviting host. He's boiling a pot of tea, offered smoked mackerel, and made good on his promise of aspirin.

She can't help but smile as he walks into the living room carrying a tea tray. Reminds her of Mr. Rogers. Maroon sweater and khaki pants. Button-down shirt with a tie. His gray hair is thin and in need of a barber, but he has combed it over for his guest. Complete opposite of the paranoid recluse she met an hour ago.

"How do you take it?" Karavayev asks, setting the tray down between them on the coffee table.

"Two cubes."

The colonel drops two sugar cubes into her tea and hands her the saucer. "Careful. It's still hot."

"One second you're throwing fake grenades at me. Another you're worried about the roof of my mouth," Martinez says, laughing.

"Sorry," Karavayev says, finishing his own tea ritual before sitting. "I've crossed some serious people. Had to make sure I was safe."

Martinez blows away the steam and sips her tea. "I know it's a risk, and I appreciate you taking the trouble to meet with me."

"I don't get many visitors. This cabin can be quite isolating."

"Jackson Hole isn't far. Plenty of gorgeous women hanging around," Martinez says.

The colonel's deep brown eyes mist over. "I lost my wife after my defection. The Kremlin was . . . unkind to her."

Martinez is aware of his wife's murder and kicks herself for her callous handling of the subject. "Sorry, sir. Shouldn't have crossed into that territory."

"It was a fine suggestion, Ms. Martinez. Only, I swore Claire would be my only one." He takes a sip of his tea. "The only reason I continue is to hurt *them*."

Martinez doesn't want to let the hostility go to waste, and she jumps into her reason for meeting. "I came to talk to you about something specific, Colonel. Unfortunately, I didn't find any information about it in your debrief records."

Karavayev's emotions drain away, and his eyes go numb. He rests his saucer on his leg, which is slight from old age and inactivity. "You want to know about the *vladelets*."

Martinez places her saucer on the tray. "How did you know that, sir?"

"My debrief was thorough, and it spanned my entire career. They're the only element that was left out."

"Did you attempt to disclose their existence?"

"Yes. But your CIA wasn't interested in secret societies that I only had a loose knowledge of." He laughs warmly and mocks the Agency. "The Illuminati, they called it. Asked me if they were living in the pyramids."

Martinez doesn't share in his amusement. Defectors like the colonel don't appear often. *Any* detail he was willing to share should have been thoroughly documented. "Your debriefing officers lacked foresight."

"But you don't."

"I wouldn't call it foresight. Just learning from hard lessons," Martinez replies. "How would you characterize the Founders, sir?"

Karavayev rests his saucer on the tray and reflects. "That's a question I still struggle with, but I can tell you that they're uniquely Russian."

"I'm not sure that I follow."

"Their true origins are obscure, but their rise to power began in the nineties," Karavayev explains. "When the Soviet Union collapsed in ninety-one, it was the world's largest police state. The KGB was a key part of that apparatus.

"Overnight, hundreds of thousands of the country's intelligence officers were thrown into the streets. They were educated men, armed with information and the social networks to use it. During that time, dozens of miniature private intelligence agencies were created. Many of them still exist—take Wagner Group, for example."

Martinez is familiar with the Kremlin's private paramilitary force. They've run amok in Syria, Africa, and anywhere else they think they can challenge the U.S. for dominance. She asks, "Were they business oriented? Was their focus on criminal activity?"

"All of the above and more," Karavayev replies. "While Boris Yeltsin was president, he created his own agency known as the Presidential Protection Bureau. It had just one mission: investigate his rivals, both politically and in business. If his enemies became too strong, he used the PSB to blackmail them. And if that didn't work . . ." Karavayev shrugs.

"Uniquely Russian," Martinez notes, thinking aloud about the colonel's previous statement. "You know, half a trillion U.S. dollars was looted from Russia during the early nineties."

The colonel nods. "It was one of history's greatest transfers of public wealth to private individuals. I'm certain a generous portion landed in bank accounts controlled by the Founders."

"Can you describe how you became aware of the Founders, sir?" Martinez asks.

"It was during the operation that cost me my career and nearly ended my life," Karavayev replies as he tells a story that started eight years ago.

He was commanding operations to disrupt and dismantle arms manufacturers that were selling weapons in Eastern Europe. Countries like Estonia, Latvia, and Czechoslovakia—satellites that Russia was working to bring back into its orbit.

"The Kremlin needed to strip them of their ability to defend themselves," Martinez remarks.

The colonel nods. "I'd been able to insert a swallow into a Czech arms manufacturer's orbit. She was with him for seven months, I think, before he finally let his guard down. When my swallow was prepared to exploit him, I requested additional clearances to assassinate him."

Martinez digests the information. Swallows. Women, or men, who are trained to be professional sex workers at the infamous State School Four in Moscow. They use lust to extract valuable information from their targets, and they're said to be highly effective. Some, but not all, are also assassins.

"Approval was granted, and Marek Svoboda was eliminated." Karavayev stops to work some of the stress out of his shoulders. Old injuries, tightened by painful memories. "The swallow's final exploitation of Svoboda's computer network was her most devastating. That's when I learned he'd been a Founder. Files on his computer system had code names, business links . . ."

Martinez makes another connection: Marek Svoboda was a Founder, and he was working against Russian interests by developing weapons for the country's enemies. She draws a conclusion: the Founders are distinctly Russian, but they have no meaningful allegiance to their host government. She says, "You received commendations for your success."

"Along with the rest of my team. I was going to be promoted as well," Karavayev replies. "That's when the assassination attempt occurred."

Martinez asks a challenging question. "Do you believe your superiors conspired in the attempt?"

"General Daniil Ionov was, and still is, GRU's commanding officer. He gave me *clearance* to proceed with Svoboda's elimination," Karavayev reveals. "In killing Svoboda, he'd have been acting against the Founders' interests. There's no way he could be one of them."

The colonel gets a rangy look in his eyes. "I have no idea how my identity was compromised. I've puzzled over it endlessly, but I keep coming up short. I underestimated these Founders. They were able to discern who harmed their interests and retaliated against me."

Martinez can sense his frustration. She notices something else too. He's spent years in this cabin, alone. Wondering, worrying. The effects have been nothing short of taxing. But he's right; there's no way he'd have ever learned the truth. Powerful people in Russia let him think he was going to be knighted and thrust a dagger in his back while he bowed before the throne. "You made the right choice to get out, sir."

"I'm not so sure, Ms. Martinez. At that point I'd only made enemies with a powerful group of individuals in Russia," Karavayev replies. "But when I ran, I became a traitor to the entire state, and I lost everything, including my closest allies."

Martinez is concerned as the story finishes. The toll it has taken on the colonel is noticeable, and his eyes are drifting further away. "I have one more set of questions, sir," she says, fishing into her bag for photographs. "About a set of twins—"

"Twins?" Karavayev interrupts, excitement in his voice.

The colonel leans forward in his seat. The words reeled him back from the abyss, and he's fully engaged again. She finds photographs of Victor and the woman her Group believes is his twin sister. "Do you know who they are?"

"Elizabet? Nikolai?" Karavayev asks, locked on the twin sister's face. "These photos are recent photographs of the Ovechkin twins!"

Martinez's skin turns cold. "I need you to tell me how you know these individuals, sir."

"Elizabet's alive?" Karavayev exclaims.

Martinez is struggling to catch up, but she can only guess that they're talking about the same two people. "Yes, sir."

"My God . . ." With shaky hands, he places the photographs on the coffee table and stares after them.

"Can we start with the woman? Elizabet, as you refer to her?" Martinez asks.

The colonel can't shake his smile. "Both of the twins were exceptional, but Elizabet? She was the most talented officer I ever commanded."

Martinez gulps. "You were her commanding officer? This wasn't in your debrief."

"Until now I thought she was dead. Do you remember the swallow I sent for the Svoboda? That was Elizabet! Her assassination occurred two days after my attempt. I could take you to her grave in Federal Military

Memorial Cemetery. Nikolai was killed in Syria several weeks later. They're buried side by side," Karavayev says sadly.

That explains why their names have changed. "You used Elizabet to dismantle an arms network?"

"Elizabet was the ranking field officer," Karavayev replies. "She earned the Hero of the Russian Federation medal for her service in the operation. The Kremlin even gave her a little apartment in downtown Moscow."

Martinez tries to check her anger. The officers who debriefed the colonel were paper pushers taking footnotes on a three-decade career. When he took credit for the operation, it was attributed to Russia and shunted aside. Why should they take any interest in deceased field operatives? Their ability to harm the United States was terminated.

"Elizabet's death was one of the saddest of my career. I never had kids, but I looked upon her as a daughter of sorts. I hold myself responsible for what happened to her."

"An officer capable of earning Russia's highest honor must have been extraordinary," Martinez observes.

"Her intelligence was sublime, and she had a real Russian's wit. Cold and dry. Her attitude was . . ." He rocks his hand back and forth. "But that's because she grew bored easily.

"The assignment to assassinate Svoboda was supposed to be her last. She never believed in Russia, or our mission. Service was just her path to freedom. Do you think that she's working with the Founders?"

"I *know* she is. She and Victor Orlov—Nikolai—were an integral part of an espionage campaign that exposed some of the U.S.'s most vital assets. It was highly successful."

"I'm sorry to hear that," Karavayev says. "I know you'll think less of me, but I'm happy they're alive—just disappointed to hear of what they're doing."

"As an officer, I understand how you feel," Martinez says before clearing the tension from her throat. "What can you tell me about Nikolai, sir?"

"He was GRU, just like Elizabet, but he'd been trained as a Spetsnaz operator. Nikolai was skilled—and extremely callous. He was suited to operating alone in isolated environments, like his sister. During his final assignment in Syria, he was attempting to mark an ISIS command post for destruction. An explosive detonated on his position and he was killed. His body was never recovered."

Martinez doesn't respond. *Bombs and disappearances.* Clearly, Victor Orlov's methods haven't changed since Syria.

"Please, excuse me." Karavayev returns moments later with a stack of dog-eared files in his hands. "Some basic reading on the twins. It includes their service records, education, and some personality traits. My personal journal is also there."

Martinez is shocked as she takes the files and the journal. They represent years of the colonel's thoughts. "You've thrown me a real life-line here, sir."

The colonel sits back in his favorite chair, and a distant look returns to his eyes. "Use them well," he murmurs.

Martinez takes the cue to leave. She extracts one of her business cards. "Sir, I'm going to leave you my personal cell. If you need anything —ever—I want to be your *first* call."

"You can do something for me, Ms. Martinez," Karavayev says as she places her card on the table. There is a pained look on his face, and the mist has returned to his eyes. "I put Elizabet through hell. Take care of her if you can. Or at the very least, let her death be a painless one."

THIRTY

SLOANE IS IN THE JOINT TERRORISM ANALYSIS CENTER'S bullpen and loving every second. Entire worlds are whizzing by on the center screen: internet traffic associated with Gombe Wireless; communications from the ISP's key executives; street-level camera feeds; and even data from her investigation.

That includes info from last night's shootings and Leelee Paragno's arrest. Being involved feels like action to her, an element she missed at the start of her career.

Gabriella Martinez, the person who isn't just her boss but her inspiration, earned experience like this as a naval officer serving in the Middle East. She had the authority to gather intelligence, plan raids, detain subjects, and finally, interrogate them. Car batteries and jumper cables weren't included; it was all chess for Martinez. Intellect and intuition are what delivered results.

Martinez had them in spades.

Sloane joined the CIA as the Middle East was becoming an afterthought in American foreign policy. China. Russia. China. Russia.

Those countries became the Agency's core focus, and once that focus was locked in, there wasn't much deviation.

China was Sloane's initial mission, and it was a disappointment. Not because it wasn't important, but she'd wanted the sandbox. Her older brother had been killed in Iraq in the mid-2000s, and she wanted a piece of that action. It just felt right, but as it turns out, she was answering a higher calling. Fate delivered her to Martinez, Jen, and the Technical Access Group she's currently serving in.

Now, Sloane is compiling photo arrays of people who may have had a motive or connection to last night's homicides, and she's going to take a crack at something Martinez excelled at: interrogations.

The arrays contain images of known mafia trigger men. Eight per page. Types of guys with rap sheets longer than Leelee Paragno's and twice as violent. Ceno Lika's face is in the mix, along with several of his associates from New York City. They've gone off the grid since Sandro Lika's death. And if there was any one person with a motive to kill Vehbi and Isuf Dibra, it's Ceno.

If she can find and arrest him, he might just give her the information she needs to crack Void and link it to Gombe Wireless. Excited, she taps her foot against the desk, wishing the printer would hurry up and spit out the arrays.

Her phone vibrates. A text from Martinez with some incredible information. Her detour to Wyoming was worth the extra gas money. The photograph on the screen belongs to Victor Orlov. Young, wearing a military dress uniform.

Another depicts the woman who is now confirmed to be his twin sister. Elizabet Ovechkin's name may have changed, but her face is the same.

What a freaking hit!

Martinez is now officially ahead on bragging rights. Her printer finishes and she hops up, eager to take a crack at Leelee and get some points on the board. He's been on ice for an hour, which should have given his temper time to cool. But she stops herself before departing the cubicle. Intuition. Gut instinct. Whatever a person calls it, she senses something off about the situation.

She returns to her desk and grabs a file out of the stack. It contains photos of Victor Orlov, forwarded courtesy of Alex Varga's dossier. They depict Orlov as he tours Varga's garden, flanked by a half-dozen armed guards.

She tucks the photograph into the stack and heads for Toliver's office. She finds him behind his desk, buried under arrest reports. He's banging on his keyboard, bald head even redder than when he's fighting oversized goons. She taps on the door and waves the photos. "Wanna take a crack at this guy?"

"Bet your ass I do," he says as he rips his jacket off the back of his chair and throws it on. He also grabs a legal pad and a pen. "Paperwork is worse than hard labor."

Sloane chuckles and follows him down the hall. She shares the sentiment, in parts. She's a hacker, and from behind a desk, she's pulled off some amazing feats. "How do you want to play Paragno?"

"Hard. He's been through the system, and if we give him the chance, he'll walk on us." Toliver takes the photos from her and examines them while they walk. "This the Orlov asshole you mentioned?"

Sloane nods. "Hunch."

"Always worth a shot," Toliver says while reassembling the photos. They arrive at the interrogation room. High security, with a plexiglass window in the door that allows them to look inside. Leelee is cuffed to a metal table and he's calm. Preening his fingernails. "He's ready."

Leelee sags as they enter the room. He offers them a pout and crosses his free hand over his chest. "My titties hurt."

Sloane posts up on the back wall while Toliver sits across from Leelee. There's a bruise striping his chest, but his muscles are like a layer of armor. Man could probably walk through a blast of double-aught buckshot from Toliver's Benelli.

Toliver doesn't acknowledge the injury either. "Mr. Paragno, we'd like to ask you some questions about the murder that took place at the Chesterfield Inn last night."

Leelee gasps. "Hate crime!" He sticks his finger in the air, circles it, and makes a siren noise. "My pronouns are they, them, and their."

Toliver runs his hand over his scalp. "Do you know where we are, sir?"

Leelee shifts in his seat and serves up a huge grin. He leans in conspiratorially. "No, tell me."

"MI5's Joint Terrorism Analysis Center. You're here today because we're looking for someone associated with a terror event on British soil. It's my job to find him."

"Such *huge* responsibilities. You must be so stressed out," Leelee replies as he eases his foot toward Toliver's leg and begins rubbing it up and down. "Let me help with the pressure."

"You want to help me?" Toliver whispers as he leans in closer.

"Yes, daddy."

Toliver smashes his fist into the handcuff wrapped around Leelee's wrist. With a shocked gasp, Leelee shoots up straight in the chair. "It'll take your fucking breath away, won't it?"

Sloane averts her gaze from the table. She's not surprised, just amused, but she needs to hide it. When Leelee is desperate to get away from Toliver, she'll swoop in, play the doting mother, and get his cooperation.

"Now we've both got something in common," Toliver observes, leaning back in his chair. "Our time is precious. You can sit there and jerk me around while I try to catch a killer, but think of the consequences. Say I get up and come back an hour from now. Maybe the nerves in your hand are stone fucking dead. Three hours? A surgeon will need to hack it off."

Leelee's forehead is glistening. He's controlling his breath to mitigate the pain. It's not working, and he becomes frantic. "Fine! What? Tell me what you want to know!"

"There's a good lad." Toliver lets the pain sink in a little longer while he reviews information in his files. "Were you working at the Chesterfield Inn last night?"

"Yes."

"Did you rent suite three-two-seven?"

Leelee nods again but doesn't reply. He shuts his eyes, sucks air through his nose, lets it out through his mouth.

Sloane senses her opportunity and swoops in, spreading the first set of photos out on the table. Ceno Lika's face is displayed prominently, but she averts her gaze. Leelee is streetwise, and she won't give him an angle to play. "Did you rent the suite to one of these men? Or did you see them at any point last night?"

Leelee stoops down and scrutinizes the faces while Sloane cycles through the pages. "No—no! Now, please, loosen my cuffs. I can't feel a fucking thing!"

"We're not finished," Toliver hisses. "What time did he come in?"

"Uh, uh . . . like, ten-thirtyish. Peak hours, when johns are wall to wall."

"Did you see his vehicle?" Sloane questions.

Leelee nods again. "White Mercedes Sprinter. Parked it in the alley behind the hotel. I saw it on the security cameras, but it was too far away for me to read the tags." He starts rushing. "Was an older guy. Six two maybe. Long gray hair and a matching goatee. Blue eyes."

Sloane's intuition kicks into overdrive. She opens Orlov's file and places the photo on the table. "Does this man look familiar?"

Leelee rips the photo closer. His brow furrows. "I . . . ugh!" He rapidly shakes his head. "He's wearing sunglasses in this picture. Show me something with eyes!"

Time for Sloane's phone. She grabs Orlov's service photo that Martinez forwarded. She zooms in tight on his face before setting it in front of Leelee.

Leelee nods frantically. "It's those eyes. Can't shake them. Only difference was that his hair was gray and he had an extra fifteen kilos of fat on him."

Sloane grabs her phone and buzzes out of the room, wondering if her legs are going to fold. Victor Orlov. Mexico City's ghost. The man who put Jen through hell and left her best friend in a wheelchair for the rest of his life. Taking a heavy breath, she presses her back into the wall and attempts to steady herself.

It's a pointless effort, and she allows her hands to tremble while she dials Martinez. Her superior answers on the first ring. Sloane's words come out in a flurry. "Orlov pulled the trigger last night, and he could still be in London! I need all-ports warnings nationwide, and an Interpol Red Notice for the rest of Europe. Train stations, ferries, airports—the works."

THIRTY-ONE

WHAT A SIGHT IT WOULD BE IN THE SPRING.

Endless snow-covered hills yawn into the horizon. And this cottage? Built in the eighteen hundreds. Stone walls protect the gardens while they wait for the winter to end. For Victor, this is the life.

The cottage is in a small town thirty minutes from Newcastle Upon Tyne. There aren't any neighbors for miles, but if he wanted, he could drive to town for a dinner, a movie, a date. But thoughts like these are for another time and another country.

Instead, he looks down to the watch on his wrist. Rolex GMT with a Pepsi bezel. It lights a spark in him. Moments ago, he tore the protective blue plastic away from the bracelet. A travel piece Anastasia purchased to commemorate the end of his work in London, and she left it in the safe house for him to find. He'd been wanting to add one to his collection for some time but could never get his hands on one. Now he has one on his wrist, and when its movement is fully wound, it will beat a silent story of his escape from the United Kingdom.

More important, he's early. This safe house is a halfway point. A waystation. Roughly seventy miles from Scotland, it's the perfect starting point for his journey home. He'll leave here, travel to Scotland's northernmost shore. Ferry crossings to the Orkney Islands are a favorite amongst local sightseers, even in the winter. He'll use them to travel to St. Margaret's Hope. A seaplane will land in the dead of night, whisk him deeper into Europe, the island of several hundred none the wiser their new guest left.

It's going to be a long trip, but it's safe. Most smugglers prefer to use the English Channel—a narrow gap between the United Kingdom and the rest of Europe. It's also the preferred hunting ground of the British Royal Navy. The North Sea's weather is less forgiving. And unlike his escape from Mexico City, the aircraft he'll be traveling on will have a professional pilot. He trusts Leo, but a computer doesn't have a place in this.

Early is on time.

He walks through the vine-covered trellis connecting the cottage to the barn, which has been converted to a garage. He finds his Porsche 911 parked where a tractor once sat.

Opening the trunk, he tosses his duffel bag inside and adjusts his overcoat and suit jacket. The car, like his outfit, may be ostentatious, but he's no longer Howard Hamlin. He's a banker traveling from London to a small cottage in the Orkneys. The passport book in his jacket pocket depicts an English citizen with dark brown hair and a clean-cut appearance.

Victor has taken the necessary steps to match the image, but it won't matter. The passport won't be required to board a ferry to the Orkneys. Another reason why that departure path was chosen.

And like Howard Hamlin, his new identity is backed by employment records, business cards, bank records, and a viable national insurance number. He won't be Raine Sydnor for long, but he'll use the identity to its fullest.

He drops into the driver's seat, running through his departure checklist. Cabin is clean. Guns are properly stored in a hidden compartment in the Porsche. Ferry tickets have already been purchased online, and his space is reserved. He's all ready to go, but an unscheduled call from Anastasia stops him.

He reaches into his pocket and extracts the cell.

"Where are you?" Anastasia demands, breathless.

Victor's brow arches as he studies her face on the screen. "Have you been running?"

"Where are you?" she repeats.

"Closing down Gateshead."

Anastasia takes several deep breaths. "The British government has linked you to last night's shootings. Interpol Red Notices are spreading across Europe, and the United Kingdom has issued an all-ports warning."

Victor's knuckles whiten around the Porsche's wheel. "How?"

"Check your texts."

Victor does as he's asked. He finds photographs taken during one of his visits to Alex Varga's estate. It was the day that he'd gone to warn Varga about Jen Yates's presence in Mexico City. An hour later, he'd gone to examine the decoy hostages he used to ensnare Gabriella Martinez's Technical Access Group. "I should have killed Varga myself."

"That wasn't part of the plan."

"Plans change."

A silent debate between them begins. Victor stares at his sister, certain that the same question is on her mind: Will the ferry to St. Margaret's Hope carry him to safety?

He breaks the silence. "It's workable. Scottish law enforcement is lax at the ferry terminals. We've challenged it multiple times in the past."

"Not in a situation like this, Victor. Mandatory passport screenings could be in play. I think it's too risky. We need to wait, and when the situation cools down, we can find you another route out of the country."

Victor looks around the old barn. Hundred-year-old dust from hay bales twists in the air. Very little has come along to disturb this place, and it would be a safe location to hunker down. But his gut is pulling him toward Scotland. "The UK isn't safe for me any longer, Ana."

Anastasia grinds her teeth.

"Don't."

"How can I not, Victor?"

Last night he crossed a serious line, and he may not recover from the damage. It was his little sister's call, and she's already blaming herself. "We protected our mission. It was the only choice."

"I knew the Americans had the Likas. I should have foreseen this."

"But we didn't know about Alex. The Americans were lucky, that's all." Always thinking of what his little sister needs, he flashes the Rolex toward the cell phone. "Thanks, by the way. You've got superb taste."

Anastasia rolls her eyes. "You've got the taste, and I've got the credit card debt to prove it."

He looks down at the watch and frowns. "Now I know it's fake. You'd never pay full price for a watch like this."

Anastasia laughs. "Just stay put, Victor—please. We'll have you out of the UK soon."

Ana. Technically, the choice is hers. She's the one handling this operation. And she's never let him down. *Ever.* He chooses to put his faith in her decision. "I have no doubt."

Thirty-Two

Sandro's body is on ice. It'll be flown to Albania in another week, but today a memorial service is taking place at Isa Lika's house. Ceno is present, as he should be, dressed in his finest black suit. This service is exclusively for family, and they're all wearing the same.

At ninety-one years old, Ceno's grandmother, Luriana Lika, is the strongest in the room. Ceno has been unable to take his eyes off the woman who has lived to bury a second son. She's been stoic, dropping her head only to hide an occasional tear. This woman is the family's bedrock, and she carries the weight with true dignity.

For a woman who survived the Great War and Enver Hoxha, nothing less is to be expected.

Ceno enters the mansion's great room to find over fifty people he calls family. His son and daughter are playing with their cousins. Bright and happy. Offering the mourning family a glimpse of what the future holds, if only they can summon their collective strength to endure another tragedy.

Isa Lika, the family's new patriarch, is the last of three brothers. He's finishing the rounds, offering encouragement. Assurances that the family will take care of its own. Guarantees that the suffering will be atoned for. He makes eye contact with Ceno, cuts through the crowd toward him.

They embrace firmly, and it's not rushed. A genuine connection. Isa pulls back, grips Ceno's shoulders, and for a moment they're hard to tell apart. The only difference is their age and a few strands of gray hair. "I heard about what you did in the Bronx. I'm so proud."

"It's my duty." Ceno steps close to Isa and whispers, "What happened last night?"

"We need to talk about that." Isa turns back to the crowd, waves someone toward them.

Sandro's eldest son, Eder, approaches. Twenty-six years old. He shakes Ceno's hand, showing off his strength. He'll take his father's place at the family table. Just like Ceno did with his father, and Isa did with his own. "Thank you for coming all this way, Uncle Ceno."

"Your father looked after me like I was his son. I'll do the same for you," Ceno responds.

Isa places his arms on their shoulders and leads them to a private study. "We need to talk. Just the three of us."

Ceno finds a seat in a maroon leather chair. He's always appreciated this room. Dark wooden walls and bookshelves. Photographs that his grandmother and great-grandparents took in the old country. A collective soul lingers in here, and it's represented in these artifacts.

Isa heads to the bar, but Eder rushes to stop him. "Why don't you sit? Let me handle this."

"Such respect. One of the things that made your father so proud of you." Isa sits across from Ceno and waits for the drinks before beginning. When they've all got a vodka, he starts. "Tell me what happened in the Bronx."

Ceno looks to Isa, Eder, and his strength is building. Two generations in this room. Protecting them was the only option, and he's proud to carry the weight. He reaches into his suit and pulls out an envelope. "I found this in their apartment."

Isa looks over the matchbooks, photographs. Evidence that the Dibras were encroaching on Lika territory. "What else did you take other than their lives?"

Ceno thinks back to the storage locker. Full of money, but none of it was Sandro's. No keys to stolen cars or files either. "Fifty thousand dollars. I was planning to present it to Eder in Uncle Sandro's name."

"Thank you, Uncle Ceno," Eder replies as he takes the evidence from Isa. He reviews it but fails to offer an opinion. This moment is for listening, learning.

"How did they die?" Isa hisses.

"Badly," Ceno replies. "They spit at my feet, cursed our name. There was fear in them."

"Their blood has always carried weakness," Isa notes. He pauses to sip his vodka. "I've been speaking with the Founders while you were traveling. They have their own suspicions about who killed Sandro."

Ceno flexes forward. "Who?"

"The Americans," Isa replies. "They're concerned."

The magnitude of Ceno's secret suddenly grows. What if Americans saw the documents in that safe? *Was Sandro that lucky? Did he have time to destroy all of them? Maybe that's why I couldn't find anything in the Dibras' storage unit.* Confronting the revelation is hard, and he shakes his head, refusing to believe. "Americans have their ways. But this? Their laws would stop them."

Isa notices an antique radio with a photograph on top of it. Both date back to the early forties. They belonged to Ceno's great-uncle. A man who'd been caught by the Soviet secret police with a similar radio in his possession. He was sent to a Siberian gulag and never returned. "When a country writes its own laws, they're free to change them and manipulate them. Remember, Ceno. There's only one set of laws on this Earth: God's. Who's to say they didn't kill Sandro and stop the police from investigating?"

Ceno's gut is vaulting, but he forces a nod. Isa's opinion has the ring of hard-earned wisdom. A relic of a dying generation. If only he could ignore the truth in it. "Last night's killings make sense now."

"The Founders want quiet, which is why they stepped in to finish our vendetta." Isa leans back in his chair and gives Ceno a triumphant look. "Vehbi's son is too young to take control of his family's interests in London."

"Their struggle is no longer against us."

"London is ours, Ceno, and the feud is settled," Isa states with an air of finality. "The Founders are urging restraint from this point forward, and I'd like to honor the request. We're responsible for securing Void's networks in London. If we draw the authorities to us—"

"We could lose everything," Ceno interrupts.

His voice is faint. A widening gap is growing between him and his family, and it's being forced open by the responsibility he chose to carry alone. They can never know about his secret, and they never will. "This means that nothing is settled, Uncle Isa."

"The Americans . . ." Isa replies while shaking his head. "There are other things you can do for Sandro." He nods to Eder, then finishes his vodka and rests the tumbler on the table. He stands up and buttons his black suit. "I'm leaving this choice with you, Ceno. I'll respect whatever decision you make."

Ceno remains silent. Isa's message is clear, but it's based on a misunderstanding. He doesn't want blood. That desire is satisfied. With the Americans involved, the family's future is in jeopardy. They're the ones who shredded Sandro's files; they know the truth. Protecting what he treasures most may no longer be possible, but he is determined to find a way.

THIRTY-THREE

THE TRAFALGAR HOTEL SITS IN THE HEART OF LONDON. Trafalgar Square can be seen from its top-floor suites, along with some of the city's most idyllic shopping centers. Despite the cold and snow, locals and tourists are milling in every direction, working their way through last-minute holiday shopping lists.

'Tis the season. Jen's working in a two-bedroom suite, feeling like a Christmas gift just landed in her lap: Victor Orlov. The Bronx forced the Likas—and the Founders—to react. Now they're exposing themselves.

Couple that with Martinez's breakthrough. Jen hasn't had time to read the twins' files thoroughly, but she has the Cliffs notes. Victor Orlov—Nikolai—was an elite Spetsnaz operator who frequently worked alone in places like Syria targeting ISIS rebels. His "death" occurred six years ago.

Impressive record, only to be trumped by his twin sister's. She'd been a swallow, but that isn't what made her so unique. She studied computers, like Victor, and graduated from one of Russia's top cyber-espionage schools. She was the best and has the commendations to prove it.

Trying to stay focused on her current tasks has been challenging, but she reminds herself of the dangers ahead. The Lika Syndicate is violent; she's going to take something from them tonight. For her, it's a human being; to them, it's valuable merchandise. Chances are, they won't let it go without a struggle.

Readiness. The key ingredient for a fight. And Jen's starting with the hotel suite itself. It's undergoing a makeover. Powerful surveillance tools are being installed in both bedrooms and the living room.

Kabir will bring their candidate back to the suite, and their transaction will occur in one of these spaces. Their conversation will be illegal, and when she agrees to perform sex acts for financial rewards, this equipment will capture it.

The first bedroom is a clean space; it's full of equipment her team will use to monitor the two bugged rooms. It's also the point from which her team will ambush their candidate.

Jen is in the second bedroom, putting the finishing touches on a laptop across from the bed. When she's finished setting it up, the computer will appear to be powered down, but it'll be recording whatever transpires in the room.

Other tools have been installed on the laptop. A keystroke logger and screen-recording feature have been activated. If the candidate attempts to use it, her activities will be recorded. The computer may be used to initiate a financial transfer, or to communicate with members of the mafia. In that event, they'll need to know who she's contacting, the websites she uses to do it, and the passwords she uses to gain access.

Satisfied with the computer, Jen conducts a false power down. The screen blinks before going black, signaling success.

She steps out onto the suite's balcony. A minivan is parked on a busy street corner. Its lights flash—Animal's signal that he has a clean view of the suite along with the hotel's primary entrance. If a security element tails their candidate into the hotel, he'll be the first to spot it.

Next, Jen surveys the suite's clean room—the bedroom housing all the equipment they're using to monitor their surveillance tools. Hastings and Kabir are setting up a multi-screen computer station. Power is on; screens are glowing.

"Looking good."

"Saved the last part for you," Hastings says as he steps aside.

Jen drops into her chair and logs in. First thing she does is check the status of the surveillance network. Cameras are rolling, and no physical obstructions block their lenses. Microphone readouts are pristine. Tiny bars jump from ambient noises, and she's able to tap in and listen to them individually.

A message pops up on the screen. Animal. He has a camera mounted to his van, and it frames the hotel's front entrance.

Finally, the hotel's surveillance cameras are looped in. Jen's force multiplier. There are close to fifty high-quality feeds. Her prediction about the Trafalgar's security was accurate. Whoever designed the system was thorough; there aren't any blind spots in the hotel.

"We're set," Jen says, turning to Kabir and sizing him up. The young officer is jittery, nervous, but he's doing his best to hide it. She plucks the Bimmer's keys off the desk and tosses them to the kid. "Take the car back to your place. Get cleaned up and put on a nice suit. We'll hang out here and monitor the security situation. The Likas could try to slip someone into the space early."

Kabir fiddles with the keys. "Right."

Hastings notices the tremor in Kabir's hand. "Do you have a letter for your family . . . just in case?"

Kabir's poker face cracks. "What? No—I mean, should I write one?"

It's hard not to laugh. Even harder for Jen to keep her darker impulses in check, but she shows mercy. "The only thing you need to do is put on your nicest suit. Remember, you can afford a night with an expensive escort."

Kabir marches stiffly to the door. "I'll be back in an hour."

Jen grabs a pair of headphones and puts one of them up to her ear. She can hear Kabir's boots sinking into the suite's carpet. Rustling fabric from his jeans as he walks to the suite's door and turns the knob. "Sound is crystal."

Hastings waits for the suite's door to shut before placing the back of his hand on Jen's forehead. "You feeling okay, Z?"

Jen balls her fist and tries to deliver a straight right to his jaw. But it was too choreographed, and Hastings is too wily. He jerks back, guard up, and her personal space is restored. "I told you to take it easy on Kabir. He's just nervous. Besides, we need him to come back."

Hastings cracks up and drops onto the edge of the bed. "Don't worry, he'll be back. You've seen how gorgeous our candidate is, right?"

"That's what has me worried," Jen states. In one evening, their candidate makes more money than most people do in a month. The Lika Syndicate will be reluctant to part ways with Serai Konci, but she's not going to give them a choice.

THIRTY-FOUR

THE COSSACKS BANYA IN ST. PETERSBURG IS THE CITY'S most infamous. For nearly a century it has been the meeting ground for Russia's leaders, spies, and Bratva—the broad term for the mafia.

The building is a stone monolith. The façade is imperial. Symbols etched into the cornerstones trace back to the Romanovs. Top-floor bathing rooms are available only by reservation, and the list of men who can secure them is short.

Anastasia is in a private changing room, preparing for a meeting with her superiors. Inside of the zakonny vladelets they are lieutenants or capos—second- or third-tier men, but still important. Her brother's tenure in London was a success, but he's been compromised. His face is lighting up computer screens across Europe. This is coming after she lost Liev Frankel in New York.

They want explanations and damage assessments, but she needs to return to work. Victor needs protection and help with his departure from the United Kingdom. Every passing second increases the chances of his being captured. She already has several options available, and her team is working through contingencies associated with each one. Saving her brother is her singular priority, and she won't achieve that goal languishing in a hot tub.

Anastasia unbuttons her jeans and rips the zipper down. She sits on a dark wood bench and kicks them off while unbuttoning her shirt. She doesn't bother folding her clothes as she places them on the bench. This meeting will be brief. She strips off her panties, the only remaining article of clothing on her body, and starts for the door. A white linen robe is hanging nearby, but she leaves it on the peg as she steps into the bathing area.

Steam boils out of a bath in the center of the room. It rolls over the edges, across the tile floor, and collects along the stone walls. She takes her time crossing the room. The tile is slick, but she wants to exude calm, poise.

The first man she sees is General Daniil Ionov, GRU's commanding officer. She spent five years under his command before he recruited her and Victor into the Founders. That was a lifetime ago, and she's amused by the memory of how it came about.

Death was her only way into the Founders. They wanted one of Russia's most elite intelligence officers, and they had every intention of maximizing her abilities. As a member of the Founders, she'd be working in Russia—sometimes for the country, and sometimes against it. To be successful, she'd need to be a ghost.

A high-profile kidnapping ending in her death was the best way to achieve it. Her journey would officially end with a headstone at the Federal Military Memorial Cemetery. She'd been worried about her apartment in Moscow, along with a host of other retirement benefits she'd earned during her service. But General Ionov only laughed when she told him. He replied that in a few years' time, she would have a penthouse in St. Petersburg.

Eighteen months later, she bought a two-million-dollar penthouse —in cash. Victor's was just several blocks away, and they had trouble determining which apartment to celebrate in first. One of her all-time favorite memories.

Ionov raises his head just long enough to gauge that she's not a security threat. A relic of the Soviet era, he's a different breed of man. Many in his generation reach seventy with Parkinson's—their brains pickled in vodka. But he became harder than the Soviet Union's iron hammer, and he's maintained control over GRU because of it.

The man sitting next to Ionov doesn't show the same disinterest in her body. He stares as she nears the bath. Tomas Gulkin is a vice-president at Veneshcomm Bank—one of the entities responsible for funneling the Founders' money into Russia. At thirty-two, he's young for the position. Being an oligarch's son opens many doors.

Anastasia dips a toe into the water, and the heat sucks her in. St. Petersburg in the winter. Temperatures at minus ten degrees centigrade. And forget about wind chill. They persist so long that people forget about the frost that settles into their bones. She descends the stairs, and with every step, she feels that deep cold dissolve in her body.

Before crossing the pool, she submerges herself. Her hair was the only remaining place for an electronic device to be hidden, and now it's soaked. Anastasia slicks back her hair and sits with the others on a submerged bench at the far end.

"Ana."

She expects Ionov's curt tone. The former KGB officer isn't one for games, or disasters—which is likely how he's come to view her work in London and New York. "Daniil."

"Mind if I call you Red?"

Anastasia scoffs at the smirk on Tomas's face. *Prostitute.* It's on the tip of Tomas's tongue as he watches her nipples soften in the water. Serving Russia has had its costs, and they've followed her here tonight. Swallows are, in essence, Russia's best sex workers, and she'll never be respected by *boys* like Tomas because of it. She leans back, rests an arm at the pool's edge, and spreads her legs. "Is that what you really want?"

"Time to smoke," Ionov says, chuckling. He grabs a cigar and a long match. While he puffs the tip to a glow, he gives Tomas a contemptuous look. "I'm glad you came, Ana. How is your husband?"

"Why don't you tell me? You're probably the last person who's spoken with him," she replies, brow arched. "And your compliments aren't necessary."

Ionov laughs again and settles back into position. His cigar is glowing, and he's finally in worthy company. "Yesterday, actually. He's well."

Rebuffed, Tomas says, "I'm pressed for time, and we need to discuss London."

"I agree," Ionov says. "How was Victor so badly compromised?"

"Alex Varga. The photos are from his compound, but I'm not sure how the Americans came into possession of them," Anastasia replies. She taps her nail on the edge of the pool, signaling her impatience. "I'm working on a secondary out for Victor—"

Anastasia stops herself. They're staring, and she recognizes what's in their eyes: suspicion. They want to know if they've been betrayed and by whom. Her breath catches. This moment will decide the rest of her life.

Ionov is a brutal judge. He stares, and stares, and stares, until the silence feels eternal. She twists on the bench. Her eyes bore into Ionov's, refusing to back down and feed their suspicion. "Think of Victor, Daniil. The danger he's in."

"Stranger things have happened, Ana," Ionov replies, satisfied with her response. He begins briefing her on the situation. "You missed something critical. Members of the Federal Bureau of Investigation have made contact with Tony Mitchell. They escorted him from his office at the FCC today."

Anastasia exhales, and, as her lungs deflate, her entire body seems to follow. She'll survive her trip to the banya, but Ionov is right: she didn't know about Mitchell. News of his arrest is troubling. Plans were in place to bribe him, but they hadn't been acted on. An insider with deep knowledge is helping the Americans.

She remembers New York's final loose end and responds. "I haven't been able to confirm Liev Frankel's whereabouts, but I'm highly confident that he was killed in Brooklyn."

"Frankel is dead," Ionov nods.

"We're still not sure where the compromise originated," Tomas says. "But the most likely source is our contacts in organized crime."

Anastasia has a savage temper, and it wants out. First, for Victor and the danger he's in. Then for these men and their stupid test. Finally, for whoever exposed years of her work to the United States government. "This is going to have a wide range of consequences."

"New York's infection has likely spread to London. Victor's compromise is just a fraction of it," Tomas agrees. "The general and I wanted to meet and discuss options, but my mind is made up. We need to begin taking equipment offline, starting with Gombe Wireless's London point of presence."

"The British government would consider that an admission of guilt," Anastasia argues. "It's also unnecessary. Gombe's CEO, Erickson, is in London. His skin is clean, and if the Americans grab him, he won't be able to help them."

"If the Americans gain access to a live point of presence, we would have serious issues, Ana," Tomas replies. "We need to pull back and keep Gombe safe."

"I prefer Anastasia, or Mrs. Orlov," she says, enforcing the strict rule about her name. Ana is reserved for friends and family. Tomas is neither. "What will they get if they take London? There's no way for them to find Leo's location or sever its access to the internet's backbone. A backup Void server is about to launch in Belarus. Africa will follow. Soon, it will be completely decentralized."

Tomas's brow flicks up. "Anastasia . . ."

Anastasia remains undeterred. "Gombe's points of presence in Eastern Europe, Asia, and Africa will also remain out of America's reach. That's the beauty of a polarized world, don't you think, Tomas?"

"Our infiltration of Western nations was always a bonus. After what the Chinese did, I'm shocked we made it this far," Ionov remarks. "Don't worry yourself, Tomas. Void will keep the red ink out of your father's books."

"How is Void?" Tomas asks.

"It's still early, but user growth is exponential. Yesterday was our first full day in operation, and we cleared just over five hundred thousand dollars in profit. Of course, we expect that figure to multiply," Anastasia replies.

"We're already exceeding expectations," Tomas says, impressed.

"Good, Ana," Ionov adds. "When you and Victor pitched Void to us, we scoffed. But you saw the potential and you stuck with it."

"A decision still needs to be made about Gombe's point of presence in London—"

"No, it doesn't, Tomas," Ionov interrupts.

Tomas grits his teeth, and the muscles in his jaw flex. "Isn't that what we're discussing now?"

"This isn't a discussion," Ionov declares. He looks at Anastasia. "By springtime, we'll have troops in Ukraine, and our posture needs to shift.

Gombe is uniquely positioned to do lasting damage inside the United Kingdom."

"Damage? That's never been the objective, Daniil. And I thought we were staying out of the upcoming conflict," Anastasia says.

Ionov shrugs. "Objectives change. We're compromised in London. We also know that the Americans are sharing quantum technology with the British. This window of opportunity won't exist in six months."

Tomas snarls, "This is outrageous."

Ionov leans into him. "Do not overstep."

Tomas isn't deterred by Ionov's threat. "We need to wind down our presence quietly. Gombe Wireless cannot be used as a weapon. It will give the Americans an excuse to dismantle our entire global footprint. The financial losses would be catastrophic."

"Your opinion is noted, but the decision is made," Ionov says casually. "It happened far above your and your father's heads."

Instead of striking Ionov, Tomas heaves himself out of the bath. He crosses to his changing room and slams the door with enough force to crack several tiles.

Ionov stares after Tomas, amused. He grunts and ashes his cigar. "Bankers."

"Spoiled children," Anastasia adds before quickly closing her mouth. Another game. Ionov allowed her and Tomas to argue against a predetermined outcome. Tomas exposed his position, along with his father's—far too much to reveal in a cutthroat organization like theirs.

Ionov's senses are finely tuned. He's alone with Anastasia, and his position has been made clear. Abuse is no longer necessary. Sinking deeper into the bath, he allows the water to consume his shoulders. "You're wrong."

"Sir?"

"You think you've failed; but you've performed so well, Ana."

Lies. But Anastasia understands the message hidden in his statement. She has only one choice. "It's time to find out how capable our new system truly is."

"That's what I wanted to hear," Ionov replies. "I've set up a new out for Victor. Consider it a gift for your successes—past and *future*."

"I don't know what to say," Anastasia says, blinking past her surprise. Ionov isn't known for generosity, but he has also broken protocol. Victor's departure is a tactical decision, which *was* exclusively hers to make.

"Say thank you. You'll find the plans in your dressing room. I also left a detailed target package for your inspection."

"Thank you, sir," Anastasia says. She eases off the perch and wades to the pool's steps. "I'll begin immediately."

"Oh, Ana . . . congratulations. I wanted to be the first."

Anastasia arches an eyebrow at Ionov and nods.

In the changing room, she dons her robe and sits next to a stack of files that have been left on the bench while she was in the bath.

Victor first. He's still her priority, despite the meeting she just endured. She grabs the file related to his extraction. The Lika Syndicate has prime smuggling routes into and out of the United Kingdom. They'll be used to transport her brother to safety. Ionov's plan is exemplary, and as she reads, the tightness in her chest disappears.

Thank you, Daniil.

This time, she means it.

Curiosity guides her hand to an envelope sealed with wax and an ornate ribbon. The reason for Daniil's congratulations. Sacrifice leads to rewards in her organization, and hers have been tremendous. But it's all been for this tiny envelope.

Pulling the ribbon away, she tears it open and reads a message written in cursive—a hand lost to modern times. This came all the way from the top of the zakonny vladelets:

Your time has come.

Anastasia trembles as she returns the card to the envelope. Soon, her life is going to take a giant leap forward. Victor's too. This is the opportunity they'd both hoped for, and as it rests in her lap, it feels earned above all else.

One file remains: the target package. But Anastasia doesn't open it. Daniil's assault against the British government is going to be devastating. The consequences will be too. There will be plenty of time to think about those after this is all over.

Thirty-Five

I T ' S B E E N T H R E E D A Y S S I N C E S E R A I K O N C I H A S H A D A D A T E, but that will change tonight. Her phone pinged several hours ago, forwarding the details. They include only a time and location; refusal isn't an option. If she doesn't confirm receipt of the message within sixty minutes, men in a nearby apartment will arrive with very direct questions about why she's uninterested in working. If necessary, they'll provide the motivation she's lacking.

The thugs have a limit though. She's merchandise, and they're forbidden from harming her too badly. Clients aren't bound by the same rules. If their pockets are deep enough, they're entitled to treat her however they please. Her most recent date was a bad one, but she's lucky enough not to remember.

Arm unfolded in front of the bathroom mirror, she covers a bruised injection site on her arm with concealer. The reason her memory is so hazy. The john had been a member of the Saudi royal family. Taking a casual break from Wahhabism while vacationing in London.

She woke up sore, unsure of how long she'd been unconscious, and struggled to return to her apartment. Raised in a religious home, she'd prayed for several days to recover before receiving another date. It was answered. *Mercy is shown when it's needed the most.*

After applying her makeup, she goes to the living room, which is set up like a giant closet. There are several dressers. Stacks of shoeboxes. Expensive dresses hang on clothing racks. Records are kept for each item of clothing. If anything goes missing, she, or her roommate, must pay for it.

The clothes were here when she arrived in the apartment, and so was her roommate. Another girl, kidnapped like her. She'd only been in London a month before Serai arrived, and together they adjusted to the hardships that their new lives brought.

In the beginning, their mornings were filled with tears and hugs and warm tea—if only to take the edge off drug and alcohol hangovers. Now they're both seasoned. Tears aren't necessary, and neither are the hugs. Whenever something terrible happens, they sit silently on the sofa, comforted by each other's presence. Everything is different now; in a way, it's easier.

She selects something appropriate for the date's location. Black dress. Matching coat with a belt and gold clasp. She completes the ensemble with hose and stilettos. Classy, and the advertising is subtle.

Her phone chirps, signaling it's time to leave. A GPS function is already active and linking her phone with tonight's client. It will allow her to walk straight to him and make the introduction without seeing his face first. Anonymity is built into every aspect of her service, and she'll only know who she's meeting when she arrives.

Leaving is effortless now, but a block of butcher knives stops her before she reaches the door. How their silver handles glint in the light. Resisting johns or her captors wasn't possible in the beginning, but she's changed. Fear can't control her any longer.

Approaching the block, she snaps open her purse and conceals one of the blades inside. A taxi is waiting as she steps onto the frozen sidewalk. When the driver's stare turns awkward, she just smiles and clutches the purse. "Take me to the Trafalgar."

———

"Coming your way. We haven't made her security."

Kabir doesn't reply to Jen's call, which came from the eighth story hotel suite. Would be awkward given the uppity crowd at the Trafalgar's restaurant, but he does smile at the Whisper's vibration. Going to take some getting used to.

But the smile fades as a message flashes on his cell phone screen. This one isn't from Jen, but Lust: *Your date is approaching.*

Adrenaline crashes through Kabir's system. He momentarily forgets how to breathe, but he does remember to wipe the sweat off his palms. Stains are left on his blue suit pants, and he kicks himself. Napkins are on the table for a reason, and he'll have only one chance at making a good first impression.

He forces himself to pay attention to the radar on the screen, and he looks toward the incoming blip.

Their candidate is speaking with a hostess, but she's already found him too. The hostess guides her to the table, sets a second menu, and pulls out her chair. When the hostess departs, the candidate takes her seat and says, "Put your phone in the middle of the table, please."

Kabir stares . . . and stares.

"Peter? Your phone," Serai reminds.

"Right!" Kabir says, with one too many decibels. He jerks his hand and deposits his phone at the center of the table. She aligns her phone over his, and both devices vibrate.

Serai smiles coyly. Beautiful white teeth, perfectly aligned. Her black hair shimmers in the restaurant's lights. And her skin? Caramel, without a blemish to be found.

"Nice to *finally* meet you, Peter," she jokes, offering her hand. "I'm Serai."

Kabir gulps. This woman isn't only stunning but charming. He can't help but be attracted to her. Her hand is small, delicate in his own. She squeezes his with just the right amount of pressure. She speaks fluent English, and a sad realization dawns on him: it's probably the reason she was taken. A girl like her could survive with little supervision in London. "Likewise. What accent do I hear? It sounds divine."

Serai places her clutch on the table and blushes at the compliment. "I'm from Eastern Europe. I think maybe you are too?"

"I am! You've got a refined ear," Kabir observes as he finds his groove. "Do you enjoy cocktails? Their menu is phenomenal."

Serai opens the cocktail menu and glances at it. "These look good."

"So you'll take one of each?"

Serai's smile is gentle as she tucks a strand of hair behind her ear. "We'll start with one and take it from there."

———

Animal sweeps incoming hotel guests with a digital camera. The 300mm lens provides ample clarity. Twenty minutes have passed since their candidate entered the lobby. Since then, he hasn't spotted any suspicious activity.

He's about to activate his radio and give the all-clear, but a suspicious vehicle turns onto the street. It advances slowly, as if it's searching for a parking spot. Then the silver Infiniti stops at the hotel entrance, but it doesn't drop any guests curbside.

Animal raises the handheld radio to his lips. "Z, may have spotted our security."

"I'm watching," Jen replies. "I'd like to get a visual of the driver."

"On it."

The car swings a U-turn on the street and parallel parks opposite the Trafalgar's entrance. Perfect view of the staircase leading into the building.

Animal cracks his window, which was speckled with snowflakes, and he eases the camera's lens into the gap. The angle gives him a straight shot through the Infiniti's windshield. Perfect timing. Its wipers slash across the glass, and the driver kills the engine. Lights activate in the cabin. The shutter whirs.

Lowering his camera, he returns to the radio. "Two big guys sitting up front. One in the back."

"Got a hit on their plates," Jen says. "Registered to an Albanian national named Valon Hajriz. That's her security. I want to know the second they make a move."

———

Kabir's arm is intertwined with Serai's as they walk to the suite. They downed a few cocktails and the jitters are gone. She's giggling at his jokes, which aren't funny, all while pressing her body into his. But she's a professional. As they near the suite, her delicate fingers navigate his beltline—a romantic search for weapons. A less thoughtful man would label it flirtation, but they both have ample reason to be cautious.

"This is us," Kabir says as they reach the suite's door. He swipes the keycard, the lock turns green, and he invites her in. "Make yourself comfortable."

Serai places her clutch on a table, and Kabir helps her out of her jacket before hanging it in the closet. "You're a gentleman."

Kabir feels blood rushing into his cheeks. "Just want to make you comfortable."

Serai is amused by her date. Most men would have thrown her on the bed already. Or squeezing her tight, forcing her back into a wall. This one's shy, and she decides to do the hard work for him. She unzips her dress and lets it fall to the floor.

Kabir stares at her body, awestruck. If there was ever a perfect woman, she's standing right in front of him. Skin the color of honey and just as velvety. Natural breasts on her slender, delicate frame.

"Relax," she says before easing him onto the sofa.

Kabir's at a loss for words, but he's not looking to make small talk anymore. Her lips are on his, and she's taking him to a new dimension.

"Let's find out what you'd like." She climbs on top of him and pulls his phone out of his suit jacket. She eases down her panties and uses the camera to photograph a QR code tattooed just inches from her body's most delicate region. "Take your pick."

Kabir examines a menu displayed on the phone. Sex acts and their corresponding costs. The ten thousand dollars' worth of Bitcoin isn't enough to cover some of these services. The more expensive, the more depraved, and they make him question his desire to bring a child into this world. He settles for the basics. "I'm easy."

Serai doesn't take Kabir's phone when he attempts to return it. Instead, she listens for her own device, which is beeping in her purse. She leans down and kisses him once more. "Just give me a minute to confirm everything."

As she works her device, another message arrives on his phone. It's a countdown clock with four hours remaining. He waves it at her and smiles flirtatiously. "This is all the time I get with you?"

"It's more than enough. But you can always buy more time," she says while batting her lashes at him.

Kabir has everything he needs. They've just exchanged money for sex, and both of their devices have a record of it. He uses a preset code phrase to alert Jen. "Dreams do come true."

"They do," Serai replies. "Will you wait while I slip into the powder room?"

"There's one in the bedroom to your right."

Serai only takes a few steps before the bedroom door bursts open. Jen and Hastings fly out, weapons drawn, and order Serai onto the ground. Kabir reaches for an end table and opens the drawer, extracting his badge and pistol.

Serai lunges for her clutch and snatches it up. Too fast for the people who burst in. Her back to the wall, she reaches inside the bag, squeezing something, holding it over her chest.

———

Jen's pistol already has the suppressor attached. Her red dot is centered over the candidate's chest. Feels awkward pointing a weapon at a nineteen-year-old, but certain rules govern this situation, and she's forced to obey. The girl is a threat until she sees both hands.

"Just lower the purse, sweetheart. We're with the British government," Jen coaxes. She doesn't get a reply, only a panicked stare.

Kabir approaches the candidate from the side, out of the field of fire, with his badge raised. "I'm an officer with New Scotland Yard, *Ms. Konci*. We know all about you. You're not in any trouble. Just let us talk to you."

The candidate's body is rigid, shaking. Teeth chattering. She hasn't noticed Kabir's badge. Just the two people standing across from her with guns. "You're not here to kill me?"

"No, ma'am," Jen replies. "You're safe. Please, just drop the bag and show us your hands."

"We're with the government," Hastings adds, sensing his American accent bears importance.

The candidate drops the purse. Her right hand is clutching the red-and-white wool verore. Tears are falling down her cheeks, and she follows them to the floor. She balls up and hides her face behind her knees.

Jen quickly holsters her weapon. She retrieves a blanket and drapes it over the candidate. This breakdown is one of the saddest things she's seen in her career. This young girl has been through hell, and she's fighting to hang onto a final bit of love in her heart. She's no longer a candidate; she's *Serai*. Cinching the blanket around her shoulders, Jen feels the tremors racing through her tiny body. "I promise things get better from here."

THIRTY-SIX

In the hour that has passed since Jen and her team detained Serai, they've made scant progress. But the challenges she's facing are unexpected.

Initially, she'd thought loyalty would be the biggest factor in preventing Serai from working with the United States and British governments. Strong ties to the old country. Family members involved with organized crime in London or in Albania. Maybe an unwillingness to change or augment her lifestyle. But Serai isn't deterred by those barriers.

Her trauma is deeper than Jen had guessed, and since she's been arrested, she's been despondent. Answering questions with nods or head shakes. Staring at the floor, exhibiting signs of severe mental duress.

"How's our time looking?" Jen asks, sitting across from Serai on the sofa.

Hastings has already removed both cell phones from the room and checks his watch. "Two hours, thirty minutes."

They'll need it. The girl is still squeezing the bracelet, refusing to let it go.

"How do I get you to talk to me?" Jen asks.

Serai looks at Hastings and Kabir. She shakes, tries to hold back tears, but fails.

Men. Jen listens to her intuition and points them both into the safe bedroom. She doesn't mince words. "I want both of you to split. I can handle Serai if there's trouble. Link up with Animal and get ready to run our evacuation plan. Clock is ticking here."

"Got it, Z," Hastings replies as he taps Kabir's shoulder. "C'mon, kid."

Jen settles back into the sofa as the suite's door shuts. Asking her team to leave seems to have relaxed Serai. Her shoulders drop, and she sits up straighter on the couch. "You're not in trouble, Serai. I'm an ally."

Serai's only response is physical; she stops shaking and gazes at the verore in her hand.

Jen smiles. The bracelet. It was one of the reasons she picked Serai, and its importance is only growing. "My family means a lot to me too. Near or far, they comfort me during times like this."

Jen peels back several layers, shows off some scars. Surgeries and broken bones and near scrapes that should have been deadly had luck or fate not intervened to save her life. She catches the girl peeking at the wounds and senses compassion. "I go through what I go through for my family. I'm starting to wonder if that's what you're doing."

Jen dips into stories from her time growing up in West Texas. Rodeos and shooting ranges with her dad. Trying to raise a garden with her mom, silty Texas soil be damned. How they had to get smart and treat their plants just right so they'd return the favor. "Why don't you tell me what's going on with the people you care for?"

Serai kicks the nearby coffee table, and the outburst startles Jen.

"You don't understand! They have them. My mom and my sister. If I end up in jail, the mafia will kill them both. I can't be here with you, understand? If I help you, my family will die. Show me mercy and let me leave."

Jen thinks back on that promise she made in the safe house bedroom. Letting this young woman or her family suffer is beyond tolerable. She leans toward Serai and speaks in an even tone. "You just go ahead and tell me where they are, and we'll free them by morning. You can meet them in the United States when this is all through. I need your help, and I'll help you too."

Serai blinks past her tears and stares at Jen incredulously. "They're in Shkodra, my hometown. The mafia doesn't have them in custody. They just watch them closely."

"I can pull your family out of Albania, Serai. Set up a living arrangement in Europe or the United States—wherever you like. We will provide money too."

"You would do that? Go through all this trouble for me?"

"Damn right I would. But I need to ask you some questions first. Try to understand what you know. What you've seen."

"What if I don't know anything?"

Jen can see the terror in Serai's face, and she smiles. "Guess you'll have to keep it a secret until I get your family clear of the mafia."

Serai melts at the wry smile. She crosses to Jen's sofa and takes her hand. "I'll do whatever I can."

"Just give me a minute," Jen says. She hops up from the table, activates a spare cell phone's video camera, and places it directly across from Serai. The footage is going to be sent to Martinez and her counterparts in Britain's intelligence services. "Just so you know, your responses are being recorded."

Serai nods. "I understand."

"All right," Jen says as she returns to the sofa. "Can you tell me who you work for?"

Serai takes a deep breath and looks into the cell phone's lens. Big step, and it involves trusting a stranger. Finally, she blurts out the name of her employer. "The Lika Syndicate. Everyone knows them where I'm from. They're the ones who kidnapped me and sent me here, to London."

"Kidnapped? How long ago?"

"Thirteen months. I was walking home from school when I was taken."

"Good, Serai," Jen says, resting a hand on the girl's shoulder. "What kind of crimes have you been involved with since you've been here?"

"Just . . ." Serai looks down at her body, but her embarrassment stops her from saying it. "Seven of us survived the journey to London.

They shipped us in a metal box. Made us swim for a time. A boat came and brought us to shore."

After another pause, she exposes her arm. She wipes away the concealer, revealing the bruised injection site. "Men force us . . . Drugs give them the courage to do what they want. I'm not an addict, but I wanted to tell you the truth."

Jen looks down at the bruise and wonders what type of monster would inject a teenager with narcotics. Taking down Void's operators may not be enough to satisfy the promise she made. Maybe she'll take a crack at Lust's clientele too. "I appreciate your honesty, but you're not in trouble, Serai. Count on that."

Serai nods, wipes her tear-streaked cheek.

Jen's tone hardens. "These individuals are going to pay for the things they're doing, Serai."

"I don't want anyone to pay. I just want to get out of this with my family."

"You will. Promise you that," Jen says. "What happened when you got to shore?"

"They brought us to a mansion. Huge place. They tattooed QR codes on us and added us to their system. Told us all the rules. We were taken to our apartments and given cell phones. Work started the very next day. I haven't had much contact with the Likas. Everything is conducted through our phones."

Solid hit. Mansion where women are processed. Tattoos are applied, linking them to a governing network. That means technology and people responsible for managing it. Void's servers might be located at this mansion, and if they aren't, they'll be connected somehow. Serai's fears aren't warranted. This is the information Jen was hoping for. "Would you be able to identify that house? Or the people who work there?"

Serai's confidence fades. "I never saw an address. Just what it looked like. I heard names though."

"A description is all I need," Jen responds. A message flashes on the cell phone that isn't recording. MI5 is working in the background, analyzing the conversation. She opens a series of photographs. "Are these your family members?"

"My mom and my sister," Serai says, nodding. She begins relating where her younger sister goes to school. That her mother enjoys going to the market every morning and searching for the freshest vegetables for the evening supper. "I'll give you their address too."

"We'll have them by morning," Jen says, beaming with confidence, hoping it bolsters the girl. "I'm not comfortable sending you back to your apartment."

Serai recoils at the idea. "I have to! If I don't come back after the timer ends, they'll know something is wrong."

"There's no way you're leaving my custody," Jen states. "You mentioned additional services to my undercover officer. That's a good excuse to keep you here with us."

"Don't give them another pound. I'll be fine, I promise."

"I'm not too worried about the money, Serai. Besides, I intend to ask these boys for a refund." She pauses so Serai understands the weight behind her next words. "I respect your courage."

Serai blushes. "I've never felt I had that."

"You've got it in spades," Jen says. She grabs her phone once again. "I'd like you to record a few personal messages for your mom and sister. You should let them know why all this is happening, and that they can trust the people who come to help. Make sure to include personal details that only you could know."

Serai takes the phone and follows the directions. She uses nicknames for her little sister. Words of encouragement her mother passed down to them as children. References to the last time they saw each other. She hands back the phone. "That will work. I'm sure of it."

Jen forwards the videos to Martinez. They'll be analyzed for any code phrases before they're deployed, but she doesn't expect any problems. She extracts an American flag patch from inside her jacket pocket. Carries it everywhere she goes. "Hold this up and let me photograph you. We'll show this to your family too."

Serai runs her fingers over the threads. Well-traveled, like her verore. "This means something to you."

"Means something to a lot of people. Won't be long before you feel the same way."

Serai holds up the flag and offers a genuine smile. The cell phone camera snaps, and she returns the flag. "When you're ready, we'll add more time on my phone."

"We've still got time," Jen replies as she hops up to fetch a soda out of the small refrigerator. "You've already done well, so just take a minute to relax. And if something comes to mind—an important detail about your family—just let me know so that I can forward it to my superiors."

Serai opens the soda and takes several big gulps. Sugar takes the edge off her shock. "I don't need to relax, and I have plenty to tell you. Let's keep working."

Jen is starting to respect this girl more by the minute. When she gets out of this mess, she'll have a bright future ahead. "All right, Serai. I'm all ears."

THIRTY-SEVEN

ABOUT AS QUICKLY AS THE SURVEILLANCE EQUIPMENT WENT in, it's coming back out. Jen is working double time to clear the suite while Serai rests. The girl was more forthcoming than could have been expected, and Jen can't extract any more information—at least until she honors her side of the deal.

Jen is nearly finished screwing a socket cover in place when her cell vibrates. Martinez has an update on the extraction mission spinning up in Albania. CIA Ground Branch operators attached to the U.S. Embassy in Tirana are being tasked with the mission. Light team but capable. She would have liked to have more operators on the task, but given the timeline, it's not possible.

With the cleanup finished, she takes a seat on the sofa. She has a straight shot into the bedroom where Serai is relaxing. She dials Martinez while hooking in a set of earbuds, and the video call connects.

"Excellent work tonight, Jen. Everyone who watched that interview echoed the same sentiment," Martinez says while aboard a flight to London. "Are we confidential?"

Jen shakes her head. Serai is beaming back at her, expecting an update on her family. "How are we?"

Martinez has a legal pad stuffed with notes on the upcoming extraction, and she begins rattling off details. "Our team will be in contact with Serai's family within three hours. Expect an update within that timeframe. How's your security situation?"

Still three guys parked out on the street, and she's got them covered. "Solid." She checks her watch, mind on Serai's countdown. "We may need another round of cash."

"You have full discretion there. Serai's worth it." Martinez pauses. "How is she?"

"Stable. What's your ETA?"

"I'll be in London in time for Serai's debrief. Meantime, I'll keep you apprised on what's happening in Albania. Again, solid work."

The line clicks off, saving Jen from another bland response. She gathers her tech and proceeds to the bedroom. She stows her gear inside a duffel on the dresser.

"How did you get so good with all of those gadgets?"

Jen turns to Serai, who is now sitting cross-legged on the bed. She lied to Martinez earlier; the girl is better than solid. Once her team left, Serai's walls went down. Now she has a thousand things to say, and they don't involve the Lika Syndicate or prostitution. She's just a kid looking for a friend, and Jen is happy to oblige. With time to spare, she sits in a nearby loveseat. "Usually start by breaking a few of 'em. Get better from there."

Serai's face lights with a huge grin. "No!"

"If you only knew!" She laughs, switches to a more important subject. "Tell me about you. Do you like school? Or working?"

Serai nods, excited by the question. "I like school. Literature is my favorite. Have you ever read Dante's *Inferno*?"

The question triggers a flashback in Jen's mind. Montana and Harrison Lowe. A man who worked in her first Technical Access Group. Was his favorite piece of literature, and the coincidence isn't lost on her. He's always been the person she failed to save, and suddenly Serai has taken a special place in her heart. "I have, actually."

"I've read it so many times. My mom says—" Serai suddenly stops, her features clouded.

Jen kicks herself. She walked Serai into a landmine.

"When will I know what happened with my family?"

Now they're both standing on a pressure switch. Serai's family is in danger, and if bad news comes, this room won't be the right place to share it. But deceit has never been Jen's strong suit, and it makes her wonder how she got her job at the Agency. "We'll know in three, maybe four hours."

Serai kneads her hands. "Long time."

"It'll pass before you know it. Just try and relax."

"What about you? You're probably tired," Serai says.

"I've got to keep my eyes on things," Jen replies with a smile. Serai's family is at risk, and she's worried about a stranger. Thoughtful and considerate. Funny how hardship brings that out of a person. "But you need some rest."

Serai drops back onto the mattress and eyes the laptop that has replaced the computer station.

"That's right where I'll be," Jen confirms.

She drops in front of the computer and sends a special request to Martinez. Copy of the *Inferno*. Simple gesture that could end up meaning a lot to Serai. With the request acknowledged, she returns to monitoring security on the laptop. They still have a lot of time to kill, and the Lika Syndicate's security could react at any time.

THIRTY-EIGHT

ENVER HOXHA, AND THE BRUTAL DICTATORSHIP HE RULED with, marred whatever it touched. The housing project that Abe Nash is facing is a prime example. Drab and gray and heartless, despite the thousands of people that live inside the complex.

The Ground Branch operator is a member of the extraction team sent from the U.S. Embassy. He's inside a work van, which is double-parked by his target structure. Using dim streetlight, he reviews photos tucked in the quarter-back sleeve on his left wrist. Mira Konci. Elina Konci. Lefter Cenjar, the housing complex's superintendent. Tugging open his sleeve, he accesses a map of the building, which is marked with two separate apartments.

"Hammer Two, this is One, we're set."

Before replying to the radio call, he checks with his teammate in the passenger seat. Matt. A Ground Branch member, like him. "Last looks."

Matt closes the Velcro flap on his sleeve and presses it shut. "Set."

Abe rests his suppressed Heckler & Koch MP7 submachine gun on his lap, thumbs his mic. "Hammer One, this is Two . . . Kill it."

"Going dark, Hammer Two. See you in five."

Lights shudder before the six giant buildings of the housing project go dark. He flips down the night-vision goggles attached to his helmet. He also drapes a hood over his helmet while his teammate does the same. "Let's go."

The green-eyed reapers step into the cold and sprint toward their target building. Clock is ticking. They need to get in and out before the mafia or the building manager realize what is happening.

Finding the back door locked, Abe removes a small crowbar from under his hoodie. The baggy garment is also concealing a low-vis plate carrier along with spare magazines. Wedging the bar into the door, he breaks it open.

It's late, and the interior hallways are desolate. Like the outside, the inside is decrepit. Cement blocks are painted gray. Leaky pipes tick water onto the concrete flooring. Scents mingle in the air—odors from humans who have sat dormant for too long, oily cooking, and mildew.

Using infrared flashlights, they navigate to the super's apartment. Target number one. Intelligence from London indicates that he's instrumental in monitoring the families of kidnap victims. If something unusual happens, he reports it directly back to local Lika Syndicate members. Unfortunately, his services are no longer required.

As Abe kneels, he pulls a small can of WD-40 out of his kit while keeping an ear close to the metal door. Zero movement on the other side. After a spurt of the good stuff, he begins picking the lock with a Lichi kit.

The lockpicking tool makes short work of the door's locks, and it's almost noiseless with the WD-40 seeping through the tumbler.

A call echoes in Abe's headset: "Hammer Two, we're inside. Progressing to the package's apartment."

Abe stays focused on the tumbler while Matt depresses his mic's transmit button twice. No voices, not now, and the two bursts of static will be the only acknowledgment.

The Lichi's rake falls on a final tumbler, and Abe twists the tool to unlock the deadbolt. Matt angles his MP7 at the door; he'll take point during the breach.

Abe eases his left shoulder into the cinder-block wall, keeping his body clear of the door. Too many years in special forces have taught him a hard lesson: no matter what it's made of, doors aren't adequate cover.

Exposing only his arm, he slowly turns the knob. Hinges groan before the door catches on a chain. Prepared, Abe clips it with a set of pliers and pushes it open.

Matt peeks at a far corner with his MP7 before making entry. Unable to find a threat, he rushes in. Abe doesn't waste a second raising his own submachine gun, then follows his teammate inside. They fan out across the living room, using night-vision and IR devices to find their way in the pitch-black space.

They survey the super's living room furniture and listen. Ears are one of a soldier's greatest weapons, and their patience rewards them. They detect heavy snoring from the apartment's single bedroom.

Abe gives the kitchen a quick peek while Matt locks the apartment door. The operators won't take kindly to any interruptions beyond this point.

When they regroup at the bedroom door, the snoring is louder. Peeking through a crack, Abe finds an oversized man on the bed. The super is a side sleeper, and his back is turned to his enemies.

They enter. Clothes on the back of the door prevent it from smacking against the dresser. Matt progresses to the room's far side, then clears the other bedside while Abe's IR laser stays plastered to the side of the super's head. Thorough, Matt drops, checks the underside of the bed.

IR light splashes Abe's feet, and the absence of a gunshot means that the room is clear. His MP7 is down and a Winkler Tomahawk is in his hand by the time Matt is on his feet. This shitbag won't report a thing if his head is caved in. And despite its brutality, the hawk is virtually silent.

Orienting the hawk's rear-spike toward the super's temple, he raises it while Matt prepares to deliver a potential safety shot. Not a second before Abe can swing the tomahawk, the fat man rolls over, eyes wide open.

Bottleneck rifle cartridges are known for one thing in particular: speed. They solve problems before they start. The super barely has time to gasp before Matt's MP7 delivers a single shot to the side of his temple.

Neurons fried, the super is courteous enough to remain still as several more shots penetrate his skull.

———

Sensing a presence, Mira Konci awakes with a start, but a pair of powerful hands wrap around her head and mouth, stifling her scream. Petrified, she looks over, finds a silhouette with four green eyes kneeling at her bedside.

The silhouette speaks in slow, steady English. "My name is James Kelso, and I'm with the United States government. I'm here to help you. Do you understand me?"

Mira nods her head. She knows some English, but she's not fluent. Even if she was, she'd be too terrified to make use of it. Another man steps into the room and shakes his head at Kelso. That makes two, and it adds to her confusion.

The second silhouette is more helpful. He speaks Albanian fluently. A local maybe? "My name is Levi. We're with the U.S. government, ma'am. Serai sent us to help you."

"Shh," Kelso whispers as he slowly removes his hands from her mouth and pulls a cell phone from his kit. A video is already cued up, ready to play.

Mira takes the device and finds her firstborn daughter in a compromised position. Gone a year, they've only spoken a handful of times. Seeing her like this takes away any confusion she had, and she becomes laser-focused. Serai's directions are clear, and by the time the video finishes, Mira understands what the next several hours will bring. Her small family will be reunited in London and then the United States. But they'll have to get there first. That means leaving this apartment behind for good.

Kelso grabs his phone and activates his mic. "We're passing Blitz."

"Copy, Hammer One. Cameras are confirmed down. Ditto fat man. Moving to you," Abe replies.

"Double-time it," Kelso orders.

Levi kneels at Mira's side. "Ma'am, where is your daughter?"

Mira scoots her back against the wall. Sitting up is helping her think. "What do you mean? She's in her room."

"No, ma'am. We're the only ones in the apartment."

Mira sighs. *Sixteen-year-old girls.* And people wonder why she's got bags under her eyes. "Are my car keys hanging by the door?"

Levi slips away, returns in seconds. "No, ma'am."

Mira runs her hands through her jet-black hair, wanting to pull it out in frustration. Elina, her second daughter, just had to pick tonight to be a teenager. Parents can't ever take time off. "She probably went to a party on the outside of town. An old train station. Local kids go there to drink."

"Does she have a cell phone?" Levi asks.

"Yes." Mira grabs her phone off the nightstand and hands it to Kelso. "There's no password."

Levi translates the update for Kelso. There's a brief exchange. "Ms. Konci, you've got two minutes to grab your essentials. We'll get your coat."

Mira doesn't hesitate as she throws off her covers and hops out of bed. This will be the last time she sets foot in the apartment. Everything she'll ever need is already gone. But she does grab a wad of cash in her dresser along with the family's photo album.

Kelso and Levi are waiting at the door when she arrives, along with two new men. Kelso drapes a heavy winter coat over her pajamas, and Levi says, "We don't have much time. Let's go get your daughter."

THIRTY-NINE

MIDNIGHT. LONDON'S TRAFFIC IS MINIMAL, AND THAT MAKES surveilling the Trafalgar easier. Hastings is sitting in the passenger seat of the minivan. Animal is behind the wheel. When a black Lincoln Navigator turns down the street, their antenna goes up. Once it flashes its headlights toward the Infiniti, antennas are traded for DSLR cameras. Shutters whir, and the vehicle's license plate is forwarded directly to Jen.

"Something tipped them off," Hastings mumbles as he lowers the camera onto his lap. Since he's been in the van, the Infiniti's suspension has barely rocked back and forth. The men inside haven't even left to piss. Like his own team, it's a sign that they're locked in.

"Could be the mound of cash Jen deposited in their bank accounts," Animal guesses. He reaches for his 2011 and toggles the safety. Off. On. Perfectly aware of the weapon's condition, he rests it on his knee. "Maybe they're looking for more."

"Did we miss something in the hotel?" Kabir questions. He's kneeling between the two front seats, wearing holes in his nicest suit—and maybe his meniscus.

"Got to be tech related," Hastings says. "Something through Serai's phone."

The Navigator stops, waits for a lone vehicle in the oncoming lane to speed past before swinging a U-turn. It stops next to the silver Infiniti. The passenger window drops, and Ceno Lika's face becomes visible.

Hastings raises his DSLR and snaps a half-dozen photographs. When he lowers the camera, his ice-blue eyes are wide, and he's wearing a vicious grin. "Call New Scotland Yard. London's entire most wanted list just parked in front of the Trafalgar."

Animal nods back at the kid. "Got all the limeys we need. Think we should handle it from here, Sergeant."

"Right . . ."

Kabir doesn't bother interjecting his opinion. He recognizes the sort of men he's sharing space with; they're lunatics on the verge of doing what they're best at. To stop them now would simply mean putting himself in harm's way. His hand flies to a nearby radio, and it shakes as he raises Jen. "Zero, we've got a visual on Ceno Lika. There's a situation developing street side."

"Solid copy," Jen replies. "I have a visual."

Another vehicle turns down the street. A Cadillac CTS V. When it stops next to the Navigator the three vehicles are blocking traffic. Its window drops, and the gangsters conduct their powwow in the middle of the street without an ounce of concern about London's traffic laws.

Ceno's control over the situation is clear. He directs his ire toward the Infiniti, then the Caddie. His men react to the orders as quickly as he gives them. A large man steps out of the rear passenger side of the Infiniti and waits by the Cadillac for a second man to join him. Together, they cross the street toward the hotel.

Kabir gets back on the radio. This time with more urgency. "Z, two hostiles are entering the hotel lobby."

"Marking them now."

With its cargo deposited, the Cadillac tears off down the street and disappears. Moments later, the Infiniti does the same. The Navigator parallel parks in the Infiniti's spot, which gives it a perfect view of the hotel's entrance.

Hastings tosses his camera in the back and grabs his brass knuckles. Twirling them on his index finger, he stares at Ceno Lika in the Navigator. "We're in for an exciting night, boys."

———

All Jen can do is watch as pieces fall into place. The two men who entered the lobby are checking in. When the clerk slides them their keys, they split. One heads for the elevator, the other the hotel bar.

She cycles the camera feeds and searches for more activity. She spots the Cadillac first. The vehicle has pulled into the hotel's subterranean parking garage and parks in a prime spot. When the engine shuts off, they've got clean sightlines of the elevators and emergency exit. Moreover, they're in position to block vehicles as they exit the garage.

The Infiniti is a little tougher. It's parked in the Trafalgar's back alley. There's no streetlight, but the cameras pick up its silver paint, which is glinting under the moon. The men in the vehicle have a perfect view of the hotel's back door, which is used for service vehicles and deliveries.

There's no way to escape the hotel without these men seeing it. Extracting Serai just got complicated, and Jen kicks herself for letting this problem develop. The safe house is only twenty minutes away, and it should have been used. Abandoning Serai's phone and its link to Lust kept her in place, but that error is only hindsight now.

Jen flips the camera feed and returns to the thug as he steps into the elevator. She whispers toward her laptop screen. "Bet my last buck that asshole comes this way."

She knows better than to call it a jinx as the thug steps off the elevator's eighth floor—the same one that she's on. He proceeds down the hallway toward her suite.

Jen looks back to Serai on the bed. A bundle of nerves, shivering from the stress. "Need your help."

Serai rushes over, prepared to do the best she can.

Jen zooms in on the thug's face as he stalks the hallway. "Recognize that man? Or any of the vehicles in the photographs?"

Serai shudders as the thug approaches their suite. He stops and presses his ear to the door. She should be moaning. Mattress springs squealing. Headboard knocking the wall, disturbing neighbors. Silence is a very, very bad sign. He shakes his head as he texts an update. He meanders toward a room several doors down. "I don't know him—same with the cars."

Green light on the lock. The thug steps in and they wait for things to get weird. He doesn't disappoint. He flips the metal latch between the door and the jamb, leaving a gap. Moments later, light fills the crack. Then a shadow consumes the lower half. He's sitting on the floor, watching.

Jen delivers a quick status update to her team before hopping out of the office chair. She paces momentarily and asks Serai, "Why would they make a move like this?"

"I've seen it before," Serai replies. "They know something is wrong, and they're making sure they can use it."

"What do you mean?" Jen asks.

"Sometimes guys hurt girls. Kill them. The men who hire us have money, and if they're caught in an embarrassing situation . . ." Her voice trails into past traumas. "There's money to be made for the Likas."

"The response seems too strong," Jen observes.

Serai shrugs. "Rich men have their own security sometimes."

The logic passes muster, but with one major wrinkle: the intelligence officer occupying the room with this woman. Murders in the Bronx. More in London. The Likas are suspicious for multiple reasons, and if they catch wind about what's happening in Albania before Jen departs, this hotel will turn into a hellscape.

FORTY

THE VIEW FROM INSIDE THE ABANDONED LOCOMOTIVE ISN'T ideal. Abe's night-vision goggles are up. A giant bonfire provides more than enough light to see what's going on at the old rail yard. There are over one hundred teenagers at the party, which is centered in a large, open garage that would have serviced steam engines. If the flames aren't keeping them warm, liquor is. And worse than the free-flowing booze? Guns.

Occasional muzzle flashes lick up at the edge of the crowd, accompanied by cheers and hurrahs. The scene is wild, and he can't help but wonder how he survived his own teenage years. Maybe he wouldn't have if he'd lived in Albania.

Alone in the locomotive, he's the one who will make contact with Elina. Walking into that maelstrom isn't a possibility. He's a stranger, like the rest of his team. They'd root him out, and interrogations conducted by mobs of rowdy teenagers aren't pretty. This'll require some tact, but his team's got it handled.

Abe activates his radio. "Hammer One, I'm in position."

Kelso replies from the team's van, which is half a mile away. With him is Mira, and he won't leave her side until she's safe. "We have a lock on our target's cell. She's in the central atrium."

Abe raises his binoculars. That should mean she's close to the bonfire. Easy to see their faces in the light, provided her back isn't turned to him, or she's beyond the flames. Scanning the crowd only makes him more uncomfortable. "One, I'm noticing older males mixed into the crowd. Ask our package to advise."

"Hold, Hammer Two."

He keeps searching and finds Elina sitting on an old car seat thirty yards from the fire. Like her mother, she's a carbon copy of Serai. Red cup in hand, she looks tipsy. The team has tried calling her repeatedly, and this is likely the reason she hasn't answered her phone, along with the music and screaming kids.

"Two, package states that Lika Syndicate members may be present. New recruits, probably in their early twenties."

Bad to worse. Abe keeps his binos pegged on Elina and responds. "I have eyes on. Try her cell again."

"Dialing now."

Abe watches the girl in frustration. Tonight should already be over, but here he sits. Murphy and his ever-present laws. That a team in London is depending on his success adds another layer of urgency. He's half-tempted to loose a machine-gun burst over the crowd and grab the girl.

"Two, no joy."

No shit. Before Abe can reply, Elina rises from the bench and walks to the edge of the crowd. She's staring at her cell with an indecisive look on her face. Her mother has been calling, and she knows a confrontation is waiting when she gets home. Now or later? *C'mon, just be a good kid and press Accept.*

Elina presses a button and raises the phone to her ear. Abe's adrenaline is firing as Kelso's transmission comes in. "Got her."

———

Mira's heart is racing as her daughter's voice comes through the speaker. She refuses to let the girl speak or enter a longwinded excuse about why she snuck out of the apartment. "I need you to stay calm. Serai is safe, but she's in trouble. I'm with a team of Americans. Don't let on, but you need to leave *now*."

Elina's response comes through the phone's speaker, allowing the others to listen in. "Mama . . . I . . . What do I say? I drove your car. My friends need me to get home."

Mira looks to Levi for guidance. He shakes his head.

"Leave them behind," Mira replies. "No one can know what is happening."

Elina's voice breaks. She's on the verge of tears.

"Honey, I'm five minutes away. You're okay," Mira says before pausing. "The Americans are waiting by the rows of abandoned train cars. All you need to do is walk in their direction and they'll find you."

——————

Abe is still watching Elina, and she's looking at the trains with a newfound wonder. Time to pay close attention. The girl isn't under his control, and she's armed with newfound knowledge. This is when people get flighty, make mistakes.

Elina pockets her phone, takes a few deep breaths, and turns back to the crowd.

Damn it. Before Abe can update Kelso, the girl starts talking with her friends.

While he can't hear, the hand gestures are obvious. *Be right back. No, stay here. Just a minute.* The girl's friends stay plastered to the car seat, but an older boy drapes an arm around her shoulder and starts walking with her to the abandoned trains.

"Just had to be a good fucking friend," Abe curses.

The young man is real trouble. He's wearing the trademark black leather. More facial hair than a teenager should have. If that doesn't give it away, the nickel-plated Saturday night special under his belt does. The boy shoots a look, and another junior predator slinks after them. Just some date-rape amongst friends.

Abe updates the team. "Package Two moving toward the trains. Two males in tow. One confirmed armed."

Kelso's reply is automatic. "You're authorized to use deadly force if necessary. Keep it quiet."

Matt's call comes in next. "Copy your last, One. Hammer Three is in position."

Abe looks through the locomotive's window. The group is moving farther from the firelight and into the shadows—his domain. They're within twenty yards of his position and falling. Two static bursts are all his teammates will receive as they get into earshot. He slips from his position and prepares to engage.

———

Sheer ineptitude caused a passenger car to derail, and it settled in a jackknife position along the tracks. Matt is inside, his cheek against the stock of a B&T SPR 300 Pro. The entire twenty-inch barrel of the bolt-action rifle is essentially a suppressor with lands and grooves. If he depresses the trigger, it'll be dead silent.

The thermal optic mounted to the rifle glows brighter. Three people just entered his field of view. He catches Abe peeking out of the locomotive's entrance. The experienced operator takes down his hood, and an infrared strobe attached to his helmet glows in the thermal optic. Friendly marked.

Matt reaches up and hits his mic. "This is Hammer Three. I've got eyes on and I'm prepared to engage."

———

Elina is running out of time and she knows it. Ismael, the man with his arm around her, is a member of the Lika Syndicate. The same people who took Serai. The same people who take whatever they want in this town, and she hates them for it.

Train cars loom on both sides of her. Window shades are pulled down in some of the passenger cars. Others sit at crooked angles. Doors are yawning open, darkness beyond. Up ahead, a derailed car will stop them from going farther, but she's not sure her legs will carry her that far. They're weak, and Ismael's hands are already getting frisky.

Elina's voice is shaking, like her legs. "Please, I want to get back to my friends."

The boys laugh.

Risto, the other boy, undoes his belt, and he's inching down his fly. "Who's first?"

Ismael gives him a cutting look. "You already know."

Elina feels his hands lock onto her hips. Ismael shoves her toward a nearby passenger car and pins her back to it. She tries to push him off, but he forces her hands over her head. "Please! Please, I don't want this!"

"You sure about that?" Ismael hisses.

Elina tries to pull her arms free, but he's too strong. She jerks her head away to avoid his lips.

Then she spots a figure approaching from behind. She's the only one who can see him. *Very* large. With four green eyes and a metallic object in his hand. An American.

"Stop!" Elina shouts, more firm.

Ismael matches her tone: "Don't fight me! We will hurt you."

———

Professionalism is tattooed to Abe's psyche, but he's ignoring it tonight. The tomahawk he's holding feels appropriate for the situation. And it is quiet, isn't it? All those impressionable kids nearby . . . Why taint their minds with violence?

Abe's approach is rapid and silent in the snow. He uses his thumb to check his tomahawk's orientation, and when he's close enough to smell the fire on the predators, he swings.

The hawk's rear spike impacts the first target's skull and transmits a message to Abe's hand. It met resistance, but the bone gave way. The target's muscles jerk, electrified in a moment of shock, but his brain short-circuits before it can process the massive trauma. Abe rips the hawk's spike out of the side of the target's head, allowing him to drop.

The great goddess of surprise is fickle, and she turns her back on Abe. The man forcing himself on Elina rips the Saturday night special out of his belt line and levels it at the Ground Branch operator.

Gangster bravado stops him from pulling the trigger. He puffs out his chest and shouts obscenities in Albanian.

Abe chuckles. Is it the gold chains flashing in the firelight? Or the pistol pointed sideways? The source of his amusement is tough to pin down, but he's certain of one thing: the pee-wee gangster is about to wish he had the stones to squeeze the trigger. He raises the hawk over his head but refuses to drop the tool. Like his laughter, that's just plain disrespectful. Then a call comes through his radio. Matt. "Hammer Two. You wearing trauma plates?"

Friends when you need them. Abe wants to reach for his mic, but he's concerned the idiot in front of him will panic and accidentally discharge the pistol. Inching his hand higher, he gives Matt a thumbs-up. Wincing, he braces himself. *This is gonna suck.*

The rapist is shouting, gesturing with his pistol, when the center of his chest explodes. The bullet that struck him passes through and smashes into Abe's chest. The ceramic plate in his carrier stops it, but the impact is a lot like getting hit with a sledgehammer.

"You good?" Matt asks nervously.

Abe gasps for air and clutches his chest but refuses to take a knee. That would send the wrong signal to his team. Hitching his hands on his hips, he sucks in air and hopes he doesn't pass out. When he feels like he can speak, he looks at a petrified Elina.

"Package secure," he rasps, still struggling for air. Reaching for Elina's hand, he starts with a standard script, just modified. "I'm American, okay?"

Elina's English is better than her mother's, but Abe's actions did all the talking. She tucks his arm over her shoulder and props him up. "Nice to meet you, American."

"You too," he gasps as they limp toward Matt's position. The van is less than half a mile away, and with every step, they get closer to safety.

FORTY-ONE

ALL HVIS SECURE. EN ROUTE TO U.S. EMBASSY, TIRANA.

Jen's response to the text message is involuntary. Her arms shoot upward, and she shouts, "Yes!" She leaps off the sofa and rushes to Serai. Grabbing her shoulders, she says, "We've got them both. Your mom and your sister are on the way to the embassy now!"

Serai bursts out in relieved laughter, and a couple of joyful tears slip down her cheeks. Yet in a flash, her mood shifts again. She wipes the tears away and sits up straight on the bed. "I'm ready to do whatever you need. Just tell me."

Since meeting Serai, Jen has felt growing respect for her. But it's shifting to admiration—for her courage and selflessness. She'd have fled long ago if her family had not been under the Lika Syndicate's control. Now that they're safe, nothing will stop her from breaking free. "Just keep our plan in mind. Go to your cell phone and get ready."

Without hesitation, Serai rushes out of the bedroom.

Jen makes her own preparations. She closes the remaining laptop and makes sure that the security camera feeds have transferred to her cell phone. With everything in place, she grabs her handheld radio and activates the mic. "Execute."

———

Infiniti first. It's parked in a one-way service alley that the hotel uses for deliveries. Only back door out of the Trafalgar, and the Albanians have it sealed tight.

Hastings peeks around the corner and looks down the alley. Clear view of the Infiniti, but he can't see what's going on in the car. The rear window is tinted and there's zero streetlight. But it's isolated. Prime conditions for a violent encounter.

"We're in place, Z. Fuzz out the security cameras," Hastings says, preparing for the assault. He flexes his fingers deeper inside a leather glove before sliding brass knuckles over them. Hard tool made for the streets. Tonight, he's going to commit a *crime*, and with knuckles like these, it'll never trace back to the British government.

Feels good too. He was glaring hard at Serai in that hotel room. He couldn't help it. At nineteen, Serai is the same age as his daughter, Kayla. People do terrible things to young women, and it hit home for Al Hastings.

"Alley is blind," Jen replies through Al's radio.

Hastings checks with Animal, who is stacked on the wall next to him. He already has his black leather gloves on. They're triple XL, and the brass knuckles had to be made custom to fit his hand. "Van is go."

Kabir's voice comes through the radio: "Moving."

Hastings peeks around the corner. The minivan's headlights are visible, and it's attempting to enter the alley from the wrong direction. But the street is too tight, and its front tire clips the curb. Kabir puts it into reverse only to back into another curb, and when he presses his foot on the accelerator, the bumper claps against a snowbank.

Any other night Kabir's driving would be pitiful. But the minivan's Xenon headlamps are blasting straight into the Infiniti's windshield, distracting the men inside.

"They're blind. Let's go." Hastings breaks into a sprint, careful to avoid patches of ice and snow as he closes in on the Infiniti.

Animal follows close behind and breaks off to engage the Infiniti's driver's side.

When Hastings reaches the vehicle, his fist is already cocked back.

He drives the brass knuckles through the front passenger window. Glass sprays a shocked goon and he recoils. But he's trapped. Hastings tattoos a dozen indentations onto the goon's face before his lights cut out.

Animal's fist moves with enough force to rock the car before impacting the back of Valon Hajrizi's head. He'd been watching his friend catch a beating when his vision went blurry. The same punch that shattered the glass puts Valon to sleep.

Hastings pushes his unconscious man forward and zip-ties his hands behind his back. Once finished, he pushes the goon back up and threads another zip tie around the headrest and the goon's neck. It ratchets tight, but he stops short of strangling him.

Animal finishes fastening Valon's hands to the wheel. Hastings leans into the vehicle and pushes the unconscious Albanian into position against the seat, allowing Animal to brace his neck. Locked in.

Both men conduct a quick search for cell phones and weapons before breaking from the Infiniti. The assault took around two minutes. They start down the street the same way they came. Kabir is no longer worried about hopping a curb. He rubs his foot into the gas and speeds up behind the operators.

"Target one is down and we've retrieved their cells," Hastings says as he clocks the van's position behind him. "Moving to the second target."

"Copy," Jen replies.

The minivan eases up beside them, and the side door slides open automatically. Both men hop into the moving van and slam the door shut without missing a beat.

————

Jen takes a last look at the parking garage's cameras before disabling them. The Cadillac is still parked near the elevators, not showing any signs of movement. She fuzzes out the garage's cameras and sends the operators a text update.

Serai is standing with her in the bathroom, cell phone in hand. There's an emergency SOS feature on the screen. Girls can use it to call for help, and she's ready to activate it.

Jen mouths two minutes, mindful to remain quiet around Serai's cell phone.

Serai nods and counts the seconds.

————

"That's right, nice and easy," Hastings says as he marks the Cadillac through the minivan's windshield.

Kabir is creeping toward the vehicle, which is backed against the garage wall. Prime location for observing the elevators—terrible for just about everything else.

"Line it up just right," Animal whispers, who is kneeling by the side door.

Hastings notices silhouettes shifting in the target vehicle. Suspicions are growing. This interdiction was never going to have the same element of surprise, which is why he has his suppressed Staccato 2011 in his hand. "Nail it!"

Kabir mashes the gas pedal. Straight to forty-five, then hard brake to zero. The minivan's tires smoke as they bite cement, and the van stops in front of the Cadillac.

Animal rips open the door, leaps across the Cadillac's hood, and lands next to the driver's side door. He points his Staccato at the tinted glass and shouts, "Show me your hands!"

"Open the fuckin' door!" Hastings shouts as he drops off the Caddie's hood and stands next to the rear passenger door, gun up.

Kabir has his Glock 17 raised as he jumps out of the van's side door and takes up a position on the Cadillac's hood. His muzzle jerks toward the driver, whose hand is inching below the dashboard. The driver corrects what would have been a terrible mistake, and Kabir repeats the directive again in Albanian. "Unlock the doors!"

Automatic locks disengage. Dominoes drop.

Animal opens the driver's side door and presses his pistol into the driver's temple, which forces him to kill the engine.

Hastings opens the back door and smashes the butt of his pistol into the rear passenger's head. Hard, violent. Flex cuffs cinch the back passenger's hands, and he rolls the body flat on the seat. He slams the door before moving to the front passenger.

The driver pleads in Albanian. Animal replies with the world's most universal language: violence. He pistol-whips the driver. Pulling back the pistol, he notices a dent in the driver's temple and wonders if his cortex can process bone chips. The driver goes limp, Animal's curiosity is satisfied, and he fastens both of his hands to the steering wheel before retrieving the car keys.

Hastings works the front passenger. Trademark style. The goon's hands are raised, pleading, *I'll cooperate!* Hastings is only too certain of that as he eases his hand behind the passenger's head and smashes his face into the dashboard. Napa leather splits, takes the form of a high-quality dental impression. Blood spurts from his nose, stains the leather. Nothing exceeds like excess, and Hastings only considers the work done when the man is limp with zip ties binding him from multiple points.

"Phones! Weapons!" Hastings orders.

"Got mine!" Animal states.

"That makes two of us," Hastings says as he slides a final phone into his jacket pocket.

The Caddie's doors slam. Kabir stays gun up until his partners are back in the minivan. Finally, he rejoins them, taking his spot behind the wheel.

"Hold!" Hastings orders before the van can take off again. "Animal, lock the car doors. Carjackings are bad in these parts."

The Caddie's lights flash and the operators laugh as they proceed to the garage's emergency exit.

———

Ceno's cell phone is screeching. It's an emergency SOS coming from Serai's phone.

But it's not the first one he has received tonight. That came from Conscript 19, the man responsible for managing and protecting Void's network in London. A high roller spent twenty-five thousand dollars on Serai, booking her twenty-four hours straight.

Unusual, but not unheard of.

Technology surrounding Serai's phone triggered Conscript's alert. There are dozens of devices that the hacker couldn't make sense of. And when he turned her phone into a listening device? Silence.

Most high rollers like to screw the women they spend tens of thousands of dollars on. There's only one exception to that rule: the police. In this case, the Americans.

Isa's words haunt him: *The choice is yours, Ceno.* But they're nothing compared to the secret that Sandro left him.

Ceno silences the alarm and sends a text to his man in the suite. He'll be the first to respond. Finished, he alerts his men covering the exits. And they already have their orders: kill Serai Konci on sight.

The Americans have his merchandise. He's certain of it. They will use her. Wring valuable information out of her head. If that happens, Lust will evaporate into pheromones. Void's collapse will cut off a multimillion-dollar revenue stream for his family. All of it will be because of his decision to hide the truth.

While he works the cell, Halit, Mirsad, and Olsi prepare their weapons. Just pistols, which should prevent them from drawing too much attention as they cross through the lobby. Slides ratchet and force rounds into battery before the pistols settle under their jackets.

Ceno looks them over. They stare back without a drop of fear. "Let's go."

———

Serai is in tears as she runs to the suite's door. Her hair is tousled and her dress is undone. When she opens the door, the man who was on overwatch storms the suite. He'd been watching from the nearby room. She'd planned to distract him for Jen, but it instantly goes sideways.

Overwatch's hands lock around Serai's throat, and he rams her into the wall. "Rat bitch," he hisses as he presses harder against her neck.

"Help! Help!" Serai gasps.

But Overwatch doesn't relent. She slaps at the goon and belches out the words. But Jen's already sprinting from one of the bedrooms.

Her leather sap smashes into Overwatch's temple. Dazed, Overwatch stays on his feet, and Jen can only assume a thick layer of dead brain cells protected the healthy ones. No matter. Another strike lands atop the first, and this time she's positive it has worked its magic. Overwatch drops, eyelids fluttering, his body locked in a seizure.

Jen snatches the pistol from beneath his jacket. While she clears it, she comes to a new realization. The Likas aren't coming to save Serai; they mean to harm her. Extracting her asset just got harder.

Before leaving the room, she checks the cameras on her cell. Men are waiting by the hotel's elevators down in the lobby, and she recognizes every single one of them: Ceno Lika and his crew from New York. "They're on the way up! We gotta hurry!"

She grabs Serai's hand and they bolt for the emergency exit stairway.

––––––

Ceno bangs on the suite's door, but the locks outlast his temper. He steps back and gives Halit a nod. With nearly three hundred pounds of muscle at work, Halit's boot folds the door, and Ceno tears through the opening.

Several paces into the room, he sees his man lying unconscious in a doorway, foam collecting at the corner of his mouth. He wheels around and points at Halit and Mirsad. "Stairs!"

They break for the emergency exit while Ceno leads Olsi to the elevators.

––––––

Cell phone screens are flashing on the van's dash. *Missed Call. Message Waiting.*

"Ceno's reinforcements are inbound," Hastings mocks as he twirls the Caddie's key fob around his finger and stares at the glowing screens. He's in the van's passenger seat, which is still parked in the underground garage. "We could be in serious trouble. Wonder what their ETA is?"

Animal is kneeling beside the open van door, watching the emergency exit. He sighs dramatically. "I knew we'd never survive. Tell my mom I love her, Sergeant. I'm going home . . ."

Kabir is blown out. He looks back at Animal, eyebrows raised. "Jesus, you two are freaking mental."

"Jesus . . . I see him," Animal whispers. "The light . . ."

Hastings fixes on the emergency exit, and his gut is talking to him. "Two minutes since Jen entered the stairway. Any time . . ."

———

Jen is struggling to manage her bag, Serai, and the cell phone. They're nearing the second floor, having just descended six flights of stairs. Needing a moment to check the camera feeds, she stops them on a landing.

Nothing has changed on the cameras. Then the screen jumps. The suite's door is missing. Ceno is back at the elevator. The lounge lizard has left his perch at the hotel restaurant and is nearing the emergency stairway. Back on the eighth floor, the entrance smashes open, and very large men begin descending the stairs.

Jen shouts, "We need to go!"

They hear shouts from above as the Lika Syndicate members spot them through gaps in the stairs.

Jen is one flight away from the ground level when the lounge lizard bursts through the door. It barely shuts before he's drawing a Beretta.

Protecting Serai is Jen's only thought. *Better me than them.* She heaves her duffel bag at the lounge lizard. It smacks him in the chest, preventing him from aiming the weapon at Serai. "Keep running!" Jen shouts as she leaps down a half dozen stairs to tackle the mobster.

The lounge lizard sees her coming. She's half his weight and he simply plucks her out of the air and locks her in his arms. Seems easy at first, like playing with a rattlesnake, but that's because he hasn't been bitten yet. As Serai rushes past, he twists and pins Jen against the cinder-block wall while attempting to level the Beretta at her temple.

Jen senses the weapon's presence and grabs the slide. When he tries to pull the trigger, it slaps against the back of the frame. "Out of battery, asshole." She raises her right hand, lets him see the stiletto's blade as it snaps out of the handle. "That one worked."

Starting at his forehead, she drags the steel across his face and down his cheek. Blood drips into his eyes. The Beretta hits the floor as he uses his hands to protect his neck. When he steps back, she drives a straight kick into his knee, buckling the joint.

Jen grabs her bag and runs as the other mobsters close in. She looks down the remaining flight of stairs as Animal grabs Serai. He turns his back to the door, putting his body and two layers of Kevlar between the girl and the incoming threats. Hero moves, and she's proud as hell to have seen it.

Hastings trades places with Animal at the door, pistol in hand.

"They're close! We gotta go!" Jen shouts.

"Got you!" Hastings replies as he angles his pistol up the stairs, covering her descent.

Jen squeezes his shoulder as she passes. Animal already has Serai secure inside the van, and the engine is running. She tosses the duffel bag to Animal and jumps in with Hastings only seconds behind. The minivan's side door slams closed, and Kabir nails the gas. They burn for the exit, leaving the Lika Syndicate stranded in the garage.

———

Ceno exits the elevator just in time to watch a minivan speed toward the garage's exit. He runs for the Cadillac, shouting, pointing. Then the vehicle's lights flash, and the horn honks. Someone pressed the panic button on the key fob. Drawing closer, he finds three unconscious men zip-tied in place.

He stops running, and his crew gathers at his sides. He can't help but laugh. These Americans; they're skilled. They're not playing by the rules either. When he sees them again, he'll remember that. They won't get this chance twice.

FORTY-TWO

First on the scene.

Constable Norman's instincts tell him that he'll be needing backup. Only, he's not sure what type yet. He was summoned to 3 Gallions Court, an industrial area, for a fire complaint. The reason for the call is within view: a smoldering steel drum twenty feet away from a white Mercedes Sprinter Van.

Grabbing his radio, Norman cancels the fire brigade's response. He has an extinguisher in his cruiser, and whatever is burning in the barrel is nearly finished. What has his full attention is the van, and it's in all the wrong ways.

Both of the van's back doors are butterflied open. He parks his cruiser behind it, and the headlights illuminate what he recognizes as a crime scene. Dozens of muddy, snowy boot prints checker the interior of the van. Valuables have been stripped from the shelves. Screws and other small, worthless items litter the floor.

The sun is still rising, and the officer hasn't finished his first round of coffee, but his imagination is whizzing. He visualizes a team of thieves ripping apart the vehicle and passing off its valuables in an assembly-line fashion.

The cruiser's engine slows to idle. Norman waits to get out. He's letting his headlights do the work while he debates his next move. He has a Heckler and Koch G36C bolted next to his shoulder. Wouldn't be too much trouble unlocking it and clearing the scene. Yet the fire extinguisher is also within reach. Only room enough in his hands for one of them.

The rifle. With a wife and small kid at home, he won't take the chance.

He takes one last look around the scene while unlocking the weapon. If someone was going to bolt, they'd have done so by now. With some effort, he exits the cruiser without getting the rifle snagged. He's qualified, but there never seem to be enough days on the range.

Stock buried in his shoulder, he walks straight for the van's driver's side. The glass is tinted, and he keeps the muzzle directed at what he assumes would be the driver's position in the seat. There's no movement. No sound.

He tears open the door and retches. The front cab is empty, but the stench of ammonia is overpowering. Hacking, he steps back and glimpses the fumes escaping the van in the morning light. Bits of hair escape with the fumes, aided by gusts of wind.

Norman lowers the rifle and advances to the front bumper of the van. Dealer plates. The only way he'll be able to trace the vehicle is with the VIN, and he's starting to wonder if it is scratched off.

With his safety assured, he approaches the drum. The flames are out, but plenty of black smoke is still rising into the air. He learned his lesson from the van and holds his breath while he peeks at the embers.

Hunks of discolored rubber and plastic cling to the metal walls: remnants of latex gloves and trash bags. The smoke burns his eyes, but he doesn't pull away. He spots a disfigured bottle of ammonia-based cleaner at the bottom, and next to it a charred respirator mask.

After taking several steps back, Norman allows himself a deep breath. His preliminary investigation of the scene is complete. He'd come expecting to call detectives to assist with a robbery, maybe even a homicide. Now he'll be calling SO15—New Scotland Yard's Counter Terrorism Branch. It won't be long before they arrive.

FORTY-THREE

THE JOINT TERRORISM ANALYSIS CENTER IS THE PRIMARY hub for terror investigations that take place within the UK's borders. The crisis center is designed to respond to threats head on, in real time. Moreover, New Scotland Yard is its next-door neighbor. When MI5 has intelligence, officers from the Yard are at hand to act on it.

When Jen fled the Trafalgar, she landed in a whirlwind. Officers from SCO19, New Scotland Yard's tactical response team, attempted to detain Serai. Handcuffs and pat-downs and fingerprints. She was a potential threat looking to penetrate one of London's most sensitive sites. Doctors with MI5's medical ward wanted Serai draped in a gown with vials of blood collecting by her arm while an IV replenished her fluids. Officers from Britain's various intelligence agencies had their lists of questions for Jen's new asset. One by one, their requests were rebuffed.

Jen wrapped Serai in her protective blanket and kept her there. No handcuffs, no needles, no probing questions. Just a subdued place for a proper debrief.

Now, Jen sits in a secure conference room with Gabriella

Martinez, who is fresh off a jet from Wyoming. Nigel Grisham is also with them. The head of JTAC, he answers to MI5's director general. He's also the national coordinator of the executive liaison group Martinez was given a chair on. He's within earshot of the UK's prime minister, with direct control of the investigation into Gombe Wireless.

Two other analysts are present for the debrief. Their laptops allow them to access MI5's intelligence database and verify Serai's information in real time. A national security threat is operational inside London, and some of the more rigid debrief protocols have been relaxed.

Grisham notes the date and time for a tape recorder placed in the center of the table. Martinez is the next senior officer, and she follows by stating her name for the record, along with the analysts. Jen follows, and they end with Serai.

When the girl has finished identifying herself, Jen takes the lead with questions. "Serai, I'd like to pick up with what we started at the Trafalgar. About the night you came to London. Can you tell us about that?"

Serai takes a sip of water. This room is chock-full of pressure, and she clears it from her throat. With a confident nod she replies, "Ask whatever you need to ask."

Another proud moment for Jen. This young woman has courage, and she feels honored to have helped her along the path to freedom. Holding back a smile, she asks, "Can we start with how you came to London?"

Serai relates the story. She and a dozen other girls were stowed in shipping containers. Several perished during the journey. Untreated medical conditions. Life-support systems had been installed. Ventilation. Food and water for the trip. Eventually, someone cracked the container open and told them all to exit. At nightfall, they boarded a speedboat and proceeded up the River Thames. "They navigated with a GPS device, but things got bad when we arrived."

"How so?" Jen asks.

"The boat that was supposed to pick us up was late. The men piloting our boat got paranoid. They forced us into the water and left us to drown. It was freezing, and several of the girls didn't know how to swim."

A bout of silence falls over the room. Part respect, part shock that this occurred in the heart of London.

Jen notices Serai's eyes becoming distant. Like she's treading water again, fighting for survival. She's careful not to coach Serai or make inferences, but the conversation needs to continue. "Remember, you're safe now. Tell us what happened next."

"The boat came, but some of us had drifted apart or disappeared under the water. It was too dark to recover everyone. They pulled whoever they could find onboard, and we headed for shore."

"Can you tell us about the boat? Maybe recall its name, Serai?" Jen asks.

"*The Good Ole Days.*"

Jen looks over to the analysts, who are hammering on keyboards. That name alone could be all she needs. "That's great, Serai."

"It didn't take long to reach the shore. We docked, and that's where the mansion was."

"Details are important here. Try to remember your surroundings. Anything can help us," Jen says.

"When I was standing on the dock, facing the house, the port's cranes were still visible to my right. I kept thinking how bright it was."

Jen looks to Martinez, gets a nod. A mansion within spitting distance of a port on the River Thames. A boat called *Good Ole Days* moored to its dock. Anne's quantum capabilities won't be necessary to find the location. "Did you see an address?"

Serai shakes her head. "I'm sorry, but I never got a look at the front of the house. They blindfolded us when we left."

Jen senses a real letdown. "Hey, that's fine. Tell us what you did see."

"I saw a plaque on the side door. It was brass, and motion lights lit up when we approached. The house was called Windham Hall."

"Hold that thought," Jen says. Analysts are passing printed documents in her direction. The first one is a thirty-five-foot offshore fishing boat with *Good Ole Days* scrawled on the back. An old sales listing provided the images. She sets the printout in front of Serai. "Is this the boat you traveled on?"

Serai studies the images. She uses her finger to trace the boat's features, as if she's again walking the deck. "This is it."

Jen hears Grisham whispering orders to a nearby analyst. He wants the address where the boat is registered. The name of the person who purchased the vessel.

Jen retracts the photograph of the boat and replaces it with images of a mansion that is likely a century old. Built in the traditional colonial style, it's got four huge chimneys, gray stone walls, and enough space to conceal a human smuggling racket. The plaque that Serai noticed is key. "Do you recognize anything from these pictures, Serai?"

Serai doesn't hesitate. "This is where I was." She settles on a picture of the dock. "You can see the port I was talking about. That's where we came in from."

"That's Port Tilbury. London's largest," Grisham remarks.

"Awesome work," Jen says, handing back the photographs. "Describe what went on inside the home if you can."

"It's been turned into a prison," Serai says coldly. She recalls details about holding cells for women in the basement. Where they wait until they can be processed and hooked into Lust's network.

"How many days did you spend at the mansion?" Jen asks.

"Around twenty-four hours. It's like I told you. They started us the very next day."

"This next part is important, Serai. Will you tell me about how they entered you into their computer system?" Jen asks.

"It didn't take long. It was also the last step before I left," Serai replies and continues recollecting the journey's details. A technology specialist arrived. He was also a tattoo artist. He generated a QR code on the computer. A printer spat out the image, and from there, he tattooed it onto her body. "After tattooing me, he scanned it and sent it to his laptop. It looked like he was making an account, and it included a picture of my face, my name, details about where I was originally from."

Jen is trying not to fidget or lean forward in her seat. These are the details she needed to crack Void, and link it to Gombe Wireless. Windham Hall is hiding powerful technology, and a raid can't happen fast enough. Containing her excitement, she says, "A name would be huge here. Even if it doesn't make sense, or it's just a nickname."

"The guy who did the tattoos and computer work went by Conscript. He was a wiry guy in his late thirties. Maybe even forties.

Kept taking pills when I was with him, and I think they were amphetamines."

"Conscript?" Jen asks, brow raised.

Serai nods. "Yes, I'm sure of it."

Jen glances to Martinez, then Grisham. Like Jen, they both recognize the name. Conscript 19 is a notorious Eastern European hacker affiliated with multiple ransomware groups. Strange where men with Interpol Red Notices turn up. "Do we have a mugshot?"

An analyst prints another image and slides it across the table for Jen.

Serai recognizes him, just like everything else she encountered on her journey. "That's the man who tattooed me."

Jen knows she has just put Serai through a wringer. Dredging up this much trauma has taxed the girl. Almost a year later, it festers like an infected wound. It's unlikely to change, no matter how much time passes. "That's enough for now. Why don't you rest? We'll talk again later to verify some details after we explore what you've told us."

Serai gives Jen a pleading look. "I really need to talk to my mom."

Jen helps Serai up and leads her to the door. "That won't be a problem."

Grisham rises as well. "Ms. Yates, we have an office reserved for you. Why don't we let Serai use it for the call? I'll show her the way."

Jen puts up a hand to stop him. She won't let Serai think that she's being pawned off. Government officials tend to make people feel used, and that's not an option here. "I'll take her, sir."

Grisham is a gentleman, and he nods before graciously stepping out of the way. "Of course, ma'am. The office door is open, and we even left a fancy sticky note with your name on it."

"Thanks," Serai whispers as the briefing room door closes behind them.

Jen puts a hand on Serai's back, guiding her through one of the world's most sophisticated counterterrorism divisions. The girl is shaking, and her troubles have nothing to do with the environment. A lot of time has passed since Serai last saw the people who care for her. Jen hadn't thought this part through, but the big reunion is another reason she's here to offer support. "It's what we do."

FORTY-FOUR

HEARING A CRASH AT THE END OF THE HALLWAY, SLOANE presses her back into cover. She's not one to shy away from danger, but officers from New Scotland Yard's SCO19 are breaching the apartment linked to Victor Orlov. After finding his abandoned Sprinter, she traced the VIN number, and it led them to this flat in central London.

Power has been cut, and the drywall is vibrating as she presses her ear to it. A dozen black-clad officers swarm the flat with submachine guns at the ready. Sloane's pulse races, and she squeezes the 2011 in her hand. Calls for movement are transmitted through the walls. *Clear right. Left.*

Before long, the tactical team members find trouble. Sloane's radio buzzes. "Post, this is Charlie One. Electronics present. Something improvised."

Sloane looks over to Toliver, who is just feet away. Charlie One is the team's leader. Walt Graves. Met him only an hour ago, and he didn't give her the impression of someone easily rattled. But there's an edge on his voice. "Explosives?"

"Working the problem. Give me a few."

Sloane surges forward. Toliver reaches for her Kevlar vest as she rounds the corner, but misses. He calls after her; she's already too far gone. Waiting on the bomb squad is the smart choice, but she knows Victor. Whatever technology he deployed will be working against a half-life. Counting down a few precious seconds before accomplishing its goal and obliterating itself. This is an opportunity she can't pass up.

Nearing the door, Sloane tastes chemicals. Ammonia. Sharp and biting. "Entering!"

"Got you!" Graves shouts.

Wood splinters crunch. Fumes curl around Sloane's boots. Pools of ammonia have collected in depressions on the floor. Windows were left open, turning the apartment into an icebox. Ammonia can't freeze, but it won't melt in these conditions either. Impossible to judge when Victor departed.

Sloane erases the thought and focuses on the technology. Exposed wires sag against the wall, away from a motion detector's angry red face. Graves is kneeling by a table, searching the underside for explosives. Another man is covering him, which prevents her from seeing more of the setup.

"Step aside!" Sloane orders.

"We're not clear of explosives yet, ma'am," Graves replies.

The warning doesn't sway Sloane, and she charges forward. "Give me space!"

Graves taps his teammate on the shoulder, and they step away from the table.

Screens are glowing. *Still time.*

Familiarizing herself with the setup doesn't take long. It's a long-range radio wired to a digital cooking timer. Zeros stretch across the timer's face. When time ran out, the system activated itself.

A warning system triggered by movement.

Sloane is certain the radio began blasting static the second Graves's point man stepped in front of the motion detector. Cutting the building's power was supposed to deactivate hazardous devices, but Victor wired the motion detector to a large battery.

He thought of everything, and there's still more to learn.

She kneels in front of the radio's glowing orange screen, careful not to rattle the table. All nerves, she reaches for the device. One hand to steady it. The other to cycle through the menu.

The battery still has juice. There's still a chance.

When she attempts to find the broadcast frequency, the screen dims. One shade, then two, until it blinks. Maybe it's the adrenaline, or her delusion, but she swears she can feel the circuit die through her fingertips.

That's the ballgame.

Sloane rests her forehead on the table's edge. The system was riding on fumes when the team entered, and it's officially out of gas. She laughs away some of her tension. "You mention something about a bomb, Walt?"

"Think we've passed that, ma'am," Graves replies with a nervous laugh of his own.

"We sure are." Sloane sighs. Rising to her feet, she gazes down at Victor's work. Entire setup is worth fifty bucks. The antenna attached to the radio is two feet tall. Damn thing could blast a signal to the Arctic. She winces—that's generous. Same goes for the chance she was giving herself.

Even if she found the broadcast frequency, Victor would have detected the transmission and severed his line, along with the possibility of tracking him. That's if he's even still in the United Kingdom. Mexico City's ghost doing what he's best at: disappearing.

"Couldn't have lasted long," Toliver remarks as he stalks into the apartment.

Sloane turns back to the ammonia pools. She clocks Toliver's agitation but ignores it. Job's done, and to her, the risk was worth taking. For Jen. For Terrance. And everything else Victor put her Group through. "Battery like that? Just a couple of days."

"Walt, what happened when you approached?" Toliver asks.

Graves settles his hands atop his MP5's stock and shoots Toliver a wild grin. "I saw the motion detector light up and made peace with God. A few seconds passed, I didn't evaporate, and I noticed the radio's screen started glowing."

Sloane nods. The radio was set for a single burst, and once it happened, the job was through. Victor was here. And now he knows that she's standing in his apartment. His turn to move again. Create more open air between him and the authorities.

Toliver starts for the door. "I'll get forensics teams started."

Sloane holsters her pistol and sighs. The pools of ammonia in the floor are deep enough to swim in. Trash is strewn about the apartment, along with enough human hair to complete a genome project. Forensics experts are going to have it tough, but he's leaving her the hardest job: calling their bosses and delivering the bad news.

Well-deserved after the stunt she pulled.

FORTY-FIVE

JEN SLIPS OUT OF THE INFIRMARY AND ONTO THE operations floor. Time to let MI5's doctors work their magic on Serai. Information is falling into place on Conscript 19, and Windham Hall has been located. Surveillance assets are closing in, and she has her sights set on MI5's tactical operations center to assist with the planning phase.

Before she can reach it, she passes a glass-encased conference room. She notices Hastings inside, going through his debrief. A lot happened last night. Brass wants answers.

Martinez waves her into the room.

Frustrated, she complies. She'd hoped to start cracking Windham Hall. Become so integral that she couldn't be pulled away. Serai's debrief was important. But this? Not so much.

Hastings is standing to leave as she enters. He gives her a fist bump and a wild grin. "Almost."

Man says what's on his mind, superiors be damned. She's forced to give him credit, despite the awkwardness it generates for her. She sits down in front of Martinez, Grisham, and several other members of the executive liaison group.

Martinez shouts after Hastings, "Get some rest, Al."

Grisham looks over the rim of his glasses. "Don't worry, Ms. Yates. We won't keep you long."

"I'm at your disposal, sir. Take as long as you need."

A DSLR clicks on at Jen's side, and she begins walking the room through what transpired at the hotel. Why she made certain decisions; key insights; crimes she witnessed or may have committed herself. To her surprise, few questions are asked of her. Sure sign the ELG is pleased with the outcome.

When she finishes, Grisham screws the lid back onto his fountain pen and rests it on his pad. He exchanges looks with the other officers present. They're satisfied. "We'd like you to look at several photographs, Ms. Yates. Please tell us if you recognize these men, and from where."

A mugshot sails across the desk. She recognizes the face in the photograph. Overwatch. Last time she saw him, his body was decorating the Trafalgar's carpet. "This is the man I encountered in the suite, sir." She begins relating more details. Specifics of the assault. The fact that he was armed and tried to murder Serai.

"Good, Ms. Yates." Grisham passes the mugshot on to a member of New Scotland Yard. Another comes after. "This man?"

Jen gets a sudden chill from the next mugshot. Lounge lizard, and the Beretta that he put to the side of her head. She can see blood dripping down his face, the terror and struggle in his eyes. Didn't have time to feel scared then, but she does now. It was close. "This is the man who assaulted me in the stairwell."

Grisham gives her a clinical nod. "We have both men in custody at the Royal London Hospital. With these identifications, we'll add some assault charges to their treatment protocols."

"Do you have IDs on the other individuals my team encountered?"

"Your people are efficient, Ms. Yates. Seven members of the Lika Syndicate have been in and out of surgery since, oh . . ."—he checks his watch—"five a.m. We don't have IDs on them all, but we're working on it."

Jen doesn't reply. She's just grateful that these guys are being taken off the streets. They'll face serious charges and long stints in British prisons before they're expelled from the country on one-way flights back to Albania.

"One more," Grisham says. He slides the photograph along the table. "Did you see this man at the Trafalgar last night, Ms. Yates?"

She saw him, all right. Waving a pistol at her minivan as she escaped the garage. "Ceno Lika. He was traveling with several other members of his New York crew."

"We'll draw up arrest warrants for Ceno Lika within the hour," Grisham replies.

"Anything else, sir? I'd like to get in the mix on Windham Hall."

Grisham shakes his head at Jen. "Sleep. Have you heard of it, Ms. Yates?"

"Tried it once. Didn't agree with me."

Grisham chuckles. "Well, you'll be able to *rest* assured that your team will have first crack at the mansion. Surveillance is online, and we're already generating a target package. Warrants to search will also be in hand soon."

Jen nods. "Great, sir."

Hearing a frantic tapping on the glass, Grisham waves a secretary into the room. "What is it, Ms. Swinson?" She relates Sloane Hamilton's update to the room, and a collective disappointment settles on the space.

"We've got Orlov in Europe, Jen," Martinez says. "Only a matter of time until Interpol—or someone else—picks him up on their radar."

Yeah, like Conscript 19, who is working in London. Jen stops short of saying it. The news is oddly devastating, and it zaps what's left of her energy. She stands, dispenses a round of handshakes, and says, "Think I'm going to take you up on your offer, Mr. Grisham. Wake me when you have a complete target package on the mansion."

FORTY-SIX

EARLY IN VICTOR'S CAREER, HE WOULD HAVE SCOFFED AT meditation. A ritual for cowards and people who'd deviated from Russia's one true religion: Catholicism. Intensity was a hallmark of Spetsnaz training. Live machine-gun rounds snapping over his head while he crawled through obstacles. Physical abuse—and not just PT until he puked his guts out, but the practiced fists of his training cadre. Their knuckles would bury into his stomach. Challenge him to remain at attention while he struggled to keep down his breakfast.

Not until he reached GRU's selection program did he learn how essential the practice could be. Here, he learned to infiltrate hostile areas, observe what was taking place inside their borders, and escape unseen. Like most training academies, the cadre had rigged the system.

Victor was captured while trying to map a small town for an upcoming assault. Determined to extract information from their new prisoner, the cadre placed him in a drum. It originally held motor oil, but it had been repurposed for torture.

The cadre banged the metal lid into place above Victor's head. The drum vibrated. His ears rang. He looked up toward a metal grille roughly the size of a paperback novel. Air, he assumed. *This is only training. There's a limit.*

Then he saw the garden hose. Something an old lady would use to water her roses. One of the training cadre directed the nozzle toward the opening and let the water flow in. Slow. Steady. And freezing cold.

Victor expected the interrogation to begin as water filled the drum. Yet he heard the cadre walk away. He figured that they'd return, but the water level kept rising. Death's fingertip inched up his spine, and he shivered. By the time water covered his mouth and nose, the cadre had not returned.

Growing desperate, he pressed his lips against the metal grille and sucked up as much air as he could. Call it basic geometry, laws of physics, or maybe a lack of willpower, but the effort failed. That was the first time Victor died, but it wasn't the last time he'd be inside that drum.

During those torture sessions, and the subsequent rounds of interrogations, he learned to harness his mind's true potential. Humans aren't lightbulbs, and turning himself off wasn't an option. But he developed the capacity to become blank when terror consumed him.

The effect was as miraculous as it was liberating.

Several hours ago, he received a radio blast from his apartment in London. Authorities no doubt found his Sprinter, and it led them to his previous safe house. British intelligence services might be able to approximate his travel routes based on those two pieces of intelligence. His current location would be next in line.

These are the moments when men break. In their solitude, anxiety takes over their mind. Racing thoughts filled with lies, delusions. Every shift of the wind brings with it a team of federal agents, stampeding through the front door. And then they run. Make mistakes that are impossible to recover from.

Not Victor. He's using the only tool capable of overpowering his mind: his body. With every deep breath, he feels his chest expand, stretching the intercostal muscles between his ribs. He focuses on those small connective tissues before a breath fills out his belly and his lower back pushes into the wall behind him.

Guarantees are meaningless in his business, but surety is. Mr. Orlov is sure that he was careful, and the chances of him being tracked are minuscule. He's safe. Period.

The phone beside him on the floor vibrates. The update he so desperately needs. But he doesn't rush to answer the call. He takes several more breaths and casually reaches for the device. *Whatever.*

Victor answers the video call. "What's going on?"

Anastasia's head cocks to the side. She squints, trying to piece together the face in the darkness. "Move into the light."

Victor doesn't feel like arguing with his worried sister. He passes from the living room to the kitchen and stands by a glass door. Snowflakes tumble out of a gray sky. They hang in the air before settling onto the pile blanketing his backyard. It's delicate, divine. "I'm stable. What's happening with my exit?"

Anastasia goes straight to business. "Your paperwork is clear at Port Newport, and your passage is secure. Cast-off is at twenty-two-hundred, local. Be there an hour early."

Victor's grin is slight and mischievous as he angles his head toward the phone. New hair. Short and black, like the beard glued to his face. Third identity this week. "Did I miss anything?"

"I see a gray patch on the side of your head."

He left a bottle of hair dye next to the kitchen sink, along with a mirror. His impromptu barber shop. He doesn't look toward either of them. Complete confidence. He's ready to step into the United Kingdom's cold one last time and make the journey home. "You know, I'd been happy to get a call from my little sister, until just now."

"Happiness is fleeting."

Victor's eyes remain on the snow. "My radio scanner picked up static. Do you have anything?"

"Ceno Lika didn't follow our instructions . . ."

"What does that have to do with my question?"

"One of his men encountered Jen Yates at the Trafalgar last night. Got a look at her before she carved his face in half," Anastasia replies. "They kidnapped an escort associated with Lust. They've linked the Likas to Void, which is what I'm sure they're targeting. They're very, very far behind you."

Victor nods. The Americans are busy chasing hookers. Safe, and he *knew* it. "How did they stumble onto Void? That's *ours*, Ana."

"Someone made a mistake that they haven't answered for."

Victor notes the treacherous look in Anastasia's eyes. She mentioned Ceno and the instructions he failed to follow. Going after Jen Yates was out of bounds, and he'll suffer for it. Just like Alex Varga. "We went through all of this to protect it."

"After today, Void won't matter."

Victor is stunned. Void is *their* project. They pitched it to their leadership. Brought it to life. And the money it would have made them? He doesn't understand how she can so easily write off their efforts.

"All that I can say is that you'll have more help with your departure than you realize." She beams at her brother. "It's our time, Victor. Enjoy the rest of your stay in Europe. We'll be busy when you get back."

Our time. Victor lets out a heavy breath. "I'll see you."

"I'll bring the champagne and caviar."

Victor is overflowing with pride as he returns to the kitchen table. Whatever questions he had have disappeared. He grabs a suppressed SIG 553 lying amongst maps, cash, and passport books. The rifle's stock is folded, and he slings it over his shoulder. People yammer on about American weapons, but the Swiss ones? They're a lot like the watches he adores. Returning to the window, he wonders which one he'll buy first. Tough choice, but he's certain of one thing: it'll match his family's ascent into Russia's royalty.

FORTY-SEVEN

THE CELL PHONE SCREEN IS STILL GLOWING FROM Anastasia's call with Victor. His face when she told him the news? Priceless. This is *their* time, and she's going to earn her new place in the Founders' hierarchy today. Standing, she exits her barren high-rise office and makes the short journey to her operations center.

Certain that her brother is safe, she'll be able to complete Ionov's task with absolute focus. In less than an hour, one of Great Britain's most powerful intelligence agencies will be hobbled. She'd been serious with her brother; he'll have cover during his departure from the United Kingdom. Jen Yates will soon forget about him, Void, and anything else they've learned about her organization.

They'll be too busy fixing everything she's about to destroy.

Anastasia carries that intensity into the operations center, focus instantly locked on Alexander Gribov, her number two. He has a legal pad in hand. Several pages are folded over, and the one he's reading from is heavily marked with ink. Her tone is curt, demanding. "Are we spun up?"

Alexander takes a breath, consults his checklist. Pages tremble as he leafs through them. He nods, looks up with a face that says: *Are we seriously doing this?* His superior's icy stare is confirmation. "You said you wanted to break some shit, and at this point there's nothing stopping you."

"Return to your station, Mr. Gribov," Anastasia orders. She addresses her other hackers. "Everyone sufficiently caffeinated? Our tasking is delicate, and every milestone is time sensitive. Once we start, you can't pull away until it's over."

They nod.

"Prepare." Anastasia notes the clock. Gives them sixty seconds to pull up the tools they'll be using to conduct their cyber assault. When they're ready, she begins, and she won't need a list like Alexander. "Let's bring London completely online. I need our full suite of command-and-control servers, and I want us logged into Gombe's point of presence from our administrative account. From there, show me routing tables."

"Both C&Cs active," Kamila says.

"Working our back door now," Roman adds.

Finally, Alexander completes his task. "We'll be seeing London's complete routing tables . . . now."

The hackers move with a precision that could rival a special forces team. They understand their tasks, and they know them by heart.

Anastasia reviews the work that is collated on the center screen. "Mr. Gribov, I want you to handle the routing tables. Bring Gloucester-shire's internet traffic to Gombe's headquarters in London. Ms. Vistin, Mr. Dyatlov, once we're rerouted, I need internet transfer speeds and latency tests for our target. Leo, isolate our target's traffic and begin your encryption analysis."

She lets her command filter through the team. "No mistakes! There won't be enough time to recover."

"We're ready, Mrs. Orlov," Alexander states.

Anastasia doesn't hesitate. *Their* time. She's going to earn it. For herself and her brother. "Execute."

Their cyber assault begins. The Border Gateway Protocol routing tables change first. Their target's internet traffic is now passing through servers located at the Gombe Wireless's point of presence in London. This act was likely detected the moment it occurred. It will trigger a response. The only question is how soon it will arrive.

Multiple analyses begin, each as critical as the other. Leo has started analyzing the target's internet traffic, which is heavily encrypted. When the Chinese government attempted this feat, encryptions were what stopped them. In the most sensitive cases, they had reams of data they couldn't make sense of.

Leo will save Anastasia from that failure. Strands of encrypted data are displayed on the center screen, and the quantum computer is working rapidly to decrypt them. The computer is learning as it works, and it only becomes faster.

"Speed test complete," Kamila says. "Target's internet transfer speed is fluctuating between ninety-seven and ninety-eight-point-nine megabytes a second."

"Latency is also good, Mrs. Orlov. We've only added three milliseconds to the target's data transfer time," Roman adds.

Anastasia nods. When she changed the routing tables, it began taking longer for the target's data to reach its intended destination. This is all about distance. Although it might seem like a small fraction of time, it could make or break her attack, and it must be accounted for.

"Mrs. Orlov, I have developed a reliable decryption key for our target," Leo says. "Standing by for re-task."

"Run a test, this time for speed. Decrypt and repackage a data transmission before forwarding it to the target. I need a one-megabyte data sample."

"One moment, Mrs. Orlov," Leo replies.

Anastasia observes the test. Leo isolates a small piece of data in route to her target and executes the command.

"Test complete. Seven milliseconds, Mrs. Orlov."

Anastasia wants to curse, but she holds back. Up to now she's tallied up ten milliseconds to execute the next phase of her attack. An impossible sliver of time for a human being to process.

"The install will take too long—"

Anastasia throws up her hand to cut Alexander off. She knows what he's going to say; despite the advances in their technology, there's a strong chance that their attack won't succeed. Leo broke an encryption that would have taken a standard computer months. Still, he's too slow.

But this is a one-shot opportunity. Success is her only option.

Anastasia initiates a two-step process. From here, almost everything Leo does will be automated. This attack will happen faster than she can blink—the power of quantum. "Leo, continue live decryption of our target's data. Run Specter."

"Specter operational. Waiting for Harbinger," Leo responds.

Alexander has turned around to face Anastasia. "Ma'am, Leo needs more time to perfect his decryption. We can do this—just not now."

"Don't interrupt me again," Anastasia snaps. At this point, his hesitation isn't only unacceptable, it's jeopardizing their mission. "Face your station and prepare to splice our malware into the target's data stream."

Alexander does as ordered. He plugs an external drive into his station and unlocks it. Leo's system is now exposed to a strand of malware stored on the drive. It had been isolated for safety reasons. "Leo, Harbinger is online."

"Harbinger security protocol activated," Leo confirms.

That security protocol is an important one. If the malware is accidentally installed on this system, it could do serious damage. Leo has been trained to handle it.

"Execute," Anastasia orders.

The center screen erupts in a series of flashes. Leo's work. Specter was the command to isolate email transmissions. Small, under one megabyte. Harbinger was the malware. When Anastasia gave the order, an automated process began. Faster than her mind could process. Not quite as fast as the atom—or Leo.

Leo splices Harbinger into a single email transmission, re-encrypts the data, and forwards it to the target. Small, it was made to sit in the email's letterhead and serve as a back door for their entry into the target's internal computer network.

But those extra milliseconds ... Anastasia's breath hangs as she waits for confirmation. *Was Leo fast enough?*

"Our transmission successfully breached the target's firewall," Leo updates.

"Phase one complete. GCHQ's headquarters in Gloucestershire is compromised," Anastasia says, clapping her hands together in sheer excitement.

GCHQ, America's version of the NSA. Leo took its scalp, and it's a trophy like none other. But phase two is next, and the target's response is certainly coming. This is just the beginning of her fight. "Mr. Gribov, listen for our malware's signal. After we log in, we'll escalate our privileges inside the target's network."

FORTY-EIGHT

GCHQ's internal security arm has unfettered access to its computer systems, and they monitor them with one goal in mind: security. Their responsibilities include basic employee logins, activity logs, internet speeds, and live scans of downloaded information. On the surface, the tasks sound simple, but "The Doughnut"—aptly named for its exterior appearance—has thousands of employees and reams of data.

The people in this room are soldiers, only their training doesn't involve machine guns and fragmentation grenades. They're hackers, armed with world's most powerful computers and the software to fight with them. Sirens are wailing as they respond to an attack on their system.

William Burns, one of GCHQ's senior cybersecurity specialists, is monitoring the attack in real time. Multiple attack vectors have opened and are currently being exploited against GCHQ's network. He's snuffing them out as they arise, but he's behind. "Where is traffic being routed to? I want an IP address. Match it to a GPS coordinate."

"I have an IP address. Check the map," Cal Giles says, another cybersecurity specialist.

William watches a map of London swirl. Globe on its axis. The pin settles on a location in central London: Gombe Wireless. He's not surprised. Warnings have already flashed because of this internet service provider. "Log it. Everything. I want documentation."

A nearby analyst begins recording Gombe Wireless's actions. Within the hour, the recordings will be sitting on the Crown prosecutor's desk. New Scotland Yard will be knocking on Gombe's doors shortly after.

"Mr. Giles, you're go on the routing tables. Let's restore order to London's internet," William orders.

"Returning the routing tables to the original configuration, sir."

William looks at another cybersecurity specialist. Up until now, his team has been on defense. That'll change with his next order. "Ms. Morrison, proceed with our DDOS attack."

Maurine Morrison initiates a dedicated denial-of-service attack on Gombe Wireless—their new enemy. It will bombard the internet service provider with data requests, slowing its servers. It may also knock its internet servers offline completely, preventing them from capturing sensitive intelligence.

"Sir, I'm detecting signal interferences. We have data incoming thirty percent slower than average," an analyst says.

William draws in a sharp breath. This was the real threat. When Gombe Wireless began intercepting GCHQ's data, it was a serious compromise. But the manipulation of incoming data streams carries deadly consequences for the network he is protecting. His team constantly monitors transfer speeds and latencies to combat this issue. It becomes his priority. "Ms. Morrison!"

"Gombe Wireless is flagging, sir! I need another two minutes," she replies.

"That's our enemy, and he should not still be on his feet," William says. "Where is the incoming data landing, Mr. Giles?"

Giles replies, "I've got three, no four computer stations on Floor Three, Section Two."

"Lock those stations immediately!" William orders.

Before Giles can complete the task, he shouts, "We've had an update request on one of our computer stations. The user accepted it. Something was installed."

Another analyst pipes in. "Foreign access attempt detected. It's coming from a website. Looks to be a command-and-control server."

This is where William loses the fight. That update request allowed his enemy to install malware on the target computer. That means direct access to GCHQ's network. "We know what to do—"

"I've got half a dozen more installations, sir!"

"Another command-and-control server has just been detected! They're also working to gain access!"

"Crash the system!"

Before William's hackers can respond to the command, a digitized skull pops up on the screen. Cyrillic letters and a one-eight-hundred number to call for tech support. Ransomware. Whoever initiated the attack on GCHQ has succeeded. Great Britain's most powerful intelligence agency is now completely compromised.

FORTY-NINE

ANOTHER PERSON RUNS PAST JEN'S OFFICE.

Reluctantly, she sits up on her couch, wipes the sleep out of her eyes, and reads the message on her computer screen: *ACCESS RESTRICTED*. Experience tells her that something serious happened. More trouble is coming her way, but now she's prepared. Reaching over, she cracks the blinds in time to catch two suited men run past her. They disappear into JTAC's situation room.

Jen grabs her phone to see how long she's been out, but Martinez is already calling. She answers. "What happened, Gabby?"

"GCHQ was just hit with a successful ransomware attack," Martinez replies.

"Why are we locked out?" Jen asks as she further examines the office's computer.

"Safety. MI5 doesn't appear to be compromised, but we're still uncertain," Martinez says. "Office?"

"Yeah."

"Grisham and I are coming."

The call clicks off, and Jen hardly has a moment to prepare before the two executives careen through the door.

Grisham shuts it, pulls the blinds shut, and sits nervously on the couch.

Martinez leans against the wall, arms crossed, and picks up where she left off. "The attack was initiated from Gombe Wireless's headquarters in London. They conducted a BGP hijack and inserted ransomware into GCHQ's data stream."

"Warrants to raid Gombe's London point of presence are incoming," Grisham adds. "We have everything we need to take them permanently offline."

"Anything happening inside of France or Germany?" Jen asks.

"We're unsure, but we're checking into it," Martinez replies. "This is less than an hour old."

Grisham cuts back in. "I'm terminating your intelligence-gathering efforts on Void, Ms. Yates."

Jen settles on the edge of her desk and runs through the potential ramifications. When Gombe Wireless gets hit, it'll be like a guillotine fell on Void. The dark web's servers will stop functioning—at least in London. From there, finding its servers, or other access points, could become impossible.

"No," Jen argues. "Not yet."

"What are we missing?" Martinez asks.

Grisham doesn't wait for Jen to answer. "Frankly, I could use your help triaging the situation, Ms. Yates. Resources are going to be extremely slim over the next forty-eight hours."

Jen delivers her argument, putting some force into her words. "We're missing an opportunity if we let Void go. The Founders are going to do this again, and we need to learn how. If we can access Void's servers while they're live, a lot of possibilities open on our end."

Martinez follows the logic. "A lot of money flowing through that system. Andrew told me the user base has doubled in the last twenty-four hours."

Grisham taps on his leather portfolio. His feet are pointed toward the office door. Only thing keeping him in place is Jen's sofa, and the fear of a potential heart attack if he stands too quickly. He shakes his head. "Void isn't a national security concern, Ms. Yates."

Jen isn't going to let him out of the office—not until she's got permission to hit Windham Hall. "How long until the raid on Gombe?"

"We've had plans in the works since we were notified of the threat. Shouldn't be more than five, maybe six hours."

"Give me that little bit of flex and I'll be back to help you pick up the pieces when I'm through."

"Void will have redundancies in place," Grisham remarks. "Servers in other countries. Different administrators. Your efforts won't have a serious impact on its network."

"We'll plan for those contingencies," Jen says. "I'm confident we can do serious damage to Void's network if given the opportunity."

"Void isn't a national security threat, but the people profiting from it are," Martinez says. "I agree with my officer's assessment, Mr. Grisham."

Grisham takes off his glasses and rubs the tension out of his eyes. Finally, he sighs. "Ms. Yates, SCO19 will be maxed out, like the rest of us. Uniformed officers will either be securing the areas around Gombe Wireless, or pulling their staff members out of bed. You won't have tactical support."

Jen wants to smile, but she won't rub it in. Her and Martinez are a tough tag team to beat. "My team is all that I need, sir."

"I'm keeping Kabir attached," Grisham says as he heaves himself off the sofa. He buttons his suit jacket and checks his watch before leaving. "Six hours, Ms. Yates. Make the most out of them."

FIFTY

MI5'S ARMORY IS ABOUT THE SAME SIZE AS THE AVERAGE GUN store in Texas. Despite the compact space, Jen still gives it the thumbs-up. The available weapons are high quality—Heckler and Koch, Knights Armament, Glock—and the armorer is a big help. But they've come to collect the bulk of her team's equipment, which has been kept there since they arrived in London.

Windham Hall is going to be a hard target, and they'll have the tools to match.

The team is assembling their individual kits, selecting bits of gear from long black Pelican cases on a center table. Gear is as personal as a signature, and customized to each operator's preference. Jen, Hastings, and Animal will be running suppressed Knights Armament PDWs in .300 Blackout. The rifles are jewels Coco picked out, and they forced Jen into breaking up with her B&T APC 300.

Kabir was issued an MP5SD, and he's just gotten his Glock 17 back from the armorer. It required a modification to accept a suppressor, and all the bureaucratic machinations to match. Work orders. Signatures. Receipts.

Hastings is muscling a low-vis plate carrier over his chest. With a red face, he pulls the wings tight, melding it into his body. He shakes his head at Kabir while he fiddles with his *upgraded* Glock. "Jesus."

Jen's vest is concealed by her leather jacket. She's tweaking the holster on her duty belt, making sure it's aligned with her draw preferences. Multiple pistol and rifle magazine pouches also hang on the belt, including a small med kit. She, too, shakes her head at Kabir's Glock 17. "You know, my mom stores cupcakes in Tupperware like that."

"Heard they sell real guns on Void," Animal adds, fixing a retractable breaching sledge to his leg via a drop holster. The sledge is five pounds, with a hydraulic shaft that extends with the turn of a collar.

"You should place an order before we take it down," Hastings says, who is now replacing the batteries in his weapon-mounted light. Fresh, always.

Kabir doesn't even blush at the insults. The team has officially broken him in. Finished with his Glock, he makes a small adjustment to his Kevlar vest and slings his MP5SD over it. "I'll have you know I qualified as a marksman during Selection."

That draws a round of laughter. Probably the last time he shot a gun, but no one finishes that thought out loud.

"Marksman, huh?" Jen says while rummaging through one of her hard cases. She lands on a small bag and slides it across the table toward Kabir. "Guess you'll need the right tool to match to your *elite* skillset."

Kabir hesitates before grabbing the bag. Who knows if it'll detonate or bite him? He realizes he doesn't have an option; the three others are watching him, expectant. He unzips the bag and pulls out a Staccato P. Just like Jen's. Fully custom, with a red dot sight, light, and suppressor.

"That one's on me," Jen says with a grin. "Can't let you embarrass us with your piece of fantastic plastic."

Kabir gingerly puts the gun aside on the table. Something else has caught his attention in the bag. A unit patch. 47/110th Technical Access Group. Jen's namesake, complete with a digitized Grim Reaper clutching a scythe. The numerical designation is a play on Whitefish, Montana's GPS coordinates. It means even more than the pistol to him. Carefully, he extracts the patch, places it inside his jacket, over his heart. After he zips it shut, he places his hand over it. "Thank you."

"Last one's from all of us," Hastings says casually. Kabir is just another part of the team now. No big deal.

Animal tosses a spare holster for the Staccato across the table. "That one's on me. It's sixty-five dollars."

Kabir laughs. "Mate, it's not on you if I have to pay for it."

Animal stares back at him, deadpan.

"Sixty-five it is." Kabir hides his grin while he exchanges the holsters.

Jen watches him prep the weapon. Clumsy, but he can handle it, and she's satisfied when he flicks up the safety before holstering it.

The gifts are generous but earned. Not only did Kabir roll with her Group, but he picked Serai. His judgment is the reason she's about to break the Lika Syndicate wide open and put a nasty hook into Void. That deserves recognition, and now he's got it.

One last rundown. After making sure they're not forgetting anything, they stash their cases and head for the door with five hours on the clock.

FIFTY-ONE

THE BRITISH GOVERNMENT WILL NOT BE FORWARDING Anastasia and her team a multimillion-dollar lump of Bitcoin to unlock GCHQ's computers. That's a pipe dream, and Anastasia's vision isn't hazy. Never would a government as powerful as Great Britain's make ransom payments to Russian hackers. They'd rather lose their data and replace the systems than surrender.

But that's not what has her worried. GCHQ's network is still online. They haven't unplugged their system, which means Britain's best and brightest are working to resolve the issue. They still think they can win.

It's possible with the Advanced NeuroNet Engine, Jen Yates, and Andrew Xiao in their corner.

The same skull that shocked members of GCHQ is glimmering at Anastasia, calling on her to make a decision while there's still time. "Mr. Gribov."

The hacker turns in his station and faces his superior officer. "We're at a stalemate, Mrs. Orlov. Gombe's London PoP is limping, and the routing tables are back in position. They took one of our command-and-control servers offline with a DDoS attack, and I'm certain that the others will follow soon. We're running out of time."

"It's time to break shit," Anastasia replies.

Alexander smirks. "I thought we already did that."

Anastasia trades a knowing look with her subordinate. She'd been hard on him earlier, but for good reason. Still, she'll make amends. "You know what to do, Mr. Gribov. Take the reins."

Alexander hesitates, if only to process Anastasia's compliment. Beaming with pride, he rises out of his station and stands next to Anastasia. It will be his privilege to harm Russia's enemies. Bragging rights inside of the global hacking community won't be so bad, either. "Leo."

"Yes, Mr. Gribov."

"Initiate New Dawn."

Several moments pass before Leo responds. "New Dawn is underway."

Anastasia watches the center screen. IP and MAC addresses associated with the infected GCHQ computer systems switch from green to red. One after the other. Like a rolling blackout. The ransomware she installed is no different from its contemporaries; failure to pay means punishment.

When Leo finishes, every infected computer at GCHQ Headquarters in Westminster is torched.

Alexander issues the final order. "Pull down our remaining command-and-control servers. Erase their web histories and corresponding domain registrations."

Leo works while the other hackers cover their tracks, insulating St. Petersburg from the crimes they've committed a thousand miles away.

Fifty-Two

Subzero temperatures seem to have frozen Windham Hall's doors and windows shut.

A personal drone is fighting to stay airborne over the chimneys jutting out from the slate roof while gusts of wind slap it around. Curtains of snow block its lens. Between the disruptions, Jen and her team analyze the feed on the BMW X5's dashboard information display.

MI5 didn't have much time to generate a package on this target, and some of what they've developed was disproven by Serai. Floor layouts didn't match blueprints on file in City Hall. Building permits and inspections weren't the Lika Syndicate's priority when they modified the home to suit their needs.

They also face the possibility that the structure will be heavily occupied. A new group of women could have recently landed at the mansion, and a guard staff would be needed to keep them contained. Conditions like that could complicate the raid, and the team is relying on their judgment to make the final call.

But there are zero signs of life from the outside, and it appears their worries are unfounded. These guys aren't the type to carve out snow angels, but they don't see any footprints leading to the single vehicle parked in the driveway. Snow is piled high enough that Jen can't even discern the make and model, which means it hasn't moved in days.

"Their cell phone still up?" Hastings asks.

"Wait one," Jen replies. During MI5's workup, they detected a single cell signal on site. Only sign that the structure is inhabited. She checks a map on her cell phone and finds a red pin hovering over the mansion. "Hasn't moved. There haven't been any calls either."

"I like it, Z," Hastings hisses, his focus shifting to the silhouetted home in the distance. River Thames flows past its backyard, and beyond it, Port Tilbury. Like Windham Hall, nearby homes sit on large, *private* lots. "Weather conditions will cover our approach. Cancel out noise we generate on target."

Animal points at the periphery of the drone feed. "Doesn't look like the *Good Ole Days* has moved in several days either. Won't be any women on site."

Jen looks to Kabir, who sits behind the wheel. Subzero temperatures aren't stopping sweat from beading on his forehead. Nerves have wired his mouth shut. "Thoughts?"

Kabir takes a breath and reflexively clutches his MP5SD. "Leaving it to you, Z."

Jen doesn't hesitate. Void is a cancer, and in her mind, it has already festered for too long. Plus, she's got a silent promise to keep. This will be for Serai, and for the other women still trapped in the Lika Syndicate's custody. "Let's go."

Without another word, the team steps into the cold. The mansion is several blocks away, and they'll be in contact shortly.

———

Black and white, color. No less than a dozen old televisions are stacked up. One has just turned to static, while the others continue to broadcast security camera footage into Conscript's tattoo parlor. Stereo speakers blast Russian death metal. Several laptops, each covered in stickers, are placed next to a tattoo chair at the center of the room.

Conscript 19, also known as Jonuz Mitrovica, sits shirtless on a rolling stool. Using a homemade tattoo gun, he attempted to ink himself when he was eleven. Left forearm. Shot the ink into his skin like a kid sitting and reading a book. Crooked and poorly drawn, it's still one of his favorites.

But after over seventy unique, individual tattoos, it is drowned out in chaos—which was his goal. Conscript, like his music, *is* chaos. Dirt poor as a kid, he used to pick cigarette butts out of the trash to get his nicotine fix. Now he's a coder, accomplished ransomware designer, and multimillionaire. Half a dozen cigarettes burn by his tattoo station. If he wasn't busy, he'd light more. Cancer, pollution, greenhouse gases; the earth is overcrowded, and these are his remedy.

Conscript dips his tattoo gun into a hopper of black ink, bobs his head to a guitar riff. Normal people would experience instant sensory overload in the space. Prolonged exposure would likely bring seizures and permanent brain damage. But this is where he finds his equilibrium.

Before touching the needle to skin, he wipes excess ink away from the QR code he's tattooing. The woman in the chair is stripped nude, his favorite canvas. Her skin is raised from the cold—and fear. She's freshly shaved, which allows him to apply the mark to her body's most sensitive region. Satisfied with his muse, he begins tattooing. The gun buzzes, the woman shivers.

Before topping the ink off once again, he calls out. "Von!"

A large man barrels up the stairs and into the second-story tattoo parlor.

Conscript 19 doesn't look up. He's selecting another playlist from the bank of laptops next to his tattoo station. After a moment of contemplation, he pops the top on a bottle of Adderall and downs a couple of tablets. "Go grab another girl. I'm almost finished here."

"Five minutes," Von replies.

"Fuck your mother, five minutes. How hard is it to shave a pussy?" Conscript mumbles. The needle buzzes in the ink pool. He checks another laptop. The girl's details are displayed, along with her new QR code. Irina. Twenty years old, blonde hair, green eyes. Recently taken from a small town in Russia. After a few more blasts of ink, he'll have her QR code finished. Linking it to Void will be simple, and she'll be ready to begin working as one of Lust's escorts.

———

Breaching the mansion's perimeter wasn't a challenge. The wrought-iron fence is more for show than stopping intruders. The team is assembled near their desired entry point: the cellar, where girls are held. Located on the side of the home, it's an ideal place to begin clearing the target structure. Start at the bottom, work up, make sure they don't get pinched by threats.

Jen is kneeling with her team in a thicket of unkempt bushes, prepared to take a shot at the surveillance camera over the cellar door. The rifle's safety is down, and the trigger has already touched the breaking point. A .300 Blackout bullet spits out of her suppressor and smashes the lens at twenty-five yards.

No time to admire the handiwork.

Animal breaks first from cover and sprints to the building. Upon arrival, he begins clearing snow from the cellar door. Finished, he uncovers the pad lock and mangles it with a set of bolt cutters. "We're ready to breach," he whispers.

Jen's back is pressed to the wall opposite Animal. She's directly under a window, trying not to expose her position. "Do it."

Animal pulls up on the cellar's door handle. Old wood groans. Snow tumbles off in a long slab.

Jen hurries inside with Hastings at her back. The red dot is her guide as she descends a short staircase. Serai's intelligence was accurate; this is a prison. Makeshift holding cells have been welded together to her left. Plumbing wasn't included in the design process, and the stench tests her focus. She counts half a dozen women between the two cells.

Surveillance didn't count for much.

She veers right along the cellar wall and comes upon a small communal shower, which doubles as a delousing area. A wet, freezing woman stands in the shower with shaving cream between her legs. The man supervising her turns with a shocked look on his face. Driven by instinct, he reaches for the pistol tucked into his belt.

Images flash in Jen's mind; Serai, standing naked in that same shower, shivering from the cold. The choice to drop the weapon's safety is an easy one. She redecorates the stall with a double tap to his chest.

When he falls to his knees, she puts a final shot between his eyes. "One down."

Behind her, a suppressor spits.

"Camera down," Hastings informs.

Jen keeps moving; she never stopped. The girl is shrieking. There's a body at her feet, and blood spatter is dripping down her chest. Jen lowers her weapon and quickly calms her. Once she's manageable, Jen grabs a towel, drapes it over her body so that she doesn't freeze to death in the cellar.

"How many are upstairs?" Jen asks, leading the girl across the room.

The girl doesn't reply in English, and Jen decides to let it go.

"We're clear to move upstairs, Z," Hastings says as the team takes up a security position by the stairway.

When they draw closer to the holding cell, the woman panics again. Jen puts a finger over her lips and quiets her. "You're safe now. Just stay calm."

Jen forces the girl back in the cell, hating herself for it. Security is essential, but it still doesn't sit right. At least her captivity won't last much longer. Jen rejoins her team at the foot of the stairs and prepares to ascend.

———

Conscript's tattoo gun has been replaced with a code scanner. Red light flashes over the tattoo, and his laptop beeps. Irina is officially synced with Void, and her listing is immediately available on Lust's webpage.

He trades his scanner for a tube of disinfectant cream and a bandage. When he turns back to apply the dressing, he notices that the woman is looking toward his bank of televisions—the security monitors. Following her gaze, he finds three of them buzzing, static.

Their eyes meet, and he realizes that she's seen something he did not. Ceno Lika warned him about trouble earlier this morning. It forced him to rush through tattooing the rest of the women in the holding cells. *Get them out*, he was told.

Furious, he labels her silence as a betrayal. He rips her out of the chair and grabs the pistol lying by his laptops. If she didn't want to help him before, that's fine. She'll be more than helpful with what he must do next.

———

The stairs from the basement deposit Jen and her team in a kitchen. Cigarettes are smoldering next to half-eaten sandwiches. Break time was interrupted, and their enemy is getting a chance to react, prepare. Heavy metal music blares from the top floor, preventing her from hearing any movement. This is where the mission gets dangerous.

They fan out. Hastings and Animal work as a pair, clearing the kitchen's far side. Kabir angles his MP5SD up a nearby set of stairs. Jen takes up a security position, orienting her rifle into what was the formal dining room.

Now it's a trash heap. Empty packages for clothes and sex toys and power tools are stacked to the ceiling. Whoever lives here doesn't want to draw any attention, and throwing away trash is part of remaining concealed.

"Clear on this side," Hastings says.

Jen doesn't take her eyes off the mess as her Whisper buzzes. She hasn't detected any movement on her end, either, but there's plenty of refuse for an adversary to hide behind. "Push to the front of the house," she directs. "When you've got the front set of stairs, we'll ascend together. Seal off the top floor."

"Got it," Hastings replies as he takes point with Animal on his six.

———

Slow and methodical, Hastings and Animal clear what has become a dormitory where the Lika's soldiers sleep. Cheap bunkbeds accompanied by footlockers remind Hastings of his first barracks. But the hygiene standards wouldn't pass muster. Soiled sheets are crumpled on unmade beds. Half-eaten plates of food have become petri dishes. HAZMAT teams will need to decontaminate this place once the team is finished evicting the occupants.

They reach a threshold that feeds into the living room. Taking separate sides of the door, they clear the far corners and make entry. Bored men spend a lot of time in here, and it shows. Flies buzz over a coffee table littered with beer and liquor bottles. Each bottle is bone dry and stuffed with cigarette butts. Televisions and gaming consoles sit across from dingy sofas.

Hastings is clearing behind a sofa when something stops him cold: screeching. Loud enough to penetrate the music wailing above them. Metal on metal—something being dragged, adjusted. It's coming from a long hallway that adjoins the living room. "Let's check it."

Animal raises his rifle to high-port, allowing Hastings to take point. "We've been here before, Sergeant."

"Someone's building something," Hastings agrees as he reaches the hallway. The area looks like it was an addition. It shoots off the house, creating a couple more bedrooms or offices. A tattered oriental rug runs the length of the hall. Shadows play against the walls before a single lightbulb cuts out.

Screeching resumes. From experience, Hastings knows that someone is erecting a barricade. The type of obstacle that gets men killed, and only one type of person hides behind them: cowards.

He signals his advance to Animal and progresses toward the noise. The hallway's first door is on his right. He tucks into the wall, studies it. A padlock seals the room from the outside. Animal leapfrogs him while he tests the lock. Doesn't budge.

Hastings falls in behind Animal, who is closing on the remaining door. It's open, and a black tarp hangs in front of the entrance. Impossible to determine what's on the other side. Tough barrier to remove as well. What's it attached to? What's it made of?

Animal is on point, and it's his responsibility to address it. With his back pressed into the wall, he reaches, cinches the fabric in his hand. He pulls. Metal rings clap against a support bar like a shower curtain.

"Going to my knife," Animal whispers as he steps in front of the curtain to cut it.

Electric energy grabs Hastings. Call it a sixth sense or a warning from guardian angels. It drives his hand into Animal's shoulder, shoving him away from the curtain.

A shotgun blasts rip through the fabric. Bits of black fiber hover in the air.

Hastings orients toward the shotgun blast and fires through the curtain. Rapid, vengeful shots. Six, seven, eight shell casings arc past Animal as he recovers his balance on the opposite wall.

Hastings stops firing when he hears a body drop. Without hesitating, he slings his rifle and tears his karambit out of its sheath. It arcs across the fabric, and the bottom half drops to the floorboards. He trades his knife for his rifle and peeks into the room.

One dead. He's lying in the far corner with a shotgun splayed over his body. King size bed, tripods for cameras, professional lighting setups. He recognizes the bedspread—Serai's pictures were taken here. *Yeah, the extra bullets were worth it.*

Hastings swallows his anger and storms down the hall. "Moving to the front set of stairs, Z. Bottom floor is clear."

————

Waiting for Hastings isn't an option. The shotgun blast reverberated through the entire house. Someone on the second story heard it and responded by cranking up the music. Wailing guitars and a lyricist screaming in Russian blot out Jen's senses.

The situation worsens as she climbs the stairs. Plaster rattles, and she can hear chunks of it falling behind the walls. Gray winter light from the kitchen is fading, turning her and Kabir into shadows. She's focused on the final stair—a precipice dividing her and the unknown. Five steps . . . four. She can almost see over it but stops short.

She holds a fist up to stop Kabir. Peek first before committing. Returning her hand to her rifle, she rests her thumb on the weapon's light switch. Driving up, she glimpses over the final stair. A tangled silhouette is standing in the hallway.

Jen activates her weapon light, illuminating Conscript 19 with his arm wrapped around a hostage's neck. The pistol in his right hand is pointing at her flashlight.

Bullets chase Jen back into cover. The impacts splinter the floorboards. Bits of debris rain down on her and Kabir. "Eyes on Conscript! He's got a hostage!"

When the incoming gunfire breaks, Jen drives up and reactivates her light. Conscript. The naked woman. This time a smoking pistol is pointed at the hostage's head. His right arm is out, bent like a chicken wing.

Jen puts a bullet through his elbow. Blood explodes out of his arm, and it falls limp, along with the pistol. Another flashlight beam hits Conscript, this time from behind. Hastings and Animal. Realizing that he's trapped, Conscript throws his hostage on the floor and sprints into a nearby bedroom.

"Stay down!" Jen screams as she pushes into the hallway and nears the hostage. There's a strong chance that the woman doesn't speak a word of English, but she doesn't need a translator. She remains flat, arms covering her head.

With a boom, glass breaks and cascades across the floor.

Jen's rifle is angled toward the doorknob as she approaches. Without breaking her stride, she dumps several rounds into the lock, rears back, and kicks it open. Past a tattoo station and rows of television sets, snow drifts into the bedroom through a shattered window. Beyond it, River Thames.

Jen runs for the window and regrets it. Someone is ducking behind a speaker, pointing a weapon directly at her. Too late. She's committed, but her teammates are too. A suppressed weapon spits behind her. Rounds eviscerate the speaker, and the music dies in the middle of a guitar riff. Another Lika soldier erased.

Jen reaches the window, locked on Conscript 19. He's limping toward the dock, leaving a trail of blood behind him in the snow. Another member of the mob is aboard the *Good Ole Days*. Mooring lines are cut and propellers are churning water behind the craft.

She rests her weapon on the windowsill. Stalagmites of glass crunch under the suppressor. As her red dot finds Conscript, he leaps over the gunwale and disappears behind the hull.

The mobster behind the controls throttles up power to the engines, and the *Good Ole Days* surges forward. Whitewater froths behind its twin propellers. Fenders on its starboard side smash against the dock and the pylons shift. Jen depresses her trigger, putting several rounds into the vessel's engine compartment. Bits of fiberglass fling into the air, and the compartment door is dislodged, but the engines keep churning water.

When the boat crosses the hundred-yard mark, she considers her weapon ineffective. Standing, she watches the boat as it's consumed by the snow-dusted horizon. Conscript is in the wind. Judging by what he left in this room, she'll be catching up before long.

FIFTY-THREE

JEN EXHALES SUPPRESSOR SMOKE AS SHE SCANS THE bedroom—or tattoo parlor, or cybercrime lab, or madman's playground. All the operators have their weapons cradled in their arms, waiting for her orders. She nods at the dead man laid out behind one of the giant speakers. "Who took the shot?"

Hastings nods respectfully toward Kabir, who is still shaking.

"First time for everything," Jen says as she eases up and gives him a tap on the shoulder. "Owe you one."

Kabir gulps, trying to keep his lunch where it belongs. He vaguely points at Hastings and Animal. "If it wasn't me, it would have been one of them."

The two operators give her confident nods. That was the classy response.

"Help! Help!"

The pleading reminds the team that they're not alone in the mansion. The woman in the hallway. She needs medical attention. The others will too.

Jen tells Kabir, "Get on the horn with New Scotland Yard. See if you can get someone here to assist." The rest of her orders fall to Hastings and Animal. "Finish clearing the target. Find someplace warm to get the girls settled."

As the team clears out, Jen begins tracing wires.

———

A shaft of dull light illuminates a section of soiled carpet at Ceno's feet. He didn't return home after last night's failed intervention at the Trafalgar. New Scotland Yard is printing arrest warrants, and he took cover in a vacant apartment his family uses for escorts.

Ceno is sitting in a lounge chair when his cell phone buzzes on the end table. Blocked number, but he answers. "Yeah?"

"It's Conscript," the voice says on the other end. "Those motherfuckers came to the mansion. Shot the place up. I'm hurt and I need to get to a hospital."

"Did you take the mansion's computers offline?" Ceno demands.

"No, there wasn't time!"

Ceno momentarily rests the phone on the arm of the chair and rubs his forehead. Contact with the Founders has been sparse since the Trafalgar. He crossed a line. They've turned their backs on his family because of it. Their guidance has always been critical in situations like this, and it's notably absent now. He'll decide how this ends, alone.

He raises the phone. "Where are you now?"

"On the water." Conscript pauses, begins hyperventilating. "Ceno . . . you've gotta get me a doctor, man."

"Shut up," Ceno hisses, decision made. Void and Lust are lost, along with the wealth they would have provided. But the most important thing remains: God's law. The Kanun. *Hakmarjja*—revenge. "I want you to get to Void. Take it offline before the Americans can access it."

"But my—"

"Don't complain to me again."

"Where will you be?" Conscript demands.

"I'll be seeing you shortly."

———

There is Founders tech in Windham Hall, but it's not the type Jen is searching for.

The Wi-Fi router Jen has discovered in the tattoo parlor is sophisticated, sleek, and unlike anything she's ever seen before. Alex Varga had equipment like this strewn across Mexico City. While it isn't a bank of dark web servers, she is betting that it is networked with Void.

Hacking it won't be easy. If she causes the aluminum box's power or internet connection to be terminated, she'll be booted from the network, ending her shot at success.

And that's just the first obstacle.

The router has no exterior ports—save those for fiberoptic cable and an ethernet line, which are in use. Ports for USB cables or other auxiliary access points have been deleted. Hardware used to assemble the box is also unique. Screw heads with unusual patterns are recessed in the aluminum housing so that they can't be easily manipulated.

Jen opens her stiletto and taps the tip against the metal. Thick aluminum. Too dense to cut. She pauses at thundering footsteps outside the door. Animal bursts in, having just ransacked the place to find a power drill and spare bits.

"Need an assist," Jen says.

"Tell me where you want me," Animal replies, handing her the tools.

"Wait one," she says, taking a second to match a drill bit to a screw head. "Put some weight on the box. When I start drilling, make sure it doesn't twist out."

"Easy."

Jen pushes the cables hard into their ports. After, she lays the box flat on its side. "All right."

Animal locks his hands around the box's edge, pressing it into the table. Jen angles the drill between his arms and pushes the trigger before contact. The bit is spinning at full speed before it bites into the screw head, reducing the chances of it snagging. Flakes of metal and smoke arc past them. She presses hard; whoever built this thing used hardened steel for the screws.

When the bit bites into aluminum, she stops and blows metal shavings from the crevice. The screw head is toast, and the router is still transmitting its signal.

"Okay," Jen says with rising confidence. "Three more."

Animal responds by putting his weight down on the box. Jen works the drill. The remaining screws are demolished in short order.

"Let go," Jen instructs.

Animal removes his hands from the box and steps back.

Jen slips a fingernail into the seam circling the router. It splits, but she doesn't take the bait. Instead, she grabs a flashlight and shines it into the gap. Inside, she finds a wire attached to the router's housing. It connects to a kill switch on the circuit board.

Palms sweating, she lifts the housing panel until the wire becomes taut. She takes a second to steady her hands, then feeds a set of tiny wire cutters into the opening. Snip. The wire separates and she lifts the panel, fully unencumbered.

Deep breath and a happy nod to Animal. "At least the hard part's over."

"Onto the easy part."

"No, the next hard part."

Animal chuckles but stops as a commotion erupts downstairs. Distressed women. "Z?"

"Go," Jen says. "I'll call if I need you."

She picks up her cell phone and photographs the router's guts. The images go straight to Andrew, who calls the second he receives them.

Andrew's face appears on her screen. He looks pumped, ready. "Took that as my cue to call."

"I never doubt your genius," Jen jokes. Using her flashlight, she takes an up-close look at the router's circuitry. "Not seeing any IP addresses or backup passwords printed in the interior."

"No, but there is a single USB port that was hidden under the housing. I think it's our only move," Andrew replies. "Waiting on your signal."

Jen sighs. She noticed the port, too, but she's nervous about connecting Anne to the router. If she meets a quantum-resistant encryption, she won't have time to break it. She unfurls a USB cable, sticks it into the exposed port, and connects the other end to her laptop. "Signal inbound."

Jen's computer beats Andrew by a couple of seconds. A barebones diagnostic program appears on the screen. Information for administrators or technicians about the unit's status. But there's no revealing data. Characters are in Cyrillic. Access to other features is closed off.

"Running a translation," Andrew states.

A still image flashes on Jen's laptop. English words have replaced the Cyrillic characters, but the translation reveals nothing of value. "I'm going to try to map the network, see who this router is talking to."

"Second that."

Jen starts a program called Hot Wire. The tool will allow her to work backward through the router and see other devices it's communicating with.

Searching...

Searching...

The screen populates with a map of the network. There are three locations in total, which includes Windham Hall.

"Andrew, let's geolocate the unknown IP addresses."

The locations pop up on her screen, and the lines connecting them look like branches, marking how the data is flowing. The lines start at an edge server, commonly used by internet service providers to decrease signal latency to far-off customers. They then travel to Windham Hall and a second location on the outskirts of London.

"The edge server is just a few miles from you," Andrew says. "It's in an office building under lease by a company called Digital Service Solutions. Just hiding in plain sight."

"The last one is a warehouse. What do you have on it?" Jen asks, eyebrow raised at a Google image of the old brick building.

"It looks like the warehouse is condemned," Andrew replies. "There isn't a single utility bill registered to the address."

But it's got blazing fast internet.

"That's where Void is hiding," Jen states. "Forward everything to JTAC, and get me directions to the warehouse. We'll be mobile in five."

FIFTY-FOUR

A FLASHLIGHT BEAM SWEEPS A SECTION OF CHAIN-LINK fence.

"Is anyone there?"

Victor ignores the trucking company's security guard. He'll get his answer shortly. The guard continues patrolling the fence, searching for the noise he heard. Victor stays crouched behind a stack of chassis trailers used to transport cargo containers. He watches his opponent, who isn't scoring too high on tonight's critical reasoning exam.

At this stage of the break-in, police assistance would be too much to ask; nothing has been confirmed yet. But the guard should be reaching out to someone—maybe a superior. Phone a friend, demand a lifeline, because he's in need. Instead, he's plodding along the fence Victor just hopped, hoping a gust of wind caused the commotion.

A burlap sack snaps in the wind, drawing the guard's light to the concertina wire overhead. He's seen that trick before, and he knows what it means. When the guard turns back toward the storage yard, Victor gets his first clear visual of the man. Big, brawny guy. Add fifteen imaginary pounds of muscle from a winter jacket. Pepper spray on his belt, along with a Taser.

The guard settles his Maglite's long barrel on his shoulder and uses it to sweep the rows of stacked chassis. Grease and oil glint against the beam. Keys rattle. A duty pouch snicks open, and the safety pops on a can of pepper spray. "Cops are on their way!"

Victor flips off his rifle's safety. *Not yet they aren't.*

The flashlight beam jerks toward the sound and settles on Victor's position. A bullet spits out of his SIG 553's suppressed barrel and impacts the flashlight's head. It screams through the lens, the batteries, and exits through the butt cap. The aluminum body bursts like a sausage casing, peppering the guard's neck with metal shrapnel.

Perfect dope.

As the guard gasps and takes an involuntary step back, another bullet strikes the knee supporting his weight. He drops in the snow and frantically tries to right himself, but he doesn't have the strength. He begins pleading with the shadow twenty-five yards in the distance, but Victor's target practice isn't yet finished. Pressure mounts on the trigger one last time, and a round impacts the guard's head.

Victor doesn't bother frisking the guard. The area is clear, and he turns his attention to what he came for. A crane at the lot's far corner looks out over River Usk . . . and the port he'll be using to escape the United Kingdom. His departure is in two hours, and he's going to make use of the time.

He climbs the ladder of the crane. Frigid, wet wind whips him the entire way. He's relieved to find the operator's cabin unlocked when he reaches the top. He strips off his backpack, drops it on the control panel, and extracts his binoculars.

Surveillance begins.

There's a lot to digest. Port Newport is an international port, but the bulk of its cargo travels between other European countries. Timber, sand, and coal are mainstays. Mountains of each reflect against the port's pristine waters, which are enclosed and safeguarded by a single set of locks.

The port is also home to a metal-processing terminal. Cutting torches burn in the recycling plant's warehouse, giving its interior a warm orange hue.

Victor is relieved to find port operations are humming along. New Scotland Yard would have evacuated the site if they knew a terrorist was planning to ship out tonight. He doesn't see any snipers posted on rooftops. Dozens of New Scotland Yard vehicles aren't clustered behind warehouses. *They're very, very far behind you.*

Sharing his sister's sentiment, he scouts his ship, *Gladys*. It's already loaded with cargo. Castoff is at nine, and everything appears to be right on schedule. But that's still hours away. Until then, he'll watch. Closely.

FIFTY-FIVE

THE TRACING TOOL JEN USED ISN'T PRONE TO THROWING out false results, but as she examines the warehouse, she's left wondering if it was accurate. The structure was formerly used as a commercial fish farm. Got a shopping mall with an outdoor pond? This was the place to call. Within a week, two dozen koi fish would be nipping at the pond's surface.

But these tanks are no longer capable of supporting healthy livestock.

Jen is standing on a section of elevated grating. Technically, the second story that enabled employees to reach the top of the tanks and access the fish inside. Six giant, cylindrical tanks occupy the length of the warehouse, each with twenty-foot diameters. Walkways cross their openings, and she can imagine hundreds of fins slapping the surface, gripped by a feeding frenzy.

Algae has taken over the tanks. When the business went belly-up, so did the fish. Animals that weren't sold at fire sale prices were left to starve and eventually rot. The warehouse's smell is abhorrent. And if something is living beneath the surface of these tanks, the devil has a hand in its survival. Not exactly the technological marvel she was expecting to find at the end of her trace.

Jen claps her flashlight against her palm and thinks. The sun has set, and she's nearly out of time. New Scotland Yard's raid will commence soon, and she needs to find Void before it does.

Activating her Whisper, she asks, "Anything?"

Hastings is providing security on the first floor. The low-level windows are painted over, and he scraped away the paint to create an observation post. His view overlooks a wharf jutting into a wisp of water called River Medway. "Clear."

"Nothing by the front gate," Kabir replies, who is on the second level, not far from her position.

Animal is pulling security by the front door. "Nothing, Z."

"Putting out white light." She activates her flashlight, keeping it on a low-lumen setting while she retraces her steps across the grating. Everything about the warehouse makes her think it's abandoned. The building's foundation is sinking, and the old brick walls are leaking. Most important, she can't spot any source of power—a vital component to running servers.

Reaching the last tank, she finds a skeleton floating on a blanket of algae. She twists her flashlight's head to activate its highest setting. One thousand lumens, directly into the water. It glows green. The beam penetrates several feet before it's diffused by a type of fauna she'd prefer to never see again.

"Z!"

Jen kills the light.

"*Good Ole Days* is approaching the wharf," Hastings says. "I've got eyes on Conscript."

Right place, right time. Conscript is wounded, but he decided that this trash heap is more valuable than medical assistance. Jen drops into a concealed position before she replies, "Stay hidden. Let them show us where Void is hiding."

———

The shock has worn off, and the pain in Conscript's arm is excruciating. Amphetamine and the elements are his only medicine, at least for now. Frigid winds have him bordering on hypothermia, which has slowed the bleeding and numbed the pain.

He'll get inside, deal with Void, and wait for Ceno. Once the boss arrives, he's gone. Not just to the hospital but back to Latvia. Or Estonia. Someplace without Big Brother hovering over his shoulder.

Struggling, he manages to climb out of the boat and onto the dock. Drilon, the man who slipped out of the mansion and reached the boat first, is left to manage the moorings. He goes to the front gate, unclasps the pad lock, but doesn't bother opening the gate. Save it for Ceno.

Drilon lumbers across the snow-covered parking lot and meets Conscript by the warehouse's entrance. "Do you want me to get the door?"

Conscript shakes his head; it's involuntary. His teeth are chattering. He'd vomit if the cold hadn't numbed him so thoroughly. "L-let's just hurry."

He manages to scratch the key into the lock and they step inside. They use flashlights that were stored on the boat to find their way in the dark.

Conscript leads Drilon to the third tank, which is tucked in the middle of the warehouse. They stop at a tangle of piping. A water line stabs out of the tank before connecting to a liquid pump. He scans the area once more with his flashlight, refusing to trust his dulled senses, but he sees nothing changed. Finally, he reaches down and pries off the pump's electrical cover.

"I need you to do the next part," Conscript says as he steps aside.

Drilon kneels in front of the pump and shines his light onto the wires.

"Remove the wire nut from the single black wire."

Drilon twists off the orange nut and sets it on top of the panel. "Okay."

"Touch it to the open contact point."

A little spark flashes in front of Drilon. The pump spins up and water drains out of the tank.

"Keep it there until I give you the word."

The back set of stairs are closest. Conscript clings to the railing as he climbs. Wavering on the rungs, he barely manages to reach the second level. He shuffles to the third tank as the water level continues falling. Algae clings to the rungs of a service ladder made of U-shaped rebar welded to the tank's inner wall. Then a layer of algae flattens out on a sheet of plexiglass, which divides the tank in two.

"Power off!"

Another struggle ahead. Conscript settles a foot on the ladder and struggles to maintain his grip with his only good hand. He lowers himself slowly, wondering the whole time if he'll have the strength to climb back out of this contraption.

Eight feet down, he steps off the ladder and walks across the glass, slick with algae. He clears away the muck and opens a trapdoor. Air whooshes out of the opening. Vacuum sealed. The smell of baking circuits fills his nose. He looks down one more ladder onto a half-dozen servers and a computer station—the nerve center of Void.

———

Street lights provide just enough light to induce a subtle play on the shadows. As Animal closes in on the man kneeling in front of the pump, he's reminded how fun it is to hunt without the aid of night-vision goggles. Livens the senses, adds a layer of challenge.

The breaching sledge is extended, raised in his hands. He won't get any medals for this one. Odds are, he'll get a reprimand. It'll probably be verbal, but if he's lucky, it'll be a letter. Something he could frame and hang in the team room. Maybe he'll get a commemorative tattoo of the sledge's toolhead. It'll match the one he's going to give out in a few moments.

The pumps and rushing water allowed him to creep within striking distance. All he needs is the signal.

A rush of footsteps pound the grating overhead. The kneeling man looks up, grabs his pistol, and orients it to the movement. That's when Animal steps out, breaching sledge already in a full sideways arc. The five-pound head smashes into his target's gut. Animal wasn't aware that there were bones in a human being's abdominal cavity, but he feels something shatter.

The man falls, struggling through the most hideous wheeze Animal has ever heard. Before he can start barfing up whatever is leaking into his gut, Animal gives him a love tap on the back of his head. Lights out.

———

Jen jumps for the ladder. It's slick, but she doesn't hold onto it long enough to slip. She drops the remaining distance to the plexiglass water barrier. Conscript is inside, accessing Void. She needs to stop him from doing any damage before she arrives.

Rifle up, she peeks into the opening. The hacker checks his back. They make eye contact once more, and he continues hammering on his keyboard with his uninjured hand. There's only one expedient way to stop him.

Jen shoots him in the back of his knee. Conscript craters and screams as he flops on the ground. She descends the second ladder.

Her work inside Void's server room is time sensitive, but she can't help but admire the setup. The space is insulated to conceal the server's sound signature. Conduit and fiber-optic cable have been run through pipes that mimic water lines. They connect Void to the outside world, all while bringing in power from a nearby building. *Clever.*

A half-dozen internet servers are governed by a single terminal. Same one Conscript was typing on. She could have spent a week in this building and still struggled to find them. But Victor Orlov and the Founders had plenty of motivation to hide them well. Void will earn billions of dollars a year at full capacity.

"You speak English?" Jen demands. She's still got her gun up, and she won't hesitate to finish off a man like Conscript 19. Where's the mercy he showed dozens, maybe hundreds of kidnapped women? *Remove.*

Conscript nods. He's clutching his leg, trying to keep what's left of his kneecap in place.

"Turn over!"

Jen leans down and flips Conscript onto his belly. He's weak. Shivering. Without a second's hesitation, she zip-ties his hands in place, feeling the shattered bones in his elbow grind. When he's subdued, she updates her team. "Clear in here. Starting work."

Conscript has already completed a login—the stroke of luck Jen was waiting for—but the session is being displayed in Cyrillic. She has no time to call Andrew and set up her own laptop, so she chooses the most expedient route possible. Extracting a Master Key from her kit, she raises the miniature hard drive's three antennas and plugs it into the terminal's USB port.

"Anne, what's our access level?" Jen asks as the quantum computer gains access through the Master Key.

"This session has administrative authority, Ms. Yates."

Jen's smirk is longer than a country mile. Scrolling through the Master Key's list of hacking tools, she selects Vector. The strain of malware is ideally suited for surveilling broad networks, and she used it to devastating effect in Mexico City. "Install my selection, Anne. I'll stand by."

"Processing."

"Z, there's a problem out here. Two SUVs approaching," Kabir says.

Jen checks the progress. Install is at ten percent, and it won't take much longer. But she's not giving an inch until her malware is installed on Void's network. "Take up defensive positions and prepare to hold the building."

Fifty-Six

A fine Cuban cigar smolders at Daniil Ionov's side, along with a glass of scotch. Typically, they'd be divine. Tonight, he's using them to keep the tremor out of his hands. Typing messages is hard if he can't hit the right keys.

Ionov's laptop is open, and Void's interface is displayed. He knows what's happening half a world away. Ceno has failed miserably. He's closing in on Void's location, likely on a suicide mission, or hell-bent on revenge. And Conscript has just logged into his administrator account for Void. But the servers are still online. Another failure—and an opportunity he'd been looking to seize.

He takes a heavy pull off his glass of scotch and sucks up a nicotine buzz from the cigar. Groaning, he curses Russia, the zakonny vladelets, and the sacrifices he's made in their names. But it's always been worth it. Always.

Initiating a secure chat on Void's private messaging system, he selects Conscript 19's user ID and types: *Jen Yates . . . ?*

———

Both SUVs are running. Their Xenon headlamps stripe the warehouse's façade, which will give Ceno and his soldiers plenty of light as they fight for control of the building.

Ceno steps out of a Lincoln Navigator, AK-47 in hand. A drum magazine dangles ominously out of the receiver. Seventy-five rounds of armor-piercing 7.62 ammunition inside. More thirty-rounders are tucked in his pocket, along with the CZ70—the tool he'll use to square the debt his family is owed.

Before approaching the warehouse, he extracts his cell phone and tries Conscript's number one last time. It rings, rings, then adds another red call attempt to Ceno's log. Not the time to be ducking calls, but as he surveys the wharf and spots the *Good Ole Days*, he assumes that it isn't by choice.

Ceno points first at a crew of four and directs them to the back of the warehouse. They're Isa's men, and highly capable. As they disappear around back, he directs his New York crew to the front entrance.

———

The message causes Jen to freeze. It came in through Void's private messaging system. She looks back to the only possible culprit, but Conscript 19 is nearly unconscious. His blood is pooling around her boots. Did he tip off whoever is communicating with her now?

"Eight men. They're surrounding our position."

Order of importance. Her install is the first priority, and it's eighty-five percent complete. "I need more time."

"Copy," Hastings replies.

Jen calms herself and focuses next on the message. She reads through several old messages and determines that Conscript couldn't have tipped the sender off. At least, not through this medium. She types: *Who is this?*

A man with information.

Another transmission from Hastings. "Breach is imminent."

"You've got authority to execute," Jen replies.

"Going silent," Hastings states.

Up above, a crash is followed by shouts in Albanian. They're looking for their hacker, but he's no longer in a talkative mood.

Back to the text conversation. Jen asks: *What kind of information? Victor Orlov's location.*

Blood shoots through her face. Her fingers whip across the keyboard: *I'm interested.*

Bubbles pop up on the bottom of the screen. *Typing . . .*

———

Never silhouette yourself.

An old lesson Hastings picked up in Ranger School.

Bars of white light are blasting through paint-chipped windows. They make the warehouse seem like it's been shot to pieces—but it's still early for that. Clouds of dirt and dust coil around gunmen as they stream into the warehouse. They're working with light at their backs—both an advantage and a hindrance.

Hastings is kneeling under a metal staircase. Boxes stacked to his right shield him from the light. His rifle is raised, but he remains still. Olsi Kurti is creeping toward him, recognizable from his mugshots until a red dot paints his forehead.

Maybe, just maybe, the ruts in the Neanderthal's face are preventing him from seeing things clearly, but it doesn't matter as Hastings' rifle burps. Bullets strike Olsi's face, leaving him with a blank stare. Hastings dismisses it as Olsi's natural state, and searches for someone equally enjoyable to kill.

The Likas duck into cover behind the tanks as another burst of suppressed gunfire chases through the warehouse. This one was Animal's, and it disorients the attackers. Wasn't the gunfire to their left? But it was muffled, and the sound signatures are tough to pinpoint.

The confusion gives Hastings the precious milliseconds required to make another engagement.

He orients his rifle toward a figure crouching behind one of the giant tanks. Halit Voka. Overfed, and slow because of it. Halit's looking in the direction of his fallen comrade, Olsi. The rifle on the ground.

Gray matter leaking all over the floor. A funeral invitation strikes Halit in the forehead at a thousand feet per second.

One gunman remains: Ceno Lika. Hastings catches a glimpse of him as he steps out of cover and levels his AK-47 at the metal staircase. Seconds before 7.62 rounds tear into his position, Hastings breaks for cover.

———

The installation is complete.

Jen is halfway up the tank's second ladder when gunfire lights up the warehouse. She's late to the gunbattle, and she needs to get out of the tank and orient herself.

She pauses before reaching the top. Someone is running across the catwalk, and she'll be meeting him soon. She draws her pistol and points it toward the top of the ladder.

Whoever is approaching slows before coming into view. First thing Jen sees is a submachine gun's muzzle. MAC-10, like the Bronx. *Bullet hose.* A head appears just behind it. She squeezes the trigger and puts a round straight into the target's right cheek.

Gravity pulls what's left of his head forward and his body follows. She tucks herself into the rungs of the ladder, and his falling body brushes past her before smacking into the false glass bottom.

Movement to her right. She twists on the ladder and directs her pistol toward the sound. A shooter appears, pointing an AK type rifle in her direction. Before she can fire, a halo of light surrounds him. A burst of suppressed gunfire follows. The would-be shooter falls into the tank.

Jen's instincts flare. The kid was on the second story with her. Hastings and Animal are down below. She screams, "Kabir! No light!"

Hurrying up the ladder, she peeks over the tank's lip as Kabir is consumed by gunfire. 7.62 steel cores cut through the grating beneath his feet. Sparks bloom around his body and leave glowing orange half-moons in the metal walkway.

Otherworldly strength propels Jen out of the tank. She bounds across the grating and kneels next to Kabir. Automatically, she reaches for his neck to check for a pulse but stops short. The rounds were blatantly effective. "One of ours is hit!"

———

The section of barrel between the AK's hand guard and front sight is glowing orange. Ceno dips back into cover and watches the orange line recede into itself. Gunsmoke booms out of his nostrils. Cordite.

The taste.

The fucker I just wasted on the catwalk.

The Kanun and hakmarrja . . . revenge. He's just getting started. Depressing the AK's magazine latch with his thumb, he cantilevers the empty drum magazine out of the rifle and eases it to the ground. These Americans are skilled. His reloads will be silent.

Before he can insert a fresh magazine, he hears shouts from the other side of the warehouse. Orders to surrender in English, and he doesn't recognize the voices. But he does recognize the sound of rifles hitting cement. Same with the coward's footsteps as they run toward the front of the warehouse.

He'll handle this now, but it won't be with the AK. There's no time to complete the reload, and the CZ seems appropriate for those who betray their family. He draws the CZ and steps out of cover. Two members of Isa's London crew run past, hands in the air.

Now is his chance to gun them down.

But the Americans are skilled.

Ceno one-eighties, puts a bullet into the first thing he sees. It strikes the man who'd been creeping up behind him. The round hits the center of his chest. Something ignites—maybe bullets in a magazine. Or an electronic device.

Ceno keeps firing. Lets the muzzle walk upward until red mist spits out of the upper section of his target's chest, just under his throat.

Smoke is coiling around Ceno as the pistol's slide locks back. Eight rounds spent. When his target falls, he takes a moment to study him. Red hair. Short but muscular. He coughs, clutches his chest as he spits blood. Almost dead, but not yet.

———

"Hastings, this is Z. Status?"

Jen looks at Animal, who is kneeling at Kabir's side. Losing the kid is hard, but Al Hastings is family, and as the charging handle ratchets at the far side of the warehouse, they both know what happened.

Animal is locked on. He's not looking at Jen or Kabir. Only the direction of his fallen brother. He hasn't moved because Jen's word hasn't come, but she knows that he's gone. Clicked off. Full disconnect. No amount of danger will stop him from reaching his teammate.

"Go."

She's never seen Charlie Keats move so quickly or quietly. Within seconds, he's lost in the shadows. And when he's gone, a memory ignites. Like Mexico City. Beijing. She's alone in a dangerous situation, and nothing compares. This is what she started in the Bronx, and now she has a debt of her own to settle.

———

Ceno took the stairs. The catwalk has risks, but it seems to be the darkest part of the building. Hugging the wall, he allows a long strip of darkness to guide him to the back of the warehouse.

He's surging with energy. It's been years since he's felt this agile. His vision is sharp, and he's not detecting movement in any other part of the warehouse.

The gears of a transmission slam into place. Moments ago, Isa's men fled the scene in an SUV. Now the second vehicle's headlights are shifting away. Its engine revs, and the lights disappear.

Ahead, Ceno notices moonlight creeping in from the back door. He spots the first man he shot. The body is lying by Void's tank, cut to pieces. The Americans left their dead for the rats. Cowards without honor.

But he won't trust that he's alone. Not yet.

He patrols the catwalk farther. After a few steps, he stops, listens, and starts again. Everything around him is still and silent. Finally, he arrives at the back door and peeks outside. Ghost town.

Back to Void's tank. Two of Isa's men are lying on the bottom. The server space is bloodied. He descends the first ladder and finds Conscript 19 propped against the wall, semi-conscious.

"Help," Conscript whispers.

"What did they do?" Ceno asks after descending the final ladder.

Conscript doesn't respond. He's drifting in and out, and the pool of blood around his body is expanding.

Ceno takes note of the computer screen. Unlocked. There's a live session that has yet to time out. He also notices an unusual device protruding from the terminal. Not a tool he's seen before, but he's not a tech guru either. He's never liked Conscript, but the only way to know is to save him. Slinging the AK on his back, he strips his belt to tie off the wounded leg.

A thud rattles the glass ceiling. The trapdoor slams shut. Ceno's rifle is unslung as a lock snaps into place.

On his feet, he dumps the magazine. Bits of copper and lead peel away from steel cores as they penetrate the glass. Shell casings ricochet off the walls. The AK's hammer falls on an empty chamber.

Ceno reaches for a magazine but realizes he just spent his last one. On to the CZ, and if that fails, he'll use his hands. He laughs. "What the fuck will this do?" He grabs his cell phone. "Maybe I'll have a cigarette while I wait for my family to come!"

Pipes rock. Pumps have been activated. Water splashes onto the ceiling. Raindrops cut through fresh holes in the plexiglass before turning to streams.

Ceno angles the CZ toward the lock and pulls the trigger. The little .32 is no match for the plexiglass. Raging, he jumps onto the ladder and buries his shoulder in the trapdoor. It's metal on metal as the handles smash into the lock.

He fights as Void's servers pop, spark, and snap around him. Needing help, he looks at Conscript, but the soiled water is consuming his chest, and he isn't responding. The space goes dark, but Ceno refuses to stop fighting. The sacred law forbids surrender. Just like the lock. Immovable. Punishing. *Kanun.*

———

Jen sprints through the front door and proceeds for the Lincoln Navigator just ahead. Animal is kneeling by the rear bumper, providing security. When he sees her, he jumps into the driver's seat.

Killing Ceno Lika was time-consuming, and for Al Hastings, every second counts. As Jen races for the vehicle, she doesn't think about the potential loss of a friend—at least not in emotional terms. She's focused on objectives: how to adequately administer TCCC, or tactical combat casualty care; the fastest routes to the nearest emergency room; the efficacy of her assault on Void.

To think of anything else would unleash emotions she couldn't control. The deluge would be overwhelming, disastrous. She's leaving a fallen man behind. The Grim Reaper's hand is resting on Al Hastings's shoulder. A horrendous gunfight just occurred. If she were to lose control now, her entire body would quit.

Jen opens the rear hatch and jumps inside beside Hastings. Blood everywhere. Labored breathing. Animal has already begun tending to the wounds, but she still has a ton of triage to do before reaching the ER. She slams the hatch shut and removes her trauma kit as Animal mashes the accelerator.

FIFTY-SEVEN

THE MEN WHO FLEW TO ISLAMABAD TO EXECUTE OSAMA BIN Laden would have been monitored in a room like this. The tactical operations center is the most advanced in existence, and it has some serious advantages over its counterparts in the Middle East. London is wired, and the computers in this room can access surveillance cameras, law enforcement databases, and cellular equipment citywide.

Martinez is standing by with Grisham as preparations take place. Soon, members of SCO19 will be beating down Gombe Wireless's doors—a party Gabriella Martinez is dressed to attend. She's wearing a Kevlar vest over her white button-down shirt, and one of Jen's 2011s is strapped to her belt.

Progress is shown on the center screen. Uniformed officers are mobilizing across the city, their locations marked by GPS, or relayed via street cameras. Entire city blocks surrounding Gombe Wireless will soon be closed off. It'll prevent the press from reaching the scene. If a gunfight occurs, civilians will be well out of range, giving tactical teams a freer hand to respond.

London's suburbs are also seeing an uptick in police presence. These officers are assembling to arrest Gombe Wireless's upper management, along with members of its C-suite, which has gathered in London for the launch of the service.

The last element is SCO19, which is assembling its task force in MI5's subterranean parking garage. Operators are donning armor, preparing their weapons. Tactical vehicles are fueled and ready to roll.

A call comes into the TOC: Jen's cell. Martinez glances at her watch and is happy to find an hour left on the clock. Her people are always efficient.

Grisham orders an analyst to answer the call. "Ms. Yates, you're live in the TOC."

"Give us the good news," Martinez adds.

Jen's tone is forceful. Not exactly calm, not exactly panicked. "One officer KIA, another with multiple GSWs. We're traveling at a high rate of speed to University Hospital Lewisham."

Grisham dishes out several commands, and analysts begin interfacing with trauma teams at Jen's intended destination. "ETA, Ms. Yates?"

"Five minutes," Jen replies. "Animal, give me your trauma kit!"

Horns wail before trailing off in the distance, but Martinez isn't shaken by the background noise. She's making inferences. Animal is driving; Jen is providing TCCC. The team's remaining members are quickly accounted for, and she feels sick to her stomach.

"Z!"

"Got it!" Jen shouts. Velcro peels back. Seals are torn open. "TOC, something came in on Orlov."

Martinez's arms are folded across her chest, and her nails are digging into her palms. But it's hardly a distraction, and she's fighting hard not to let her eyes mist over. Leaders can't quit in the middle of a fight. "Feed us everything."

"He's at Port Newport. A cargo ship will be smuggling him out of the country at nine o'clock local time."

"Who forwarded you this information?" Martinez demands.

"Source is unknown. It came as a private message on Void. Our penetration was a success, by the way."

"Do you consider it credible?"

"Whoever made contact referenced me by name. They also possessed intimate knowledge of Orlov." Jen strains as she works. "We need to get people to the port."

Grisham studies the asset allocations on his map before breaking back into the conversation. "Ms. Yates, we don't have any resources to spare, beside local port police. I can reroute a surveillance helicopter to rendezvous with you at Hospital Lewisham. You'd be our closest responder."

Jen doesn't hesitate. "Reroute the asset."

"We'll have a helicopter meet you at Lewisham, Ms. Yates."

"TOC, I need to sign off," Jen says abruptly before the call cuts out.

The tactical operations center is hushed as the call ends.

In the silence, Martinez thinks of Mexico City. Terrance Kline. Bobby Hollice. Cameron Vinke. Everything they endured. Now they have taken more casualties, and she won't let Jen walk into trouble alone. She looks at Grisham. "I'm taking my people to Newport. Forward our information to port police."

FIFTY-EIGHT

A TRAUMA TEAM IS STANDING BY AT THE ER ENTRANCE.

Jen's hands press into Hastings's shoulders to keep his body still as Animal careens into the parking lot.

The vehicle slows, and she rechecks Al's vitals. His pulse is heading in the wrong direction. She worked to control blood loss, but nothing seemed to work. Getting him to the ER alive is a major victory, and she prays that her effort was enough.

"Clear, Z!"

Jen kicks open the hatch. The trauma team moves swiftly into place. While they work to load Hastings onto the gurney, she feeds them information. "Four gunshot wounds to the chest; airways aren't perforated. Heart rate fifty-seven, falling. Breathing is labored."

The surgeon's head is bobbing up and down, processing the information. Before the stretcher takes off, he gives her a double-take. Bloody, decked out with weapons and tactical equipment. A plate carrier and other gear cut off the patient remains discarded in the back of the SUV. If the interior weren't black, it would be stained red. London shouldn't feel like a foreign battlefield, but it does tonight.

"When was he shot? With what?" the surgeon asks.

"Around eight o'clock—ten minutes ago. Small-caliber handgun."

The surgeon ignores Jen as he gets the gurney rolling. He presses his fingers on Hastings's neck, monitoring his pulse as he moves. "Straight to the OR, nurses. Let's have him prepped for surgery before we arrive."

The surgeon continues. "Do we know the patient's blood type?"

Animal is following close behind the doctor. He wedges between the nurses and pulls a piece of tape off Hastings's boot. An old Delta tradition many would consider bad luck. "O positive."

The surgeon shouts, "Let's get a couple bags on standby!"

"Al, I'm with you, man!" Animal says as he locks his hands onto the gurney and assists the nurses with propelling it forward.

Jen slows her pace as they pass through the ER's admittance doors. She's provided all the help she can. Now the surgeons, and the heavens above, will decide Hastings's fate.

The gurney slips around a corner. Animal doesn't look back, and it's best that way. Knowing that Hastings isn't alone gives her the strength to move on Orlov. She finds the nearest elevator and selects the button for the top floor. By the time she steps off, a helicopter will be waiting on the helipad.

FIFTY-NINE

LANE NUMBER FOUR. VICTOR'S INSTRUCTIONS WERE specific, and he guides the Porsche into position behind an eighteen-wheeler, which is next in line to make entry at the port. Checking the clock, he marks the time: 8:50 p.m.

By 8:54, port security has completed the screening. Victor will know there's a hitch if his screening takes longer than five minutes. The officer raises the gate, and the eighteen-wheeler grumbles forward.

He pulls up to the gate. Smooth. Calm. Just another one of the port's many expected guests. He rolls down the window, searching for the customs officer's name. *Lewis.* The Lika Syndicate's man, standing exactly where he should be.

"Busy night," Victor remarks as he hands Lewis his phony passport.

A moment of recognition passes between the two men, and Lewis takes the passport. "Never seem to catch a break, sir." He thumbs the pages. "Shipping out, Mr. Chekov?"

"Yessir."

"The *Gladys*?"

"Right again. Just joined her crew."

"Just a moment, please."

Victor watches Lewis pocket the passport book as he enters the security booth. He punches a few keys on a computer and scans a port employee ID card. The screen flashes green. *Clear for Entry.* Had his passport been scanned, the entry would have reached computers inside multiple British intelligence agencies. Always possible they'd have missed him, but then again . . .

Lewis returns. "Everything checks out, sir."

Victor grabs the booklet and places it in his jacket. "Thanks."

"Know where you're heading?"

Victor's been studying the place for hours. He can only smirk. "I do."

"Safe travels."

Victor follows a series of signs, lines, and yellow arrows to a long-term parking lot. He parks and grabs his duffel bag from the trunk.

Upon exiting the lot, he gets a clear look at the vessel that will take him to safety. The *Gladys* is docked at Middle Quay, the farthest dock that encloses the port's waters. Thin, filmy ice surrounds the hull, and the decks are clear of personnel. Cargo is loaded, and they're just waiting for their last crew member to arrive before shipping out.

Before he can step away from the Porsche, he notices two police vehicles speeding down East Way Road toward the *Gladys*. Their sirens aren't flashing, but they're moving at a high rate of speed. One of the vehicles brakes hard and disappears behind a small warehouse. Perfect place to watch the gangways he'd use to board the vessel.

The second police cruiser keeps coming.

He looks up and notices a helicopter shifting along the gray clouds. A Sikorsky, running without any lights flashing on its airframe. Its flight pattern suggests that it's circling over the port. Must have arrived in the past thirty minutes, because he'd have seen it sitting atop the crane.

A powerful surge of anger takes hold of Victor. The fighting man's spirit that refuses to accept defeat, or failure. He's been compromised *again*—but there's no time to work through that. He takes one last look at the cargo ship and erases it from his mind. That path is gone, and it's up to him alone to break free of this mess.

———

Jen is wondering if the port constable behind the wheel of the cruiser has nerve damage in his feet. Liberal amounts of pressure are being applied to the accelerator, and she's clawing at the door handle to keep herself steady.

Minutes ago, a New Scotland Yard Sikorsky deposited her at Port Newport. Parts of the facility are still under construction, and its skids touched down on an open stretch of concrete foundation. The constable is driving her to the port's main office, and its security station, as quickly as possible.

The constable barely eases off the gas to take a turn, and he continues updating her on the situation. "The port's locks are closed, ma'am. Departures are no longer permitted."

Before Jen can respond, the cruiser's radio chirps. "Unit Three, we've just had a suspicious entry at lane four."

Jen grabs the radio. "Send the details to our dash computer."

"One moment, please," the dispatcher replies.

Images of the entry appear. Black Porsche. British plates, and the registration has already checked out. But photos of the subject grab Jen's attention. A man with dark hair is passing off his passport book with an air of confidence. As she studies the face, there's no question that it's Victor Orlov.

Jen is too pissed off to celebrate, but the thought crosses her mind before she responds. "That's our man."

After several moments the dispatcher responds. "The Yard has been informed. We're currently tracking the subject."

"Where is the vehicle?" Jen asks.

"Long-term parking. The vehicle's driver is on foot, progressing south along the land side of the port."

Jen processes the response. Victor's cargo vessel, the *Gladys*, is behind her in the rearview, and he can't reach it via his chosen route. "Continue tracking him. I'm close."

Hanging up the radio, she grabs her cell phone and dials Martinez. "We have visual confirmation on Orlov. He's inside the port."

"Alone?" Martinez asks.

"Yes. Something spooked him though. He's not trying to reach the *Gladys* any longer. I'm going to engage him."

"We're twenty minutes away."

"Better make it ten," Jen replies. "Out."

The cruiser buzzes past the long-term parking lot and nears the port's primary office building. But Jen isn't interested in watching security cameras; she's already looking ahead to the route Victor used to move deeper into the port. "Drop me here and double back to the port's exit."

"Right, ma'am," the constable replies as he strips his radio off his duty belt. "Stay in contact."

"Thanks," Jen says as she takes the handheld and slips into the cold.

———

Essentials only from this point forward. That means weapons, ammunition, and comms equipment for Victor. His Glock is holstered on his belt. His SIG 553 has its suppressor attached, and it's slung under his coat.

Law enforcement failed to apprehend him by surprise. Critical mistake. These precious few moments have allowed him to formulate a plan. He has a shot at surviving, and he'll make the most of it.

He grabs a wad of cash from the duffel and tucks it into the breast pocket of his jacket. Finished, he stuffs the bag into a nearby dumpster. All the way to the bottom. He's certain it will be found, but he's not going to make it easy for the Americans.

Before slipping out of cover, he grabs his phone. Anastasia must know. He texts her: *I'm compromised. Port exit is blown. Law enforcement is close.*

Anastasia calls him back immediately but he doesn't answer. His sister's voice will feel too much like home, and the thought of how far away it is will only soften him.

We're working it, Victor. We're with you.

"I know, Ana," he whispers before returning the phone to his pocket.

Victor scans his surroundings and confirms he's alone. He slips out of cover and runs toward the metal recycling plant, which is less than a hundred yards away.

———

Jen takes cover behind a vehicle—a squat little pickup truck used to transport bins full of scrap metal. She peeks around the edge, looking into the recycling plant through its giant open doors. Harsh environment. Even from a distance she can feel the heat. Several dozen men are using cutting torches to break down scrap metal. Slag drips onto their steel-toe boots. Sparks fly. Inky smoke collects above their heads.

None of the workers appear disturbed. Moments ago, she saw Victor approaching the building, but she's not sure if he went inside. He could have kept moving, but she'll need to confirm it.

Jen keeps her rifle under her jacket and enters the recycling plant. The employees are wearing protective glasses, and their vision is further obscured by cutting torches. None of them notice her as she passes.

An unusual sight catches her attention. A truck axle has been left unattended. It is being recycled, and a partially finished cut is still glowing orange on its frame. Someone's work has been disturbed.

She approaches on an angle and finds a man lying on the ground. The metal worker's neck is broken, but that's not what causes Jen's heart to skip.

The torch he'd been using to disassemble the axle is still burning. Its hose is coiled around the oxygen-acetylene tanks, and the torch's handle is pointing a blue cone directly into the oxygen tank. An orange blister is widening across the metal. Pressure gauges are fluttering. Something pops. Hisses.

Jen sprints toward a nearby forklift. She dives and tucks her body into its cover as the tanks explode. Fire sucks the air out of the warehouse, and she struggles for breath as the ambient temperatures skyrocket. Bits of scrap metal and debris lash the area. The lift she's hiding behind is several thousand pounds, but it pushes into her shoulder.

Everything settles into something peaceful, serene—but that's just shock. It doesn't last long. Screaming begins. Pleas for help. Panicked people calling out for their missing friends.

Jen forces herself to stand and orient herself amid the chaos. Bits of flaming debris are everywhere. Oxygen-acetylene tanks have toppled to the ground, some with damaged regulators and hoses. Sprinkler systems are either nonexistent or have failed. No way to tell with a pall of black smoke covering the ceiling.

Then the stampede begins. People rush to assist those who are in need. Wounded men limp out of the warehouse and into the cold. They're all covered in soot, coughing and struggling to breathe.

None of the people running past her look like Victor, but identifying him will be hard in a situation like this. Going against her instincts, she walks deeper into the carnage. A group of men limp toward her. She studies their faces, their clothes. No match. She shouts, "Is anyone hurt back there?"

One of the men points toward the back of the warehouse. Covered in soot, he's wearing an orange vest with reflectors on the sides. "The foreman! I didn't see him leave!"

The foreman may have caught Victor trespassing and confronted him. That fight wouldn't have ended well. There's also the possibility he was injured in the blast. Either way, Jen won't leave a wounded man behind. She sprints for the foreman's office in the warehouse's back corner.

———

"Stop! Stop the vehicle!" Martinez shouts.

Coco mashes the pedal as a series of secondary explosions rock the port. I-beams fold. An oxygen tank rockets into the sky, flames glowing behind it, before it explodes like a supercharged Roman candle. The recycling plant's roof heaves up and sinks into a pillow of smoke and fire.

The port's first responders were several minutes ahead of Martinez. They were tending to the wounded when they were consumed in the cloud of smoke and debris. A jet of water arcs over the cloud and falls into the fire—the only hint that a fireboat is hidden somewhere beyond the smoke.

"What are we doing, ma'am?" Gray demands from the back seat.

Martinez looks at Sloane. "Anything?"

Sloane terminates a call on her cell. "Nothing from Jen."

Martinez drops a New Scotland Yard badge over her Kevlar vest and ensures the law enforcement patches fixed to it are exposed. "Coco, you're with me. Sloane, take Gray. Try to punch through along the warehouse's far side."

Without another word, they grab their weapons and exit the SUV.

———

An explosion rocks the earth under Victor's feet. The orange fireball makes the reflectors on his new safety vest glow. The foreman's clothes. He smiles. Jen Yates walked straight past him in the chaos. He debates her odds of survival. Low. Tack on a handicap for the collapsed roof, and she's toast.

The port is in chaos, and Victor continues navigating through it. Alarms are blaring. Dozens of men are rushing to render aid, or simply trying to understand what's happening. Crane operators are scrambling down ladders, worried that the concussions or flying debris will collapse their rigs. He isn't bleeding or screaming for help, which means he's not worthy of a second glance.

The helicopter he'd seen earlier has disappeared; aerial debris is a hazard to its rotors. Problem solved, but more are forming up behind him. First responders are streaming into the port, choking it off. But he's not walking in their direction, and the collapsed recycling plant is stopping them from traveling in his.

There's no touching him, and there's a path to freedom ahead.

A satellite police station occupies the far end of the dock. They have several patrol boats in slips beyond the port's locks. It's for expedience; they don't have to run through the locks every day to begin their patrols. If there's an emergency on River Usk, they can respond quickly.

When he reaches the police station, he finds it abandoned. He missed them as they responded to the explosions.

No one questions his presence as he approaches a lock box filled with boat keys mounted to the wall by the entrance. Wedging his fingers underneath the lid, he uses brute strength to pop it open. Unsure of which key corresponds to which boat, he decides to take them all. If the cops can't chase him, all the better.

He steps onto the docks and finds River Usk relatively calm beyond the locks.

Numbers are written on the boat key's bobbers. Big and bold. He walks to the closest slip and boards a Targa 32 Fast Patrol Vessel. Reflective blue and gold checkering decorates its cabin, and it flashes against the fire light. *Police* is written boldly on the blue hull. Passing the boat's twin outboard motors, he grins. This'll be a fast trip, *No Wake* signs be damned.

Before severing the moorings, he enters the cabin and tries the key. The outboards roar to life. Fuel levels are good, and the GPS is functional. This is officially his ticket downriver.

While he unfastens the boat's front mooring, a motor sputters out. Half a second later, the second one follows. Frustrated, he turns to find oil spurting out of a bullet hole at the top of a motor. On instinct, he ducks for cover behind the hull.

"You should have killed me!"

"Surrender, Victor! It's over!" Jen shouts.

Victor grins and extracts his SIG 553 from under his coat. If his friend from Mexico City wants a fight, she'll get it. Some delays are worth every second. Flipping out the rifle's stock, he drops the safety. His trigger finger is itchy, eager to win this gunfight as it settles into position.

———

Jen's rifle is leveled at the area where Victor's silhouette disappeared. Her trigger is prepped, and the red dot is perfectly placed. She just needs a hunk of flesh to tear away with a high-velocity projectile.

She's in cover behind a concrete pylon, and it gives her a straight shot into Victor's boat twenty yards in the distance.

A rifle muzzle snaps up from the boat's gunwale. Just a weapon and two hands. Blind fire rakes the pylon. The rifle is suppressed and its signature is recognizable, along with its increased rate of fire. Concrete fragments zing up from the pylon. Rounds snap over her head. The tactic is effective, and it drives her back into cover.

The second volley is more precise than the first. She presses her body tight into cover as rounds begin landing. The first chips the edge of the pylon, and a second lands directly on top of it. *Son of a bitch can shoot.* A final shot rips through rope coiled around the pylon. Frayed bits spit in her face as the bullet zips past.

She reaches for her handheld radio and attempts to contact the New Scotland Yard helicopter that rushed her to the port. "Kano Six-Three, this is Zero. I'm under fire at the port's satellite police station! Do you copy?"

Static.

The radio, like the rest of her body, was damaged in the explosion. Timing saved her life. She had already escaped through an emergency exit when the concussion struck her. One of her eardrums ruptured, and synovial fluid is dripping down the side of her face. She's nauseous, and likely concussed from the explosion's shockwave, but she'll live.

Victor's fire breaks. She listens for a reload and prepares to act, but he's not finished. He was only searching for a way to increase his effectiveness. Bullets strike the pylon five feet from her position. Bits of hot lead and copper pepper her body. A steel penetrator ricochets, strikes her knee, and she nearly tumbles out of cover.

Tough way to learn an adversary is using armor piercing bullets.

Adrenaline should be helping her with the pain, but her knee is screaming. Her temper gives way and drives her to make a rash decision. Flipping her rifle to sustained fire, she falls onto her back and dumps a dozen rounds into the hull of Victor's boat.

Victor drops into cover and out of sight. With a few rounds left in the mag, she continues firing into the hull before noticing the fire extinguisher bolted to its center console. A .300 Blackout round drills through the canister, and flame retardant consumes the boat.

She hears coughing. Victor is struggling for air. His vision will be impaired too.

Jen sits up and rests her rifle atop the pylon. Activating her visible laser, she hovers the beam over Victor's position. The laser forms a red shaft in the smoke, effectively pinning him.

"It's over, Victor!" Jen screams. Quickly, she reaches for the laser's quick-detach lever and removes it from her rifle. Once it's free, she returns it to position on the pylon. "Reinforcements are inbound! You can walk out of here alive!"

Victor doesn't utter a word. Instead, he yanks back on his weapon's charging handle.

Message received.

Jen ducks into cover and performs a reload as quietly as possible. Her rifle should still be up, according to her laser beam, which is still penetrating the flame retardant. When she's finished, she peeks past the pylon once more.

The boat reminds her of a cauldron. Flame retardant is boiling over the gunwale and hovering on the water's surface. Still no Victor, and she's not interested in finding out what he's waiting on.

Jen attempts to stand, but a jolt of pain forces her back behind the pylon. She examines her wound. Blood is dripping from her kneecap. Could be shattered or fractured. She can't tell, but she knows it's not interested in holding her weight.

Too bad, because she's not giving it a choice. Gritting her teeth, she grabs onto the rope coiled around the pylon and forces herself upright. Victor won't stay whipped for much longer. Leaving her laser on the pylon, she limps toward the boat slip. With every step she gains a better angle of attack on her adversary.

She's halfway to the boat when a vibration shakes the dock's planks. The helicopter. It must have seen the flame retardant, or picked up her radio transmission. Either way, it's coming to assist, and the pilots will direct reinforcements to her position.

A gang box is posted on the dock, directly behind the boat. Jen heads for it. Five yards, no movement on the boat. Three yards. No Victor, and his coughing has subsided. One yard.

Metal clangs. The helicopter's spotlight illuminates her position, along with the boat. The white smoke becomes blinding. Wisps of flame-retardant chemicals infuse with light and slash golden ribbons into her vision.

But she can see a black streak cross the boat's deck: her silhouette. Unable to dive, Jen allows herself to fall into cover behind the gang box. Automatic gunfire tears out of the smoke and eviscerates the fiberglass gang box. She feels the bullets ricochet between its walls and snap over her body. They're getting closer, and she presses her chest hard into the dock, searching for space that doesn't exist.

The gunfire stops and there's a splash.

The helicopter's spotlight cuts off.

Jen rolls onto her back and rushes to process the situation. Jumping into the water is suicide in these conditions, but it's better than taking a bullet. Without any real cover, that's exactly what Victor was going to get. She manages to get upright, shoulder her rifle, and present it as she looks over the gang box.

Bubbles are rising next to the boat's hull.

The helicopter's rotors beat at her back, and the wind gets stronger. Keeping her rifle tight to her shoulder, she waits for the inevitable. Wind pushes away the flame retardant, and the boat's deck becomes visible.

Victor Orlov is lying on his back with a Glock pistol pointed at her. His weapon discharges; a bullet from Jen's rifle strikes his chest. She feels the pistol bullet burrow into the gang box, but it stops there. He goes limp and drops the pistol onto his stomach.

Blood is dribbling out of his mouth, and already a large pool is collecting around his abdomen. Jen realizes he was wounded during their previous exchange, and he couldn't get back to his feet.

Victor struggles to remain conscious while reaching for something in his pocket. Jen takes up the trigger's slack but holds her fire when she sees a cell phone. She'll let him make the call. Texans don't forget what's right—but it's still a shrewd decision. This will be a chance to trace the contact.

Victor speaks in Russian. Death isn't far away, but he remains calm, if only to find a few extra moments to speak with whomever he loves. The conversation drains what's left of his strength. The phone drops from his ear and rests at the side of his head. Whoever is on the other end hasn't ended the call.

Victor looks at Jen with hatred in his eyes. "When Anastasia kills you, make sure to think of me!" With a last burst of strength, he reaches for the pistol on his chest.

Jen's trigger breaks. When her bullet drills into the boat's hull, Victor's gray matter is chasing after it.

The helicopter pulls away, and the wind at her back fades. Victor is dead, but she still has a use for her rifle. Pressing the muzzle down into the dock, she uses it as a cane and boards the boat.

Jen kicks Victor's pistol off his stomach and makes sure it settles out of his reach. When she's satisfied, she reaches for the phone and leans into the railing. "Anastasia?"

After a long pause, the voice on the other end replies. "Yes."

Now she knows his sister's name, but that's not the only connection she makes: *Couldn't have done it without you, Ms. Yates.* This woman typed the message. Enjoyed watching her suffer from half a world away. She speaks plainly, lets her lack of remorse show through. "He's dead."

Anastasia's voice catches, but she refuses to let it break. "So are you, Jen Yates."

The call terminates.

Jen drops the phone onto her lap and looks back at the port. Martinez and Coco are running toward her position. Moments later, Sloane and Gray appear. She waves, signaling that she's okay, then takes a final look at Victor. *Good riddance.*

SIXTY

Mounds of cocaine are being carried in the arms of triumphant New Scotland Yard officers. The drugs were found—all too coincidentally—during the investigation into the explosion at Newport. The Lika Syndicate's drug smuggling ring is officially out of commission. Their human smuggling racket is soon to follow.

It's not the only convenient lie law enforcement is peddling. They discovered several faulty valves connected to oxygen-acetylene tanks at the steel recycling plant, and they have attributed the explosion to improperly stored gas.

Explosions are obviously big news, and the raid on Gombe Wireless hardly receives the coverage it's due. Shortly after Jen finished with Victor Orlov, Ray Toliver led an uneventful raid into Gombe's central London headquarters and disconnected its servers. C-suite executives were also apprehended. After the attack on GCHQ, there's a zero percent chance that they'll ever come back online again.

Jen sits in her hospital bed, transfixed on the morning news. The painful night has returned to the forefront of her memory.

"I wouldn't have been able to stop you from fighting that crazy Russian."

"I didn't—" Jen says, her sadness disrupted. She forgot she'd been on a video call with Terrance Kline. He's watching her with a concerned, knowing look. Same one she gives him. She smiles. "Still. Coulda used a hand, *Terry*."

"*Terrance*. And I'm busy. You can find plenty of virtual assistants online. Affordable too. Twelve bucks an hour."

Jen laughs, then stops as the stitches claw at her knee, which is fractured. Her equilibrium is off from a concussion and busted eardrum. Doesn't seem like much compared to the sacrifice others made, and it's hardly fair she'll recover fully. "I'm hanging up now."

"I've been waiting so long to hear that—"

Jen hangs up, as promised. All part of the act, but there's no one on earth she's more grateful for. Spirit rejuvenated, she takes stock of her hospital room.

The black suit hanging on the wall is a haunting reminder of her duty today. She'll put it on before being discharged to attend Kabir's memorial service. He saved her life at the mansion, but she failed to do the same for him. His death is a repeat of one of life's most painful lessons: the burden is left for the living to bear.

She thinks of the bright spots that have emerged from this ordeal. Things to celebrate and look forward to. Dante's *Inferno* sits on her nightstand. Serai is traveling stateside today. Jen will see her off before she boards the flight. She'll get the chance to meet Mira and Elina too.

Given the weight of Serai's contribution, joint payments from the U.S. and British governments combined to form one extremely healthy bank account for her family. All three of them will become U.S. citizens. Free. Proud to start their new lives as Americans.

She forces herself out of the hospital bed and reaches for the suit. Adult diapers and a blow-up doll are piled next to it. Gifts for Hastings, who is in stable condition several floors above this one. She'll drop them off in hopes that she'll be there when he wakes up. After all, the gifts will need explaining.

Diapers are to help with his new condition.

The doll will be company for the lonely nights ahead. That it's a male version is irrelevant.

None of it will be true, of course. With time, Al Hastings will return to the battlefield—if he chooses to do so.

She laughs and when she's finished, she finds that suit easier to put on. It's a sign that she'll get through. People she cares for are counting on it, and she's not the type to let them down.

Sixty-One

Vodka and laughter.

There had been plenty of both during Victor's *first* funeral.

Passing a pint between them, Anastasia and her twin brother sat in a heavily tinted Mercedes Benz, watching as people mourned over an empty casket in the Federal Military Memorial Cemetery. All the pomp and tradition of a military burial made for an amusing show to watch.

Members of Victor's Spetsnaz unit adorned the casket with unit regalia and other tokens related to his service. That was the only part of the ceremony Victor had been quiet for, but he wasn't bothered by it—just honored. Warriors are meant to perish on the battlefield, and for his brothers, the funeral was the celebration for one of the greatest they'd ever known.

Their father created the greatest amount of mutual amusement. Drunk, he stumbled up to the casket and nearly fell into the tomb grave diggers had spent the previous night preparing.

Some things never change. Maybe it was their vindictive, cold natures, but they enjoyed watching him sob over the empty box before wandering back to his Opal.

"Doesn't deserve our pensions" had been Victor's only remark.

He regretted missing Anastasia's service. Funny, because she missed it too. The thought of attending hadn't ever crossed her mind. That was a prank only her older brother would have thought of. But Victor had been too deeply embedded in Syria to return home and pitch the idea.

They left the cemetery that day giddy and excited—rarities for them. Newly recruited into one of Russia's most powerful organizations, they would become acquainted with wealth, power, and status. Work seamlessly between the government and private organizations, enjoying the fruits that both sectors had to offer.

That's the real Russia.

That's the real world—only their counterparts in Western countries need to go to greater lengths to hide their corruption.

Now Anastasia has returned to the cemetery. Standing alone, she watches as a grave digger piles dirt onto an empty casket. Her husband isn't here. Victor's Spetsnaz brothers didn't get invitations, and there aren't any twenty-one-gun salutes booming through the cemetery. Members of the vladelets, along with their condolences, are also absent. Her vodka bottle is still in the cupboard, and she wouldn't dare laugh. But the tears . . . they're oh so real and flowing endlessly.

Others will mourn too. Jen Yates will cry for killing Victor. So will everyone she loves. In time, Anastasia will make it happen. She's certain of it, as certain as the casket below her feet is empty.

Anastasia's cell phone rings. She answers, and she hates herself for it. "What?"

"It's time to return to work, Ana," General Daniil Ionov says. "Say a prayer for me. Give it to Victor, one of the greatest men I've ever known."

Anastasia wipes away her tears and forces a reply. "I will."

"Good. We're waiting on you."

Epilogue

THE HILL. ONLY ONE FOR MILES, AND IT'S ABOUT AS GOOD AS it gets when it comes to looking over the Yates family ranch.

"Whoa, whoa!" Jen says, tugging on her chestnut's reins. She leans forward and strokes the horse's neck. "Good boy, Gus."

Dogs bark in the distance. Whole pack of them. Led by the Yates family's chief relations officer, a German shorthair pointer named Huckleberry. The dog her parents loved so much inspired them to start a rescue on the ranch.

Huck barks as he leads the charge down the family's dock. He jumps into the lake, followed by Rocky and Bullwinkle. The two newest rescues have all but forgotten about their previous hardships.

Gaze returning to the horizon, she finds vastness beyond explanation. Like what she's experiencing with the Founders. There is a difference between them; the Founders are men, and this land has God's hand in it. The Founders have tried to remain a mystery, but their designs are weak compared to what stretches out before her.

There are more of Gombe Wireless's points of presence operating globally, but key points in Europe have been taken offline, including

France and Germany. Those that remain are in nations hostile to the United States. Russian forces have invaded Ukraine, and heightened Russian aggression may flat-out stop her from terminating them. It could also help tremendously.

To Jen, Gombe Wireless seems like a wasted effort. An endeavor of that magnitude requires billions of dollars. It should have been a crown jewel, but it was sacrificed, in a sense. Why use it to attack one of the United Kingdom's most important intelligence agencies? It wiped out thirty percent of GCHQ's computer network, but it also opened the door for a devastating reprisal. Not just against Gombe Wireless, but against Russia too.

That reprisal is in the works and it'll hit soon.

The malware she installed on Void was just an opening salvo in that barrage. The dark web platform remains online; a signal that more servers have launched elsewhere in the world. Her malware is spreading, and she might get the opportunity to send another message to Anastasia Orlov.

Victor.

The twins are permanently linked in her mind, and another question arises: Who betrayed him?

An encounter with Anastasia is coming, and Jen needs an answer to this question before they meet. It could help in many ways, along with another useful piece of information: Victor's burial site. He's resting stateside in a grave marked only with a serial number. Information like that is valuable, and Jen is one of the only people alive who has it.

Yes, Jen's meeting with Anastasia Orlov is coming. And she'll be ready.

Jen clucks Gus along. Old boy doesn't need much encouraging; there's a shady barn calling his name. Besides, she's had enough reflecting for the day. She'll be back in the fight soon, and that'll be the time to worry about what comes next.

WANT MORE JEN YATES?

Sign up for my email list to receive a free copy of SEVERANCE NOTICE.

Anastasia Orlov is one of Russia's deadliest killers, and the organization she represents is equally ruthless.

When that same organization sends her to Mexico, it isn't for the beaches. Armed with a weapon with the potential to kill hundreds of people, Anastasia sets out to betray one of Mexico's most vicious cartels.

But Anastasia has a past, and her mission takes a serious turn when it catches up to her.

Caught between two worlds, Anastasia must not only fight to survive, but escape Mexico before becoming one of the names on an extremely long list of casualties.

Witness the beginning of a global conspiracy that will ensnare the U.S. government's brightest thinkers, and its deadliest assassin: Jen Yates.

Click here to download:
https://dl.bookfunnel.com/twqcr7quta

Also by J.W. Clay

The Jen Yates Series:
Code of War
Code of War: Cyber Kinetic
Code of War: Partition Theorem
Code of War: Zero Day

The Founders:
Severance Notice
Unknown Variable
Siege Network
Forthcoming Title

The Forsaken Sons:
Forsaken Future
Forsaken Son
Forsaken Road
Forsaken Brand (Forthcoming)

About the Author

I've worked in chemical plants, industrial refrigeration, and everything in between. Heck, I've even done a couple of film stunts (got a bum knee to prove it). The journey has been as fun as it is inspiring! When I'm not pushing the pen, I'm on the range, under a barbell, or rewatching the first season of *True Detective*.

Jen Yates is my main squeeze. You can find her "ripped from the headlines stories" in the *Jen Yates Series* and the *Founders Series*. Her books are as fast-paced as they are thought provoking!

If you love the *Sons of Anarchy*, check out James Hayes and the Forsaken Sons. I'd say the books are made for T.V., but they're too crazy for the mainstream. Once you pick them up, you won't be able to put them down!

Want to stay in touch? Sign up for my email list. I'll keep you up to date on new releases, exclusive content, and anything else related to my work.

Made in United States
Orlando, FL
11 February 2025